PLANET OSTER

FERTILITY FUSION

J.L. LOGOSZ ✦ VERA VALENTINE

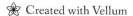

- DEDICATION -

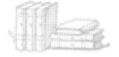

Sometimes you meet someone that changes your life –
so much so that you aren't just grateful for them, you're
relieved. You think about how easy it would have been
to miss them in the great cosmic flow of existence, if
you'd decided not to go to that place, or linger in that
chat, or go to some mutual friend's party. I know, I
know, this is sappier than our usual dedications, but I
needed to publicly express my eternal admiration for
my cowriter before this madness of ours went much
further (she said, as they plot book 5). J.L, you are
amazing and make every day I spend in front of this
keyboard one I treasure. Thank you for being not only
my cowriter, but my friend, and also my bestie in
damnation because *hoo boy* we're committing some sins
in these suckers, ain't we?

Sierra Cassidy, my beloved fellow author, editor, and
bookwife, you remain my moon and stars. Thank you
so much for your digital companionship, your help, and
your warmth – you're a truly beautiful soul and I shine
in your presence.

Thank you to the Monster Dong chat folks, especially Beatrix Hollow, Clio Evans, and Ashley Bennett, for their support and peer-pressure sprints of productivity. Thank you to Evangeline Priest for the heroic help with both formatting and advice. And finally, thank you to our Holiday Hedonism fans, who came together (har!) to pile on the preorders and make this exercise of literary insanity plausible for J.L. and I to continue. We're already starting on the next one (Sacrificed to the Freedom Dragons) for you!

P.S. As always, a very special note of gratitude to the United States Consumer Protection Agency (@USCSPC), who abruptly stopped returning our calls after the publication of J.L.'s bestselling, critically-acclaimed novel **Burning Embrace: A Sexy Fire Safety Skeleton Short Story**. You were our villain origin story, and now the meme-friendship YOU created has blossomed into torrid tales of Thanksgiving side dish gangbangs, Christmas ghostfucking smut, bisexual Valentine's Day vampires servicing divorcees in a van down by the river, and **NOW** omegaverse ovipositing Easter bunny reverse harems in space. Enjoy knowing that you're indirectly responsible for this **FOURTH**, eminently regrettable but always unforgettable, *whole-ass novel*.

- AUTHORS NOTE -

When broma pod smuggler Ch'ik Wazo finds herself -
literally - down and out on an unfamiliar planet in the
Rahnbo system, she's forced to admit she's in one hell of
a tight spot. Just as she's preparing for a long, boring,
and credit-less wait through the harvest season, an
unlikely trio of long-eared aliens makes her an
irresistible offer. Zul, Roz, and Jau promise they'll help
her save her cargo if she'll agree to carry theirs. But with
hidden dangers ready to turn a not-so-simple business
arrangement into an all-out space war, it will only take
one wrong move for this strange partnership to go
supernova.

**Planet Oster: Fertility Fusion is an explicit
Easter-themed alien romance intended for
18+ audiences only. It involves very explicit**

group activity, colorful (and frequent) explosions of "egg dye," ovipositor action, knotting, discussions of fertility, pregnancy, birth, brief mentions of stillbirth/infant loss (not directly affecting characters), allusions to sex work, allusions to drugs, vaping, pain kinks, praise kinks, kidnapping, gross vending area snacks, graphic violence, space gun violence, extensive property damage, unethical hacking, stealing, unaliving of baddies, awakening of furry tendencies you might have been previously unaware of, alien anatomy, mating bites. And finally, while neither sweet bunnyboys still carrying their V-cards for certain acts or MM interaction needs a "warning," consider this a notice this lovely stuff is in here too. (*If you have any questions about potentially problematic content, please feel free to reach out to the authors directly on social media!*)

Legal Info

An Unfortunately-Necessary Warning: If you have received or downloaded this book from a source OTHER than:

- The Kindle Unlimited program,
- A direct purchase from Amazon under the ASIN ending in CVL, or
- An ARC or promotional copy provided directly from or certified by the author (Vera Valentine / J.L. Logosz) via Bookfunnel,

you are reading a FRAUDULENT COPY, are committing THEFT, and are SUPPORTING PIRACY. Sources of income derived from pirated books often come from overseas sites that launder or provide money to terrorist organizations, human trafficking, and other illegal activities.

In addition, you are consciously damaging our ability to earn a living as authors, as this doesn't simply prevent us from getting paid for our work, it jeopardizes our ability to sell our books on Amazon. Please don't steal, promote stealing, or download pirated books - most authors are more than happy to hook you up with a copy in exchange for a simple review. We do our best to be good people - please meet us where we stand. Thanks, and sorry to get heavy about it - we really do love and appreciate our legitimate readers.

Now, onto the good stuff!

CHAPTER 1
- CH'IK -

Cʜ'ɪᴋ ᴡᴀs sᴄʀᴇᴡᴇᴅ.

The obnoxiously loud buzz shrieking from the comm panel clashed with the snapping strobe of red lights in a headache-inducing display. She growled and slammed the heel of her hand into the panel, which, predictably, didn't do a damn thing but make her palm throb.

Fuck. A wincing glance at the meter told her she was going to have to touch down. The problem was that her current location, the Rahnbo system, was a bunch of podunk planetoids. The chances she'd find the parts she'd need to fix her ship anywhere nearby was slim to none. That meant she'd be grounded for the entire harvest season, waiting for the conglom-liners to swing by for the agricultural shipments.

A nervous peek at the windowed door to the cargo hold reassured her that the substantial mound of broma pods inside were intact. Too much jostling could crack their shells, and all that fancy flying to sneak them over the galactic border would be wasted. It would all be for nothing if she couldn't finish the run, though - they'd rot in the hold and she'd have yet another mercenary gunning for her head.

She'd made a good living smuggling the restricted fruit into territories where it was banned over the last few cycles; it was the sole source of dust in the quadrant. The council preferred some of the more threatening species stay dulled and tired, conditions that broma seed powder - *dust*, colloquially - was all too happy to negate when a user hydro-jected it into themselves. While Ch'ik could claim she smuggled pods for the sake of equality among the species, the reality was that credits - and saving her own ass - had just as much to do with it.

With a fierce scowl at the meter, she tuned out the persistent buzz of the alarm and kicked the stubborn landing gear lever with her heel. Gripping one well-worn command chair arm, she clenched her teeth as the entire ship shuddered in protest but began the descent loop. Another angry alarm and a pair of orange lights flickered frantically, vying for her attention all the way down.

The touchdown was jarring, but not so rough any *important* pieces of her ramshackle ship had fallen into the parched brown soil. Another hasty look at the cargo hold confirmed that the vast majority of the broma pods had, miraculously, survived the unscheduled planetside excursion. Shoving open the exit hatch, Ch'ik popped up out of the top of the ship, checking the site perimeter. She was relieved to find the clearing was as empty as it'd seemed from high above. The last thing she needed right now was some pissed-off Rahnboan farmer tromping out here with a laser rifle.

She blew out a resigned breath as she looked around her surprise destination, finding nothing but tangled greenery nodding sleepily in the solar winds. It could have been worse. She could have ended up crashing on a sunless world, or one with an acidic atmosphere. The whine of a sparkfly made her shake her head, sweaty blonde locks tickling along her chin at the movement. She swatted at them with annoyance, instinctively closing her eyes against the burst of light when her hand made contact.

Fuckin podunk planetoids.

If anything was universal, however, it was that even the most backwater asteroids had a place to get a drink. Where there was a place to drink, there was a place to pick up a very good dick attached to a very bad decision, and that sounded like the *perfect* balm to a shitty day.

Ch'ik whistled cheerfully as she slid back down the access ladder and strolled to the sonic shower by her quarters. The broma pods would keep for a night, and she didn't plan well when she was stressed out like this, anyway.

CHAPTER 2

- ZUL -

Z<small>UL SCRUBBED AT HIS EYES, FLICKING SILKY CURLS</small> of blue-black hair off his forehead in annoyance. He'd been staring at the digital ledgers so long, the lines were starting to blur together. He felt Roz's heavy steps behind him, the larger Lapann's surprisingly gentle touch skimming against one of his long, sky blue ears. It drooped lopsidedly, brushing his shoulder, a sure sign he'd been pushing himself too hard.

Zul turned his chair to face his larger mate, who quickly took the opportunity to reach past him and click off the monitor.

"Hey! I wasn't done with that." He grumbled, shoving his ear off his shoulder as he looked up at Roz, who snorted derisively. Hulking and covered in soft pink fur, most of his impressive body was hidden under his coveralls, but his broad arms and torso belied his surprisingly gentle nature. It didn't mean he didn't *try* to look intimidating as he attempted to bully Zul into taking care of himself.

"Zul, you're practically nodding off at the console. You're going to take a break now, even if it's only to punish me for insubordination, *Captain*." The title was filtered through a warm, knowing smirk. Their cluster no longer used the titles formally on board, preferring to utter them only while dealing business or occasionally while enjoying some private time in their mutual sleeping quarters.

Their navigator and third cluster-mate, Jau, appeared in the doorway. He yawned, stretching luxuriously after his nap, tightening his eyepatch in place. His blonde hair was feathery and tousled around his pale yellow ears, shorter and more erect than theirs.

"Roz is right, Zul. We've been forced to pleasure each other without our Captain's guidance for three nights now. Grounds for mutiny, I'd think." Jau grinned and tugged one of his own ears with a coy expression.

One of Zul's ears straightened with interest, his weariness slipping away as a smile crept to his lips. "You've been bedding each other? Should have told me —you know I like to watch."

Jau grinned, moving to wrap his arms around Roz's waist from behind, peeking at their captain from around his much-larger mate's side. He seemed just as eager as Roz to coax Zul away from the consoles; the two of them constantly ganged up on him for working too much. "No time like the present?"

Zul turned his chair to face them fully, letting his legs fall open as he did. His cock was already straining against the serviceable blue coveralls - their unofficial uniform - at the thought of watching them. The tip of his tongue swept across his lower lip as he nodded for Jau to continue.

Roz sighed happily, lifting his arms so Jau could unzip the side of his coveralls. As the smallest of their trio slid the garment down off Roz's arms and down his torso, his hands abruptly froze in their descent.

A faint illumination in the dim of the comm room snuffed the lustful fire the three of them had kindled. Hurt flashed through his chest before he managed to rein in his own shock. Roz's hands gently closed over Jau's, helping him tug the coveralls down the rest of his stomach to see for himself.

There, under his short, silky pink fur, Roz's abdominal wall glowed. Jau winced as he stepped around for a better look, gaze lingering on the circles of light. *Three.* Zul blew out a tense breath, the sting of loss and longing sharper this time.

They were hard to make out through the layers of tight muscle and fur, but the three distinct glowing orbs in Roz's sket gland were their eggs. *Could have been* their eggs, he corrected himself, if they hadn't all been exiled and denied the rites of breeding. Roz's previous seasons had only ever produced one egg, save for a fluke pair several cycles ago, but never *three*.

If they weren't exiled, if they could have made it home in time, if they could have found a willing female Beta - *if, if, if*. It would have been so perfect, each egg taking on the unique traits of a distinct father, creating a truly blended family. *Three*.

Zul stood and reached for Roz, concern etched in his features. He knew as well as Jau did how deeply each lost season hurt Roz, who took on the burden of exile like it was his personal failing. In reality, it was a mutually-botched contract job for a vindictive high-level official, what felt like a damned lifetime ago.

Roz clenched his jaw, fighting the tears that shimmered at the corner of his eyes as he shrugged off Zul's touch. He pulled his coveralls back up, zipping them with an air of finality. "It's fine," he gritted out, running a hand through his hair, angrily flattening his drooping ears against his skull. "Next season."

It had always been "*next season*" for them. The mantra was a wound as much as a balm, and silence settled heavily in the control room. In that moment those glowing orbs were only potential. That was all they would ever be. So much potential, wasted again and again and again.

Jau, ever the cheerful center of their cluster, finally broke the morose quiet.

"So, hey. We have to refuel anyway, why don't we find a port with a bar? Let's have a drink, try to relax like old times. It'll be good for us, right Roz?"

It was to Jau's eternal credit that he managed to make the optimism seem genuine. Roz nodded stiffly, backing away from Zul's reach and turning towards the door. The eggs would emerge the next time he ejaculated. No matter how much Jau and Zul tried to help support him, it was always something he insisted on doing alone; bearing the sadness for the three of them as the small lights would flicker and go dark.

Roz rested the side of his fist on the doorway as he left the room, pointedly not glancing behind him. His voice was rough as a gravel landing on broken gear. "Just tell me when we're in the descent loop, guys."

Zul abruptly pulled Jau against him for comfort, and they clung to each other in unspoken grief, watching Roz move beyond the door. How many more seasons of disappointment could they endure before this crack in their world became a fracture?

CHAPTER 3

- ROZ -

Roz managed to get back to their sleeping quarters, slapping the button to slide the door closed before the tears that stung at his eyes slid free. He splayed a hand over his abdomen, keeping the room dark to watch the faint glow between his fingers.

His hand drifted down the front of his coveralls, gripping himself through the fabric, a lump rising in his throat. He *hated* this part. The thought of it made him sick. He *knew* they couldn't grow without a Beta but his protective instincts still flared. His kits. *Their* kits.

There was also a darker cloud surrounding all of it - a specter that lurked around the edges of the issue, unspoken but never forgotten. There was a high rate of failure for Lapann pregnancies. He tried to soothe the ache of the endless missed opportunities with science, but it was such cold comfort it rivaled the atmosphere outside the *Koton*. Even if he'd somehow managed to successfully lay the eggs, there was only a slim chance that the kits would all make it without an extremely rare prenatal supplement. One or two, maybe, but the odds were undeniably against a full, healthy triple clutch.

Roz was strong, with the physical presence to fight his way out of almost any situation with confidence. He could protect his mates and their ship. It was his job and he was good at it, but this... this was his job too, except his physical strength was ironically useless here. The eggs inside him left him torn - both hopeful and utterly helpless.

He moved to slide the zipper of his coveralls down and get it over with, but swallowed a sob and yanked his hand away a moment later. *Not yet.* He'd carry them a while longer, maybe forget their predicament for a night, pretend they were just a normal Lapann cluster with a compatible Beta waiting for them back home. He laid on the bed, staring at the metal bolts of the ceiling, until a gentle chime sounded from the comm beside him and Jau's voice murmured affectionately from the speaker.

"Looping now, Roz. Come on up front with us."

He grunted as he rose from the bed, taking a moment to splash some water on his face and run a comb through the hair between his ears, tying it back at the nape of his neck. He knew staying holed up aboard the *Koton* would only lead to a spiral of self-loathing. Maybe a few drinks would help numb the ache until he could work up the courage to end his season again.

His mates both turned as he ducked under the door frame into the bridge, Jau smiling warmly. Always as bright as a star, seeing him immediately lightened Roz's mood. Zul reached out for Roz's hand, squeezing it gently before kissing the back of it. Roz stroked his captain's ear with his free hand, managing a small smile. He loved them both, and they were trying for him. He could try too.

Smoothing Jau's ears back, Roz dropped a kiss on his mate's head, turning to repeat the gesture with Zul. "I'm going to see to things tomorrow. You're right, let's relax tonight." Jau nuzzled Roz's belly tenderly and nodded.

As Zul turned back to his console, Roz slid into the seat beside Jau. He proudly watched his fair-haired mate flick a dizzying array of switches before his fingers danced nimbly across the panel in front of him. Roz swore no Lapann alive was faster at charting courses, and with Jau at the helm, their landings were always whisper-soft.

Sure enough, he barely felt it as the *Koton* touched down, mood brightening further as the hydraulics hissed along the door. It had been far too long since they'd been anywhere but the ship together. The triple moons in the sky above comforted his soul, reminding him that most Lapanns didn't get to see the beauty of space the way his cluster did. So what if they couldn't join the rites of breeding? The galaxy was theirs to explore.

Jau ducked under his arm and cuddled into his side as they walked to the bar, loud and raucous even from the outside. Roz relaxed a bit, breathing in the scents of carrus smoke and the tang of spilled liquor that always fragranced a rowdy night out at one of these backwater dives. But wait - what was *that*?

Sweet.

Roz, graceful and quick on his feet despite his larger size, stumbled uncharacteristically, making Jau straighten to keep him from toppling over.

Addictive.

Zul turned to the pair of them at the scuffling sound, raising a questioning brow. Then, his pupils flared, mirroring his mates', and all three of their small pink noses twitched frantically.

Impossible.

Thousands of light-years from Oster, all three of them caught it at once: the unmistakable, burnt-sugar scent of a compatible Beta.

CHAPTER 4

- CH'IK -

"You know, you'd be a lot hotter if you grew your hair out." The voice oozed into her perception like an infected wound.

Without missing a beat, Ch'ik set her drink down on the bar and turned to look at the Lurquer who had sidled up next to her. At least three heads taller, he loomed into her personal space without an ounce of hesitation. When he grinned down at her - a condescending sneer - he displayed misshapen teeth inlaid with shiny black metal; a style favored exclusively by idiots and assholes.

Ch'ik fought the urge to roll her eyes. She leaned back on the barstool as she looked him up and down and took a deep breath. She meant to keep her cool until she could determine if he'd be a likely mark to fleece for a tow, but found herself gagging before the air could make it to her lungs. The Lurquer looked like a sulfur miner - the scales on his wrists and the side of his neck were filthy with bright yellow rime - and he smelled like one too.

"No."

"What?" He looked at her like she'd grown tentacles.

"I said..." Ch'ik took a long sip from her bottle, setting it back down on the bar with a heavy clunk. The Lurquer's eyes flicked towards it, distracted. She used the shift in attention to drop her free hand down, sliding the knife out of her boot. "No."

"What do you mean *no?*" The Lurquer took another step towards Ch'ik, his body language irritated and en route to "dangerously entitled" now that he'd processed her refusal. He hadn't put his hands on her, yet, but he was close enough now that she was going to have to shower later to get the stink off.

"All of this? Nah." Ch'ik waved her hand at him in a vague gesture that encompassed his entire being. "Nope. Fuck off."

He scowled and shoved through the barrier of rude proximity into her personal space.

A spindly triple-jointed finger stabbed the air between them. "Listen here bitch, you'd be lucky to -"

Ch'ik quietly pressed the very tip of the blade in between two of the chitinous plates on the Lurquer's thigh, the ones that were meant to protect his primary neural cord sheath. He froze instantly at the touch of the sharp blade. Ch'ik grinned as he tilted his head down slowly to stare at where the metal gleamed in the dull bar light, mouth agape like a stunned stellar eel.

She knew in a minute he would look back up at her, and she would have to stand there and wait as the gears turned slowly in his head, all while breathing in his sulfurous stench. She was pre-irritated that he was wasting *even more* of her precious time realizing that his winning personality was a wrist-twitch away from leaking out onto the filthy bar floor.

He never got the chance.

Before he could say anything at all, a glass bottle shattered over his head and he staggered - backwards, thankfully. He lurched away from Ch'ik's knife, out of range of that razor-sharp promise of a murder charge, accident or no. Good thing, too, when her only means of fleeing the law was still broken down in the dirt outside of town.

Ch'ik plopped her ass right back down on her barstool, watching as the establishment erupted into chaos around her. She took another long swig from her bottle, piecing out what had happened. Three furry, pastel-colored gents - all from an extremely rare lagomorphic-looking species called the Lapann - had apparently decided that galactic chivalry wasn't dead.

Sure, she'd had the situation pretty much in hand, but that didn't mean that she was going to get back into it *now*. Not when these guys were so clearly feeling themselves out there. After all, who was she to deny them a chance to get all hot and sweaty protecting her?

The huge pink Lapann hauled the Lurquer towards the center of the room, arm around his neck in a chokehold. Lurquers were too hard-headed for the bottling to have done much damage, unfortunately. The entitled, sulfur-stinking asshole had already started to struggle and spit at his opponent, shaking off the earlier bludgeoning. The pink Lapann, ears laid down flat to his head in rage, turned and hip tossed his opponent to the sticky bar floor with a satisfying thud.

The second Lapann - the smaller, yellow one with the eyepatch - wasted no time joining the fray. He sprang onto the prone Lurquer and started just beating the brakes off of him, a surprising explosion of violence that seemed equally defensive of the big pink guy, she mused. He was also grinning wildly as blood peppered the air around him, which was admittedly off-putting.

Most of the patrons had already moved aside at that point, watching with wary expressions or placing bets, but four other stinking sulfur harvesters had muscled through the spectators and piled on. That was going to make things more interesting, especially since the blue Lapann who had started the whole ruckus hadn't moved since the fight started. He was still standing there beside her, nose twitching rapidly. He loosely grasped the neck of the broken bottle in his hand, almost like he had forgotten that he was holding it.

Ch'ik leaned back with both elbows on the bar, whistled low to catch the bartender's attention, and held up a couple of fingers. They looked at her with a bit too much judgment for someone barbacking on a shitty planetoid, but they popped the tops off of two bottles and slid them across the countertop to Ch'ik all the same.

Ch'ik took a long pull off of one bottle, holding the other out towards the blue Lapann next to her.

"Nice coveralls." She angled the beer at him in offering.

He didn't reply. He also didn't move to take the beer, which really torpedoed her plan to pull it back at the last second and chug it in front of him. It would have been a petty bit of payback for sticking his wiggling nose where it didn't belong. But no, he just *stared* at her, a dazed awe in his expression that Ch'ik didn't understand. Did she have something stuck in her teeth?

"Zul! Little help here?" The pink Lapann shouted. One of his impressively large hands was wrapped around the writhing mass of wormy tentacles that served as hair on one of the sulfur miners. He flung his other massive pink hand out for counterbalance, lifting one of his powerful legs and kicking out hard. His foot nailed another miner directly in the chest, sending him crashing backwards through a table.

The pale blue Lapann - Zul, apparently - shook his head as if to clear it. He finally tore his strangely intent gaze away from Ch'ik, shoving off the bar beside her and absolutely *wailing* on the crowd of horrendous-smelling harvesters as he finally aided his companions.

Long frenetic moments, a few screams, and a disconcerting amount of spilled bodily fluids later, the three Lapann stood victorious and panting. The sulfur harvesters retreated hastily out a side door - the ones that could still walk, anyway - dragging their unconscious Lurquer buddies along behind them.

The smaller yellow Lapann made a beeline for the bar, the large, pinkish one following close behind him. The big one spoke first, almost shyly. "Hi. Hello. We're, I'm-sorry about the..." he gestured stiffly at the mess of blood, ooze, and worse smeared across the floor behind them.

He cleared his throat, his eyes fixed nervously on the edge of the bar. "I'm Roz. These are my mates, Jau and Zul."

Jau, the yellow-furred one he'd pointed to, was the smallest of them, only slightly taller than her and sporting an eyepatch. His good eye was bright blue, and his pale furred ears jutted up from a nest of tousled blond hair. He held his hand out, gently motioning for hers, the fur of his knuckles caked in blood. He looked nervously between Ch'ik and the exit, still ramped up on adrenaline from the fight, a strange, simmering heat in his gaze. "Please come with us, let us get you out of here. They're probably going to get more of their crew and they're gonna outnumber all of us when they get back."

Ch'ik raised a brow, finishing her bottle, flicking her fingers across her wrist comm to transfer credits for her drinks. She ignored the outstretched hand, sliding off the stool with a frown, moving to slide her knife back in her boot but thinking better of it. "Uh, thanks, but I'm good. I appreciate the assistance, but I had it handled. I need to get back to my ship, so y'all have yourselves a good night."

She was in a foul mood now, her planned evening in shambles. She'd need to repeat this outing tomorrow to get the stress relief she wanted, as well as potential exit strategies that *weren't* covered in blood and sulfur stench. Normally she'd already be trying to convince these Lapann that transporting her off-world free of charge was their idea, but their burst of stunning violence made her uneasy. This Jau guy seemed absolutely jazzed they'd gotten into a bar fight for some reason, and that sure was a red flag if she'd ever ignored one.

Ch'ik also didn't know anything beyond a few rumors about their rare leporine species, but brothel whispers insinuated they frequently fucked interspecies partners to death. *Thanks but no thanks*. She wanted a fun night, not to be turned inside-out like a stubborn glove.

The way Jau's ears drooped dejectedly, you'd have thought her refusal ripped the manifold off his ship. It didn't make her feel great, but she didn't owe the three anything for "saving" her from an asshole she had well in hand. She moved past him to the door, starting outside just in time to see the flash of laser fire melt a piece of the bar's siding a few inches beside her head. Apparently, her would-be Lurquer suitor had skittered out of the fight conscious, and was now more than a *little* peeved.

He howled in rage, glaring from at the far edge of the barren field that served as a spaceship lot. "You're gonna die, bitch! Your crew broke Jteal's - "

The translator implant tripped over the word, a pleasantly incongruous automated voice cutting into her thought stream to explain it was hyper-regional slang for a reproductive organ. Despite nearly getting her face disintegrated a moment ago, she had to choke back a snicker as she ducked back inside the bar.

She quickly reasoned that A) she wasn't likely to convince the asshole the Lapanns weren't her crew, and B) getting *potentially* fucked to death was probably more enjoyable than getting *definitely* vaporized.

She nodded tersely towards the dejected Lapann trio still leaning on the bar, making shooing motions with her hands as she herded them towards the back door. "*Right*. I've thought deeply about it and reconsidered your offer. Let's go immediately, can't wait, nice to meet you, I'm Ch'ik."

All three Lapann immediately brightened, not questioning her change of heart for even a moment as they followed her, forming a protective barrier of rippling pastel muscles in her wake. That alone was suspicious, but Ch'ik had all the holes in her body she currently cared to have, and getting out of firing range was a priority.

"I - uhm." The large pink Lapann, Roz, cleared his throat, looking pointedly away from her. These guys sure were bashful. "We could travel faster if, well, if I carried you. If you want, I mean. It's no-"

Ch'ik was many things, but she wasn't an idiot. She'd brought a knife - and an unexpected bunny brute squad - to a gunfight. Those were bad odds. These guys didn't need new body holes on her behalf either, which meant fast outweighed comfortable for a hasty retreat. She cut Roz off by sheathing her knife, turning and stretching her arms starward in agreement. "I'm down. These boots are pinching my feet anyway."

He carefully schooled a budding grin on his face back to a neutral expression, reaching for her. Ch'ik expected to be lightly tossed over his shoulder, but instead he carefully arranged her against his chest, draped in his arms like precious cargo. He gently but firmly placed one of her arms behind his neck, murmuring.

"Hold on tight, okay?"

She was used to the unsettling stomach-flipping sensation of takeoff in a smaller ship, but she let out a squeak of alarm as he crouched slightly and began powerful, stride-eating leaps across the landscape. The rapid momentum and jarring bounces were unsettling at first, but she relaxed her hold as her body learned to anticipate the lurch and rise. Roz always held her securely, though once or twice she thought he might have been discreetly sniffing her hair. It was strange, true, but not worrying.

A few minutes later they stopped, Roz's two mates thumping to a halt beside them as he gingerly set her back on her feet. The ship in front of them was much larger than her own, and in far better condition. *Maybe this wasn't a bad idea after all.*

Ch'ik caught a glance of the scrolling chyron over the port thruster; it showed the ship - the *Koton-Tayl* - was registered as some sort of independent mechanic vessel. The sleek interceptor was, however, a pirate vessel if she'd ever seen one.

Nevermind. This was *definitely* a bad idea.

An angry yell in the distance spurred Roz to press his hand to a panel that swung open on the side of the ship. He gestured politely but firmly to usher Ch'ik inside, watching the horizon carefully for danger as they all climbed aboard.

Ch'ik grimaced as they herded her aboard, staring up at the specialized pedipalp grapplers on the shadowed underside of the ship.

The last time Ch'ik had hooked up with a pirate, she'd ended up having to fuck her way off of a toxic prison planet. It had been a pretty fun fraction-cycle, but she couldn't risk a repeat of those shenanigans in the middle of broma season. She didn't have stasis equipment aboard, which meant she had a few days at most before the rare, smuggled pods in her hold were essentially compost.

This ship was much nicer than her last pirate hookup's had been, though. As Jau led her deeper into the huge ship Ch'ik marveled at the cleanliness of the corridors, how slick and well-kept everything looked. Real classy stuff - if these guys were pirates, at least they were good at it.

Finally the group of them emerged onto what must have been the observation deck, and the group of them guided her to sit on a soft bench. What was next, Ch'ik wondered, with a giddiness that bordered on hysteria. Were they going to offer her a plate of refreshments before the gang of them banged her brains out?

Zul cleared his throat. "Is your ship near here, Ch'ik?" His voice wavered slightly on her name. "We can escort you, or you can stay here with us until things cool off a bit, if you'd like."

"Yeah, so...about that." She sighed dramatically, furrowing her brow and gearing up to launch her best "damsel in distress" routine. "My ship is broken down and the - uh - *Mooravean starfruit* in my hold is about to spoil. Is there any chance you could tow me to the next port?" She turned wide, pleading eyes on Zul, considering but ultimately refraining from batting her lashes. *No need to oversell it.*

Zul and Roz's faces immediately lit up with excitement, but Jau lifted a quieting hand, tilting his chin up in the universal stance of a negotiation.

"We've got stasis equipment *and* we'll take you wherever you need to go." He swallowed thickly. "But you have to do something for us, first."

Ch'ik wanted to roll her eyes at the familiar start of a morally dubious offer, but she played the game - she knew how this song and dance went. Feigning shock, she brought one hand up to cover a gasp.

"You want me to... to satisfy you sexually in exchange for transport? And if I don't acquiesce to your lustful advances, what then? You'll leave me to wither away in the depths of space? Abandon me to the Lurquers?"

Ch'ik blinked hard as she thought about the saddest episode of her favorite holonovella, Night Beats. The one where Jordan had dumped Wendy was a real heartbreaker, especially considering Wendy had *just* found out that her entire personality was a dark market implant. The memory always made Ch'ik's eyes well up with tears, which made it a convenient go-to when visible anguish was needed.

Being able to sort-of cry on demand was a great talent to have when it came to getting out of interstellar speeding fines, or determining if your rescuers were actually scumbags. She was pissed off, truth be told. So, what, they'd hop on in to defend her honor with strangers, but were apparently fine with fucking-for-favors when they benefitted from it? Furry friggin hypocrites. At least they had the decency to look startled that they'd upset her. Good, that was how she liked her marks - horny, unbalanced, and ready to promise her all three of the moons to stop the waterworks.

"Well, I guess I don't have any other choice..." She murmured breathily, really selling it. She started to unzip her coveralls, equal parts excited and concerned over the Lapann rumors. Sometimes being sexually adventurous meant trying out a feather, other times it meant the whole damn chicken. *Time to rotisserie up, Ch'ikie girl.*

All three Lapann looked flat-out horrified. Jau actually cringed back, the barely-visible whiskers to either side of his nose flicking when she took a step towards them. Roz's eyes darted fearfully to her zipper tab like it was going to rear up and bite him.

"We're so sorry, please don't -" Zul held his hands up as he attempted to placate her, his expression so earnest that Ch'ik immediately regretted messing with them. "It's not like that. We won't leave you to die! We just thought maybe we could help each other. We really, really need..."

Ch'ik' raised her brows, shaking her head and grinning amicably. "Dude, no, it's okay. I'm only fucking with you, alright? That's actually part of the reason I got into this business, you know?" It didn't feel right to let him squirm. As weird as their sudden defense and intense interest had been, they'd been nothing but respectful to her since walking into the bar. Their puzzled expressions also told her they weren't really picking up on what she was trying to lay down.

She sighed and dropped her head back for a moment, gathering her thoughts and changing tactics before sitting up again. "I'll level with you boys. Have you ever been to Rizen?" Blank looks greeted her as they shook their heads.

She smirked. "Well, let's just say that the men on my home planet - well..." She held up a fist, extending a pinky and wiggling it. Ch'ik had fucked sentient orbs of light with bigger cocks than the males of her species. These rabbit guys thankfully seemed to be cut from the same bipedal, bilaterally-symmetrical species cloth that she was. Whatever they were packing, Ch'ik would be willing to give it a try. Certainly couldn't be any worse than what she'd had back home.

A ride for a ride was a pretty good deal, after all, as long as no one got attached.

She shrugged. "I've taken lovers throughout my travels, sometimes for favors, sometimes for funsies. Sex is something to be enjoyed between consenting, sentient beings, period. I wanted to see what the universe had to offer. You know, in its pants. So to speak." She smiled brightly, thrusting her hands into the pockets of her coveralls. Why'd they have to stare like that? They were making this awkward.

"So your...males are...poor at reproduction?" Zul ventured haltingly, mostly connecting the dots.

"Yeaaah, I guess that's one way of putting it. Definitely not a memorable event, I'll say that. Not culturally adept at *using* said equipment, either." She rolled her eyes in annoyance. "So, if you three want to make the beast with - uh - four backs, I'm game."

"We only need one back." Jau gestured at Roz, giving him a gentle nod.

Roz's jaw had a stubborn set and he looked everywhere but at her as he pulled down the zipper of his own

29

coveralls. He hesitantly revealed a taut stomach covered in a light thatch of downy pink fur, with more than enough muscle to catch Ch'ik's interest. Her attention quickly shifted away from his chest to the trio of softly-glowing orbs in his abdomen, pulsing with illumination under his reverent fingertips.

"We need you to carry them." Jau explained hesitantly. Roz cupped a protective hand over his stomach and nodded.

Ch'ik blinked. "*Carry* them? What, like, in my ship? In my hands?"

Roz straightened, tilting his chin up and looking her in the eyes at last. "Inside of you. I need to lay our eggs inside of you."

For one shell-shocked moment, Ch'ik wondered if her translation implant was on the fritz. It wasn't, obviously - no incongruous automated voice cut in to apologize for the interruption of service - but it was the first thing her mind jumped to, because, well, *what the actual fuck?*

She'd always been shit at school, hadn't even gotten to Interstellar Biology before she'd dropped out, so would have been the first to admit she didn't know crap about how ovipositor species worked. Ch'ik could see the three glowing spots in Roz's abdomen as plain as day, however, and she was 99% sure they had just asked to knock her up.

Ch'ik had been silent for too long - it was a lot to take in. The Lapann had started to shift, nervous and uncomfortable in her silence, until Roz finally broke.

"These are our eggs, Ch'ik, our future children, if - *only* if - you agree to carry them until the kits are born. Otherwise..." As he trailed off Ch'ik realized the look on Roz's face wasn't stubbornness at all, but rather... sadness. The big guy was overwhelmed with sorrow.

She blinked, staring at his stomach, still struggling to comprehend the question, let alone her answer. *"How?"*

Zul cut in now, seemingly more comfortable discussing this than anything previously. "You'll carry the eggs for seven fraction-cycles - roughly 250 day-cycles. We'll provide all the nutrients needed to keep them strong, as well as anything you'll need for your own health and comfort. When they're ready to hatch, we'll help you deliver them, and then you're free to go."

"Zul." Roz's tone was reproachful.

"What?" The blue Lapann frowned, pulling his gaze away from Ch'ik with noticeable effort.

"She's our..." Roz trailed off, swallowing hard. "She's our guest. Not our prisoner."

An affronted scowl from their leader. "Roz, you know that's not what I -"

Ch'ik held up a hand to stop their bickering, unexpectedly pleased when they fell quiet instantly.

They apparently thought that she didn't understand how pregnancy worked - *men* - but at least they were demonstrably attentive.

"I *meant* -" Ch'ik clarified, exasperated, "-how are you going to *get the eggs inside of me?*"

"Oh." The stunned syllable echoed from all three of the men.

By way of answering, Roz unzipped his coveralls further, and even Ch'ik was impressed by the complete lack of shame. *Well alright then.*

"Oh." It was Ch'ik's turn to mutter in surprise, her eyes immodestly glued to the absolute monster of a dick that his shoved-down coveralls revealed. *Praise be to the pulsar goddesses, that thing should be given an honorary gravity well.*

"The next time I - *you know* -" Roz made a vague hand motion, "-the eggs will emerge. So I would...fit into you...and that's how, uhm, that would happen."

Ch'ik blinked. If she signed up for this absolutely batshit plan, she'd be safe and cared for over the next seven fraction-cycles. That was *way* more stability than she typically enjoyed, and these guys actually seemed...nice? There was only one thing giving her pause.

"Roz, is it? Have you ever - uh - *fit* that into a vagina before?" She leaned forward, resting her elbows on her knees, doing her level best to look at his face and not his genitals bobbing placidly at eye level a few feet away.

The intimidatingly large man in front of her crossed his arms defensively on his chest, shaking his head no. The posturing was somewhat diluted by the fact his cock was flopped out of his coveralls, rudely eavesdropping.

Pressing her palms together, she rested her index fingers against her lips and exhaled slowly. She looked at Roz's dick again. A mental list of all the things wrong with her ship scrolled through her brain. A long moment was spent considering how much more she could get for the broma pods if they were preserved until the markets shifted. Then, a glance at the other two guys, both of whom were looking at her like she had single-handedly gifted them both a spaceport and an account full of credits. A final, surreptitious glance at Roz's dick rounded out the brainstorming.

She'd originally been heading for Pontrass Prime, a planet hop that balanced the broma pods' perishable lifespan and the opportunity for a passable, if not phenomenal, black market price. With the night's delay, even if she managed to get a fix or tow tomorrow, it'd still be a dicey trip without stasis equipment.

Decision made, she clapped her hands on her knees and stood. "Alright. Well. Full disclosure time, I'm hauling contraband. So, if you're fine with me shifting that over to your hold then I'm fine with you, uh, shifting your eggs to my... hold. Okay?"

"Okay?" Roz repeated her answer, hesitantly.

Ch'ik nodded. "Yeah, your translator on the outs? I said yes. I'll do it. Let's uh...fit together. I'm sure you're eager to-" She hastily averted her eyes as Zul abruptly turned away, scrubbing the heel of his hand across his cheek. Was he...crying? Was he upset about this? Was *he* supposed to carry the eggs or something?

Jau hooked a finger in one of Zul's pockets, pulled him close and angled up to press their foreheads together. They simply swayed together for a moment until... Oh. *Oh.* She broke into a grin as Jau and Zul started to kiss, locked in a desperate embrace that was broken off only to laugh joyously at each other as they pulled an equally-thrilled Roz into their huddle. *Okay, that's a good thing. Whew.*

Zul and Jau immediately started skimming Roz's coverall's off the rest of the way, tugging off his boots as he used their shoulders for balance, quickly getting completely naked. Ch'ik flushed as she took in his absolutely mouthwatering body, completely covered in short, soft pink fur that lightened around his stomach.

Plunking back down on the wide, deep couch beside her chair, she slid off her own boots and shrugged her coveralls off a shoulder. Finger-combing her fluffy white-blonde bob into something she hoped passed for sexy, Ch'ik was grateful she hadn't worn a bra that day - less to divest. A liberated sexual attitude ensured Ch'ik was completely comfortable with nudity, but the audience was a new thing for her. Ah well. *In for a light-year, in for a parsec*, right?

Her eyes widened as Jau dropped to his knees, deep throating Roz's cock like someone had a phaser to his head. Zul gripped one of Roz's ears, tugging his face firmly to the side to kiss him passionately. Ch'ik might have felt left out if she wasn't enjoying the show so damn much. Roz's hand tangled in Jau's hair as he moaned into Zul's mouth, the big Lapann perfectly devoured by both of his mates, right in front of her.

Then Jau leaned back, a silvery thread of saliva tethered between his lips and Roz's cockhead. Roz's *slightly wiggling* cockhead.

A trio of short, slender, tentacle-like appendages extended about a finger's length away from the tip of his shaft. From the way they undulated, his body was clearly pleased with whatever Jau's tongue had been doing. As if to confirm her suspicions, Jau dipped his head again, extending his tongue for the little tentacles to happily embrace for a moment. She'd hit the bunk with some *strange* looking copilots before, but this would be a new one on her. Well, *in* her, more accurately.

Zul moved back too, and she felt the weight of their attention on her naked body. Roz moved to the couch, his eyes an absolute well of emotion that left her feeling completely unmoored. This was just sex, she reminded herself - fun, interesting sex with a guy that had a

35

discernable, albeit be-tentacled, dick ready to lay some eggs in her. Just another day in the life, really. Ch'ik chuckled nervously, tongue darting out against suddenly-dry lips.

Roz reached out and cupped the side of her face, the furless palm of his hand rough but unexpectedly gentle against her cheek. His pupils were blown wide with desire; the thin halo of color like an event horizon around a black hole, the full force of his attention fixed on her. For the first time, Ch'ik noticed the notches of old scars scattered along the edges of Roz's ears, the pale white line around his throat - mostly furred over - where someone must have tried to garrotte him.

What the *fuck*. Ch'ik wasn't exactly known for falling in with winners, but this was a whole new level of dubious backstory, even for her. Those marks of past violence faded from perception as he pressed his lips to the top of her head, inhaled deeply and murmured.

"You're a wonder. We're so lucky that you -"

His voice, choked with emotion, stuttered into a moan when Ch'ik reached down and got a hand on his dick. The move was intentional, derailing him before he could reach whatever heartfelt territory he was headed for because, well, this arrangement *wasn't about that*. This was about her getting some eggs shoved in her for awhile, that was it. Getting an orgasm of her own, hopefully, and coming out the other side more financially secure and free to enjoy the riches of her broma pod haul. Resolute despite a nagging discomfort in her heart, she stroked a finger across the tip of his dick. She looked down in fascination as the tentacles unfurled ever so slightly, wrapping wetly around her knuckle.

Roz groaned, a sudden, startled sound at her touch. *Was he not expecting me to reciprocate or something?*

"Tell me - please tell me what to do." He panted, hips rolling forward to thrust into her hand, swallowing another strangled sound of pleasure.

"Um. You're the one with the eggs, big guy. You tell me?"

"No, I mean..." Roz dropped his hands to rest on her hips, color flushing in his furred cheeks. His touch was so gentle, a barely-there flutter that felt like nothing at all. "Tell me how to - touch you. How to help you feel -"

Oh yeah, right. Roz wasn't a fumbling virgin - not with the way the three Lapann had gone at each other a minute ago - but he also had no idea what he was doing when it came to *her*.

With the hand that wasn't occupied, Ch'ik took his right hand by the wrist and traced it from her hip down across her belly. She looked down, and in the faint pink glow coming from the eggs, she shifted her seated position slightly, opening herself up to his exploration. She slid two of his fingers down, dipping them into the short, soft curls between her legs. His broad fingertips felt amazing, and it was all she could do not to grind impatiently into the sensation as he curled them, curious.

Roz's dick tentacles tightened around Ch'ik's fingertips as she used her other hand to guide his fingers into her body, already hot and wet with anticipation. Gently withdrawing his fingers with a grip on his wrist, she used them to spread her labia open, slowly, teaching him. Roz stared down, rapt in his attention, as she showed him how to find and caress her clit in slow circles. She sighed happily as he proved to be a very quick study with only a few quick course-corrections for pressure and speed. The other two looked on eagerly, their quiet, intense presence an unexpected aphrodisiac.

Roz leaned forward, looming over her on the couch, his nearness crowding her happily onto the attached chaise until she stretched out on her back. He kneeled between her thighs, those delicate cock-tip tentacles still gripping and searching along her fingertips where she held him. As their naked bodies brushed up against each other, she uncurled her fingers and relinquished her grip on him, slightly puzzled at the tingling, cooling sensation left behind. He shifted his knee against the side of her leg, taking himself in hand and guiding the head of his cock against her.

They both gasped as his erection appeared to take matters into its own hands, the dextrous tentacles splaying out and firmly suctioning his cockhead against her clit. She arched into him as pleasure flooded through her, and he looked down at her with such awe and tenderness she practically glowed from the unspoken adoration. What the hell was this *moment* and why did it feel so *amazing?* They clung to each other on instinct, their mouths meeting in a sudden, passionate crash. She whimpered against him, their tongues tangling as Ch'ik was hurled without warning into the most powerful orgasm of her life.

She threw her head back, shouting in ecstasy as Roz cradled her body reverently, his warmth and size and nearness making everything even more incredible. At the crest of her pleasure, he slipped inside, his breath catching as her inner walls still fluttered in climax around him. He coughed out a few native words of worship, gripping the upholstery of the chaise to steady himself as his body appeared to carry out the mission regardless of his conscious participation.

Chi'ik shuddered at an unfamiliar sensation, deep, *deep* inside her. The small tentacles on the end of Roz's dick must have attached to her cervix. Ch'ik felt her lip curl with discomfort, grimacing despite trying to keep her expression neutral - she didn't want to give the guy a complex, not after *that* delightful performance.

He still caught the wince as it flickered across her features. "Oh no - Ch'ik? Are you alright? Did I hurt you?"

She hissed out a breath between her teeth, trying to adjust to the strange sensation. "It's okay, just fuckin' - warn a girl first, you know?"

"Sorry, sorry, I- I didn't know it would do that." Roz's voice was tight as one of his hands clutched on her hip, fluttering up ineffectively against her ribcage like he'd forgotten how to use it. He had his eyes squeezed shut, the breath huffing out of him as he apologized, apparently struggling in an entirely different way.

"There should be... you shouldn't feel it for long." Jau's voice sounded dreamy and distant to her ears, his fingertips suddenly light as a feather on her forearm, as if he was afraid to touch her. She blinked in surprise, finding Jau and Zul kneeling beside the detached chaise on either side of her. She'd been so caught up in everything she hadn't even seen the two of them cross the room. Jau lightly stroked her skin with the back of his fingers, the kiss of his own soft yellow fur against her wonderfully comforting. "The goo takes on anesthetic properties during this stage."

Ch'ik grimaced again, wanting to tell him not to call it *goo*, for fucks sake, but she stopped when she realized that he was right. She could still feel the good stretch of Roz's dick in the shallower parts of herself, but the strange suctioning and deep discomfort had faded away entirely. She was tired of being treated like a piece of Venusian glass, though - if they wanted to be involved, they could be involved. She slid her hands off of Roz's sides and let them lay beside her head instead, pointedly grabbing Jau's hand on one side and Zul's in the other.

They both squeezed her hands warmly in appreciation, Zul, lifting her hand up slightly to kiss it as well. The gesture filled her with a happy glow of warmth, but confusion, too. *Why were they being so damn sweet? Were the eggs that big of a deal to them?*

Then, Roz's cock started to swell inside of her and any further questions evaporated. She made a pleased cry at the delicious stretch and Roz's tenuous grip on self-control snapped. He answered with a low wordless sound, finally, *finally* grabbing her hips like he meant it. He hunched over her, grinding in when he suddenly stiffened. One of the balls of light in his stomach winked out of visibility.

She had known it was going to happen. Theoretically. But seeing it, feeling it, was something else entirely.

The stretch of his cock inside of her had been good - no, make that *great* - before, but the way his dick changed as the egg traveled through took her breath away. It was a slow, encroaching pressure, swelling deeper and deeper before vanishing into the strange numbness at her core.

"Oh, *ohhh*, I -" Roz dropped his head down next to her, hot breath panting against her neck, voice shaking with joy. "I can't believe - *oh!*"

He seemed to realize that his efforts to form words were futile, leaning down to touch his lips and tongue to the side of her neck instead. It was once more tentative, barely there, as if he wasn't sure he was allowed such a thing. She tilted her head away in wordless invitation, baring the sensitive column of skin to him. Inordinately pleased when his kisses against her pulse moved from tentative to passionate, Ch'ik trembled against him as he thrust into her frantically.

Roz whimpered, those big paws of hands flexing like a pleased Artinan cat's claws on her hips.

"Thank you, thank you, thank yo- ah*hh*!"

She didn't see the second light vanish, but she knew the exact moment that he started to lay the next egg by the way his voice broke. More than broke: shattered.

Ch'ik untangled her hands from Jau and Zul's twin grips, sliding one hand down between her and Roz, determined to join him in climax again. The fur of Roz's stomach was soft on the back of her fingers, which she began rubbing firmly against her clit as she felt the third and final egg descend. His flesh shifted as the egg traveled along his alien length, that moving girth that was *just* on the right side of too much as he stretched her to her limits.

That perfect pressure inside of her matched with the practiced rub of her fingers and everything went supernova. As she rode the sharp star of another orgasm, body locked in pleasure, the third and final egg passed once again into that numb zone inside of her. She had clamped down hard enough on Roz's throbbing cock that she hardly even registered the sensation this time.

The big Lapann had gone silent on top of her, body still except for the slight trembling in his muscles that revealed how hard he'd been working to hold himself back. Ch'ik let her head hang backwards off the edge of the chaise, finding Zul and Jau equally dumbstruck. They had, at some point, slid their coveralls open; hands frozen on their colorful drooling cocks as they watched their mate fuck her brains out.

Maybe it was the post-orgasm endorphins talking, but it was sort of cute how rattled all of them seemed. Ch'ik tipped a wink to her audience that sent them squirming and hastily covering themselves, as if she hadn't caught them jerking off. She turned her attention back to Roz.

"Hey, big guy. How you doing?" She kept her voice soft as she brought the hand that wasn't still pressed against her cunt up to the back of Roz's head. She curled her fingertips affectionately through the short brown hair between his ears, and was rewarded with a desperate, pleased little noise that seemed completely at odds with his hulking size.

"*Three.*" Roz finally gasped against her shoulder, as Ch'ik rubbed at the base of his ears. "Three, *three*, I... I just..."

Ch'ik's heart squeezed at the gratitude in his tone. She freed her hand and laced her arms over his shoulders, settling him to lay against her. It squished her slightly, but she adjusted her hips to lay against his side, rather than directly under him, startling herself by splaying a hand over her stomach without even thinking about it. She was already feeling protective of the eggs, ridden hard by a deep primal instinct to safeguard them.

That had to be hormones, right? Some chemical weirdness. That was all.

Roz nuzzled her neck softly, making her giggle a little from the tickle of his fur. He lifted himself up enough to bare her stomach, braced up on one arm as he clapped his other hand to his mouth, covering a joyful sob.

She followed his gaze, eyes widening as she realized it was even easier to see the orbs, now that they were inside her. They were more white now, most of the previous pink hue having come from Roz's fur. She wiggled a bit, intending to free herself, and abruptly realized she and Roz were stuck together - or rather, his dick was stuck *in* her. Panic started creeping in.

"Uh, Roz? I can't - I mean, you're kinda...stuck in me." She dug her heels into the chaise a bit, but it didn't do any good.

"Mm." He sighed pleasantly, completely unbothered as his eyes slid up her stomach to meet her gaze. "Of course, we're knotted." His brows crept up as her expression hit home. "Does your species not...knot?"

She rubbed her temple, frowning as her universal translator gave the mental equivalent of a silent shrug. "What do you mean *knotted*? Like a goddamn *ship tether*?"

Jau brushed the side of her arm in a calming gesture, seemingly the first among them to sense she was freaking out. "Ch'ik, in Lapanns, the base of our shafts swell after - well, this time it was after Roz released his eggs, but typically it happens after we..." His pale yellow-furred cheeks darkened with a blush. "Once mating is concluded."

It was a testament to the power of post-coital hormones that Ch'ik found this endearing instead of exasperating. He'd just watched Roz rail her and lay three eggs in her, and he couldn't say 'ejaculated'?

Zul cleared his throat, jumping in to save his mate further embarrassment. "It should be about twenty minutes, judging from our experience, before the knot deflates. Roz's knots release a little faster than ours because he's our Omega, and we depend on him to protect us".

Even though they didn't have them on Rizen, Ch'ik had heard of designation systems before. That wasn't how she thought they worked, though. Struggling to sit propped up on her elbows, her gaze swiveled between the three of them. "Your *Omega?* Don't you mean your Alpha?"

Zul looked at her like she'd grown another head. "Of course not, that wouldn't make any sense. Omegas produce the eggs, so they need to be larger to protect them, as well as Alphas like Jau and I." He tilted his head towards the smaller Lapann beside him in indication.

Ch'ik blinked in shock, glancing at Jau. "You? *You're* an Alpha? I'm sorry, I don't mean to be like...classification-biased or anything, I assumed because you were shorter that you were a...Beta or something. Which is fine! There's absolutely nothing wrong with being a Beta." Ch'ik chewed the inside of her cheek, feeling incredibly socially awkward, particularly considering Roz was still buried deep inside her and seemed absolutely fine with it.

Jau laughed, short ears twitching with amusement. "Me? A Beta? I'm flattered. No, Ch'ik, *you* are the Beta. Our Beta." His voice was warm and proud. "The Beta carrying our eggs." He glanced lovingly at her stomach, moving as if to reach out, but curling his hand back to his chest instead.

Ch'ik reached up and caught his hand, bringing it physically to her stomach. "Guys, it's okay for you to *touch me*, you know? I'm not going to break. If it's annoying or I don't want it, trust me, I have no problem letting you know in the moment. Why are you so hesitant?"

Zul and Jau grinned, their fingers almost colliding as they reached over at the same time to lay palms on her belly. Roz smiled softly, watching them all with a peaceful expression.

"It's not common for Betas to be receptive to that, Ch'ik, not on Oster. Our female Betas generally pair up with one another for companionship and this-" he glanced down to where they were still connected, ears laid back in a way she wasn't sure how to interpret "-is usually a business transaction. It was kind of you to let Zul and Jau participate in the ovulation. I'm - I'm sorry for kissing you, by the way. That was inappropriate. I got caught up in the moment."

"*Inappropriate?*" Ch'ik coughed and laughed. "Listen, if it didn't bother you, it definitely didn't bother me, big guy. You're a good kisser and no one said business couldn't be fun. And Zul and Jau can *participate* any time they want to."

The surreal image of the hulking pink Lapann, still buried to the hilt in her, blushing and trying not to grin was absolutely hilarious. She flexed her internal muscles, enjoying the feel of the knot pressing up against her walls, a very tight fit, even now. She was rewarded with a gasp of pleasure from Roz, his hands falling heavily to either side of her to support himself.

"Oh. Oh *wow*." His eyes were wide, his voice an awed whisper. "That...must be part of ovulation. *Wow*. Uhm."

Ch'ik smirked, folding her arms behind her head. "Yeah. Must be."

This was going to be fun.

CHAPTER 5
- JAU -

THOUGH THEIR NEW BETA HAD SEEMED STRANGELY disappointed when it happened, Roz's body freed itself from hers right around the promised 20-minute mark. After he had placed a gentle, chaste kiss on her forehead in the customary gesture of gratitude, Jau brought her to the *Koton*'s well-appointed guest quarters.

A short sonic shower later, she found her way to the cockpit, where Zul was setting the autopilot to the coordinates she'd given them. They'd thankfully be able to store her entire ship in their cargo hold; extended towing tended to cause stellar drag that could damage their thrusters.

The group climbed down into the cargo hold together, Roz crossing the cavernous room to open the hatches and get the ship ready to take on the weight. There was a noticeable spring in his step and his ears twitched attentively as he hauled down switches and pressed buttons.

Ch'ik gave an apologetic smile to the two of them as they all waited for Roz to finish. "Hey, I'm sorry you guys won't be able to do any *business* with the *Aeon Hawk* taking up your cargo hold."

Jau shared a look with Zul. The unofficial smooth talker of their cluster, he gave a wan smile and held his hands up in the customary gesture of confusion. "What do you mean? Fixing your ship *is* our business, we're a registered mechanic craft."

Ch'ik leveled a smirk at him, folding her arms across her chest. "I saw the pedipalps when Roz carried me onboard. You guys are grapplers, yeah?"

Jau didn't reply, just shifted and stuck his thumbs in the pockets of his coveralls and rocked back and forth. His ears dropped back as he whistled with faux innocence.

Ch'ik, likewise, didn't say anything, but grinned as she looked pointedly at the bay doors underneath their feet, the thick, raised, ship-to-ship sealing mechanism obvious around the edges. She tilted her head back to look up at the device mounted on the ceiling above them, conspicuous and decidedly *not* made for repairs.

Her voice was rich with amusement. "So Jau, you're going to tell me that's *not* a hull piercing apparatus?"

"Well, have you ever seen it pierce a hull?" He feigned shock while looking up at the ceiling, maintaining his act for comedic value.

"Have *you*?" She shot back, grinning wider now.

He clapped a hand over his good eye. "Nope."

Her laughter was contagious, brighter than any cutting torch, and Jau uncovered his eye to watch as she threw her head back. Gods, she was *beautiful*. How had he not seen that? It was so strange to feel his body respond ardently to a female - a *Beta*, for pulsar's sakes - but he couldn't deny she stirred something in him. He shoved down the thought, shame coiled low in his belly: this was simply their Beta, carrying their eggs. He had two mates he loved, and it wasn't appropriate to have these thoughts for a Beta, even if their makeshift contract was unusual by Oster standards.

He was just emotional they'd have a family soon, it was misplaced gratitude that she'd agreed to carry for them.

Right?

He was relieved when wind whipped around them, disrupting his thoughts as the doors at their feet opened slowly.

Ch'ik had turned away, squinting her eyes against the kicked-up dust that accompanied the short-beam attractor pulling her ship up into theirs. Jau was glad she wasn't watching his face or Zul's, because they were both wearing matching grimaces. He couldn't see Roz until the dust died down, but he suspected he'd find the same expression there, too.

How was that piece of shit even spaceworthy?

The obviously new damage would have been enough to relegate it to the scrapper - the side of the cockpit was webbed with cracks and an arm's length of one wingtip was sheared off completely. The exterior radiation shielding showed deep gouging, peeled back in ragged rips along the underside. It was the evidence of past repair, however, that gave Jau pause.

The secondary thrusters were both cheap aftermarket attachments that were better suited for joyriding around in a planetary atmosphere, nothing he ever would have trusted for deep space travel. One of the stabilizer fins on the underside was a completely different color than the rest of the ship, and when he stooped down to look at it more closely he saw that the weld around the edges was a nasty mess of purple-flared burnout.

"Did you pay someone to fix that for you?" Jau asked, hoping someone else was responsible for this travesty. He pointed to the stabilizer as the cargo bay doors sealed back together with a sigh and the wind settled, wondering which backwater chop shop had ripped Ch'ik off.

"Nope! Fixed it myself!" She sounded terribly proud of her accomplishment. Jau was filled with dawning horror as she patted the ship's scarred flank, adding, "Yep, I know every inch of this baby."

She produced a fob interface from her pocket and pressed a button. The *Aeon Hawk* chirped, then made a sad grinding noise as the access ramp started to shudder its way down. One of the support struts had been sheared in half at some point, and was now held together with nothing more than a twist of wire. He almost recoiled when he saw they'd been wound through lopsided holes hastily drilled around the break.

Oh. Oh *no*.

The three of them traded a look as they followed her up into the ship. Roz caught up to Ch'ik in a few long strides, hovered at her elbow as she strutted, oblivious, up the ramp. He was ready to catch her the moment these shoddy repairs failed, likely envisioning the same thing Jau was: the lot of them tumbling down to the floor of the cargo bay. By some miracle, the pile of terrible repairs their new Beta charitably called a ship held together long enough for them to board.

CHAPTER 6

- ROZ -

CH'IK LED THEM INTO THE TINY BRIDGE OF HER ship and Roz couldn't conceal his full body cringe at the scene that greeted them. The floor under the command console wasn't merely grimy, it was nearly ankle-deep in discarded nutrient bar wrappers. There was a worse-for-wear blanket shoved in around the edges of the cushions of the pilots chair, tattered edge dangling over an armrest.

"Ah." Zul started but quickly trailed off, likely realizing - in a rare display of tact - that there was nothing they could really say about the situation. Not without potentially getting stabbed to death by the Beta carrying their kits, anyway. "Where's your cargo?"

"Oh, right. Back this way." She waved them down a short hallway, elbowing a loose, bowing panel back into place with practiced ease.

It wasn't a large ship. Unless she had hidden compartments built in, he couldn't imagine where she was storing anything. As he followed her, his mind kept turning, trying to figure it all out as Ch'ik slapped a button on the wall. From the outside the *Aeon Hawk* hadn't looked big enough to have much more than the bridge itself and living quarters.

His heart sank as he realized he'd been correct. The ship was, in fact, just big enough for a bridge and living quarters, but she'd converted the living quarters into a makeshift cargo bay.

The room that should have held a proper bed and her belongings had instead been stuffed from end to end with stacks of agricultural transport crates. That explained the state of the cockpit, at least - she'd been sleeping in there, pulsars knew how long. What the revelation didn't explain, however, was the sharp stench of burning that stabbed at their sensitive noses immediately after Ch'ik activated the door.

Roz coughed, fanning a hand in front of his face as the distinctive note of singed wiring and something faintly familiar wafted through the retrofitted living quarters. He frowned and poked at a nearby panel, wordlessly shutting down the main power cell of the *Aeon Hawk* and hopefully staving off an electrical fire. The main lights dimmed for a moment before the backups kicked on, bathing everything in a harsher glow.

"Thanks! It does that sometimes." Ch'ik yelled over her shoulder, disturbingly unbothered by the telltale signs of imminent electrical failure.

Jau had set his hands on his hips, staring intently into the makeshift ship's hold as Zul joined him to look at the contents. The source of that unique fragrance that had puzzled Roz, the undercurrent of scent beneath the worrying burning note, suddenly made sense.

"Ch'ik? I - uh, I thought you said you were hauling contraband?" He scratched at the base of one of his long pink ears, brain whirring into calculations of credits and all the favors this could buy. The *welcome home* this haul could secure them.

She grimaced as she joined them at the doorway. "Yeaaah. I'm not a huge fan of enabling the dust trade, but gigs were hard to come by in my end of the quadrant. I don't sell the finished product, mind you, just get the -" she made air quotes with her fingers, "-*Mooravean starfruit* to worlds that would otherwise have trouble getting it. Processing and sale's on their heads, not mine."

Jau and Roz shared a puzzled look before Zul spoke up, voicing what had stunned his entire cluster. "But - those *are* broma pods, right? That's not a holographic overlay or something?"

"Yeah?" Ch'ik gave him a questioning look as she shouldered through the pack of them, snagging a large brown pod from the nearest crate. She held it up, turning it in the light to examine it. "They're harvested and dried off-world and used to make dust. Big no-no in the council's eyes, lets some of the big bads tap into their focus and potential, but also tends to cause uncontrolled, murder-y rage. Bit of a tradeoff." She carefully set the pod back down in a pile. "Why do you ask?"

Zul's stare went a little wide as they collectively gawked at the sheer *volume* of pods. "Ch'ik, this is a notoriously fussy crop back on Oster; only the biggest agricorp clusters can manage to grow it in our climate and soil. We have a weak genetic strain in our seed stock and haven't had new strains to introduce for generations. It's used to make a rare delicacy used to strengthen eggs in Omegas and kit development in pregnant Betas."

"So...you're telling me that your entire species is a bunch of *dust heads?*"

Roz didn't miss the way her hand skimmed protectively over her stomach. He wasn't entirely sure what she meant by *dust heads*, but it was bad enough that instinct was driving her to protect their kits.

He held up his hands in a placating gesture. "No, we don't even know what this *dust* of yours is. On Oster, the fruit of the pods is mixed with the sap from a native vine and formed into a paste we call *laht*."

She looked at him dubiously. "Uh huh. And I suppose this *laht* is bright white, right? Hydro-jected into the olfactory glands?"

"*What*?" Jau startled at the thought. "No! It's dark brown, almost black. It's cooked and eaten, like food."

"Oh. Huh." Ch'ik seemed like she wasn't sure what to make of that. "Does it even *taste good*?"

Roz shrugged, looking over at Jau, who mirrored the gesture.

Zul looked suddenly uncomfortable, his voice dropping to a mutter. "Yes. It actually does."

Roz's stomach dropped at the sickening revelation. Jau gasped, clapping a hand to his mouth. "Zul! You took *laht*?"

Zul's ears twitched, his gaze dropping to the deck with embarrassment. "Yes, I did. It was once, a long time ago, at one of my family's parties. There was a lot of pressure, alright?"

Roz scowled angrily, folding his arms across his chest as he turned to Ch'ik, explaining. "*Laht* is *supposed* to *only* be for pregnant Betas and Omegas carrying eggs. It's *very* rare, and it makes a huge difference in survival rates for the kits. It's considered decadent and wasteful-" at least Zul had enough shame to wince at the look Roz cut his way, "-for an Alpha to consume it, but some wealthy *warren-wreckers* consume it as a status symbol."

Roz shrugged off Jau's gentle, calming hand on his shoulder, his pink-furred jaw ticking angrily as his voice grew terse. "I need to go tend to a few things on the ship. I'll stop by and see you later, Ch'ik."

Turning abruptly, he stomped down the boarding hatch, a concerning creak of metal following in his wake.

CHAPTER 7
- ZUL -

Jau sighed, running a hand over his face in the universal gesture of exasperation. Zul, brow creased with concern, started to say something, but Jau cut him off with an impatient gesture. "Just...save it, Z. We're fine, I'm not happy but we're fine. Roz is the one you need to apologize to. Help Ch'ik get her stuff on board and go make amends, I'll get the stasis field set up in here."

Zul nodded morosely, his face a mask of defeat. Stepping gingerly past Jau, he headed up to the bridge of the *Hawk*, a wide-eyed Ch'ik trailing behind. He felt terrible about exposing her to those unseemly parts of his life. He wasn't ashamed of their pirating, but taking *laht* as an Alpha was a shallow, stigma-carrying act back on Oster, one that would have made finding an Omega, or even a cluster contract for a Beta, difficult.

His secret had thankfully *stayed* secret until now, though, which meant he'd found not only his Omega and an Alpha mate, but a Beta that knew nothing of their cultural stigmas. Knowing their eggs were safe in a Beta had loosened his tongue in a rush of emotion and he'd probably broken his Omega's heart in the process. He'd been a father-to-be for all of five minutes and he'd already managed to stick his foot firmly in his mouth, a realization that soured his stomach. Roz was *furious*, and he had every right to be.

Blessedly ignoring the uncomfortable subjects that had been aired in front of her, Ch'ik pulled open a storage hatch in the floor and wrestled out a bulging black duffle bag. Large silver-taped Xs barely covered up the numerous rips and tears in the dark material.

She shoved the heavy bag to the side, reaching back down into the compartment to pull out a green plastic bag. Much smaller, it was emblazoned with a faded, three-eyed alien smiley face on the side and an advertising logo for Night Beats, a popular holonovella series.

She kicked the hatch shut with a bang as Zul reached for the big black bag. It looked heavy and he wanted to help, but no sooner did his fingers brush the material than Ch'ik snapped at him. "Don't touch that."

"Well, can I touch *this*, then?" Zul snarked back before he could stop himself, pointing to the green bag that she held. It wasn't like him to be so flippant, but he was on edge with guilt and not quite sure what to do with himself.

"Uh, sure? Knock yourself out." Ch'ik handed the bag over to him before she shouldered the big black duffle with a labored grunt. He wasn't crazy about the fact his Beta was exerting herself, but it wasn't his place to tell her what to do.

Unfortunately for him, the plastic bag in his hand was old and weathered, and the bottom seam split wide open as Zul followed her down the ramp. He growled a curse and apologized profusely as the contents scattered on the cargo bay flooring. Small half-full bottles of soaps and liquids, a few lacy, strappy pairs of underwear that immediately made his cheeks flush a dark blue with inappropriate images, and a pair of coveralls. He crouched, gathering up everything but the underwear, which he studiously avoided.

He plucked a battered old notebook up off the floor, the covers entirely obscured in arrival seals from different stations, ports, and planets around the galaxy. A familiar one caught his eye.

He stared at it like it owed him credits as he tried *very hard* not to watch her pick up those delicate confections of undergarments off the floor. *Fuck him*, why the hell was his *knot* swelling?

Much to his annoyance, his voice cracked nervously as he tried to talk about something, anything, to stop his mind from ceaselessly imagining what she'd look like in that lingerie. "O -oh, hey. You've, uhm, been to Daucus, huh?"

"Yup. Ran a shipment through there a couple of seasons ago. Nice place, but the night markets were kind of crowded." She shoved a fistful of lace in a side pocket of the duffle and Zul found his mouth had gone dry. He forced his thoughts to linger on more neutral topics.

"They are. Did you try the sookrut while you were there, by chance?" The sweet and savory vegetable dish wasn't easy to find in the quadrant, but their cluster thankfully didn't need to leave the ship to enjoy it.

Her eyes lit up as she grinned, zipping the bag closed again. "Heck *yeah* I did. That stuff is amazing - it was my favorite part of the markets. I swear one of the food vendors knew me by name by the time I went off-world - I ate so much I thought I was going to stain my teeth orange."

Mate-pride bloomed in Zul's chest. "That's actually one of Jau's specialities."

"What's one of my specialties?" Jau emerged and carefully made his way down the ramp, engine grease smeared along the fur of his cheek.

"Sookrut. Ch'ik's a fan, apparently." Zul pulled his hand into his coverall sleeve and used it to gently swipe away the smudge on Jau's cheek.

The yellow Lapann grinned and nuzzled Zul's hand as he withdrew it, tilting his head at Ch'ik. "Oh, yeah. I could totally make some for you later if you'd like."

She laughed softly. "Don't trouble yourself, I can put flavor crystals on a nutrient block as easily as the next gal."

Jau clicked his tongue, admonishing. "As if I'd keep nutrient blocks in *my* kitchen. I'm talking actual planet food, the whole dirtside freshness experience."

Ch'ik stopped, stunned, shifting the bag strap on her shoulder as she looked at him in disbelief. "Seriously? How the hell do you manage that?"

"Oh, you know." Jau's nose wriggled mischievously. "We have our ways. Come on, we'll drop your stuff in your room and later I'll show you where I work my magic."

He took the awkwardly-bundled items and torn bag from Zul, gently shooing him back up into the *Koton*. "Go on, Z. We'll catch up later."

Zul only hesitated a moment before nodding, bounding up the considerably sturdier ramp that led to their hydroponics bay.

For the most part, rations for space travel came from specialized fungi farms where genetically modified mushrooms recycled waste into biomass at an accelerated rate. The constantly-regenerating caps were shredded and compressed into layers, folded into planks and blocks of cheap nutrients that were easy to store. They tasted decent enough, and additions like flavor crystals staved off just enough monotony to keep folks from losing their minds. Things like *variety* and *actual flavor* were reserved for going planetside, not the long hauls between point A and point B.

To have even a small hydroponic garden onboard a ship was an unbelievable luxury. The one that Zul stepped into was far beyond anyone but the most extravagantly wealthy spacefarers - which, coincidentally, was exactly who they had stolen it from. Family was everything in Lapann culture, but Zul's cluster was his family now. In the wake of his exile from Oster, Zul hadn't felt even the smallest vestige of guilt for pirating his extended relatives.

The hydroponic system was one of the first things the three of them had hijacked together. It had been more of a statement than anything - they hadn't even had anywhere to put it after they'd gutted his uncle's private biodome. Room was always at a premium for spacefarers and the equipment had clogged their cargo hold until Jau figured out that the huge empty cylinder at the interior of their gravity core could be retrofitted with a door.

These days, anyone entering the hidden hydroponics suite at the center of the *Koton* would have thought that they were having a fever dream. There were no shadows here, not with grow lights glowing from every direction on the towering racks of white substrate boxes. They lined the edges of the cylindrical room, held in place by the residual gravity that radiated through the ship's surrounding walls. The center of the column, however, was completely zero G. If they stayed in that weightless lane, they could drift up and down the beds, skim fingertips past dark leafy greens and the ruffled rows of sook tops and medicinal lahtvine in endless variety.

Roz was there in the middle of the room, upside-down from Zul's perspective, his ears swaying gently with his movements. Tools hung around him in a field, tethered to the racks of vegetables with thin lines of filament to keep them from drifting away. Zul's chest ached at the sight of him, like his heart was also bobbing, tetherless and uncertain, in mid-air.

With the ease of long practice, Zul pushed himself off from the inside of the doorframe and leaped towards Roz with practiced momentum, slowing to a stop as their heads were aligned. Roz had studiously ignored his approach, wordlessly applying fertilizer to the organic beds even as the tips of Zul's ears obscured his line of sight.

"I'm sorry." Zul felt his throat burn with shame; the words were inadequate, but he didn't know where else to start.

J.L. LOGOSZ & VERA VALENTINE

Roz left the fertilizer bottle to float near a rack of sookrut. Reaching up towards Zul, he simply pushed his ears out of the way, returning to work at clearing stray stalks with a little pair of shears.

Zul's stomach flipped uncomfortably, a sensation that had nothing to do with the lack of gravity around them. "I'm so sorry, Roz, I really -"

"Don't. I don't want to hear it." Roz's jaw ticked again, and Zul noticed the red rims around his eyes before his mate abruptly turned away again.

Zul pressed on, desperate now. "That was cycles before we met. I was a different person then. You know. You *know* what my family is like."

"Yeah. I know what your family was like. That's *why*, Zul. Your family is why you didn't have to care. You could have been taking laht every day! Your family still would have bought your way into a full cluster and guaranteed that your kits came out healthy. With the mortality rate, you know what a difference the laht makes, and yet you still-." He clenched his jaw, cutting off his words as he angrily tied a nearby filament around the shears to keep them from floating off.

He spun to face his Captain, voice cold, practically spitting the syllables out. "If you hadn't been exiled with me, would I even *be* in your cluster? Or am I just an Omega conveniently cast into the black with the wayward prodigal son?"

68

His long rosy ears snapped down with irritation as he pushed off the shelving, going chest-to-chest with Zul, furious now. "Well? Was *I* bought, Zul? Did they arrange to have us captured together, hoping you'd put down roots?"

Zul recoiled as if he'd been struck, kept in arms' reach only because of the gravity. "Is that what you think, Roz? You think we've been through all of this because you're *convenient*? We are a *cluster* and I would have chosen both of you in *any* circumstances. If my father sent a beam tomorrow telling me to come back alone I'd tell him to launch himself into the twin suns."

He reached out, firmly grasping the back of Roz's neck and forcing him to meet his eyes. "I love you, you big stupid bastard, and Jau does too. We're going to have a family together and it's all because of you. I'm sorry I was a fuckup in the past, but believe me, that is *not* who I am now, and that's because of you too. You've inspired me to be a better Lapann from the day we met, Roz, and now our kits will too."

There was a long stretch of silence as they both tread air, Roz's eyes downcast, Zul's grip keeping him close. When he finally spoke, his voice was quiet and strained. "Really just the once? You promise me? Even though it was in the past, I'm not sure I could be with someone like that."

Zul's shoulders sagged in relief. "Pulsars take my ears if I'm lying, Roz. I swear to you, just the once, and the smallest possible piece, cycles before I knew you even existed. I only did it to get my cousin to leave me alone, but I knew it was wrong even then."

Roz's face softened, his eyes closing. "Alright. I can forgive you for that. But no more secrets, alright? It really hurts to know you kept that from me."

Zul grabbed his mate's hands, squeezing them gratefully. "No more secrets. I swear it."

Roz swallowed hard. "If we're being honest, it should go both ways. I had a...strange reaction to Ch'ik, Zul. It was more than laying my eggs, she felt *good*. I wanted to make her *feel good*, far more than what was necessary for the ovulation. Even now, I find myself wanting to... interact...with her again, even though my part in that is obviously over. I'm having trouble knowing how to act."

"When we were getting her things, she had her coveralls pulled down and tied around her waist, and I could see-" Zul stopped, swallowing hard. He didn't have to say it, they both knew what he had meant - the eggs, glowing. *Their* eggs, glowing in *her*. "I felt strange too. I'm sure it's only nerves. We're all anxious to imprint on the eggs, that's all."

He left out the part about her underwear, and how badly he wanted to see her wearing them for him. That didn't fit with this tidy little version of things, that complicated tangle of urges that made his knot swell, even now.

Shoving it from his mind, he grabbed Roz by the shoulders and hooked a foot in one of the hydroponic racks, rotating them both against the curved edge of the room, where the fringes of the gravity field drew them slowly back to the floor. It had stopped being disorienting long ago, but Zul still let himself press his head against Roz's chest as he tried to settle himself.

Not much chance of that happening.

The higher O2 saturation in the hydroponics suite always made him feel slightly giddy, but he hardly needed the help right now. The thought of it all - their eggs, Roz's forgiveness, Ch'ik's presence - lit Zul's soul on fire, for better or for worse. And here, with Roz, and all this photosynthesis happening all around them, it drew out his primal nature. Here he didn't need to dwell in the failures of his past or agonize over the uncertainties of the future. Zul could let himself get lost in the scent of wet dirt and new leaves, the layers and layers and layers of life. Verdant and green. Radiant. Glowing.

Zul remained quiet, needing more grounding than gravity provided. Roz reached up, gently stroking Zul's ear. "It feels good doesn't it? Knowing that we did that?"

Zul nodded wordlessly, his brow still resting on Roz's broad chest. He was fully erect now, beneath his coveralls, the thought of *his Omega* and *his Beta* completing their family filling him with a nearly feral satisfaction. He ground against Roz's hip, fingers curling in his coveralls to pull him closer.

Each male Lapann, no matter where he wandered in the galaxy, kept a clear tube-like bottle among his belongings. Simple and outfitted with a hydraulic plunger at the base, they were used for procreation after the eggs were transferred; eggs themselves still needed to be delivered body-to-body because of their fragility. Because Oster's female Betas only mated with one another, the bottles were used to deliver genetic material when cluster contracts were finalized.

"I know you have your bottle here, Roz. You're too sweet not to have it close. Where is it?" Zul's voice was a pleasant growl, full of heat and promises.

Roz groaned happily. "In the toolbox, under the first tray. I...I never thought we'd ever get to-"

Zul kissed him suddenly, pressing him hard against the racks behind him, shoving his hard cock against his mate's with nothing but thin canvas separating them. "Seeing you fill one is going to be so fucking sexy. I've *dreamed* about this." He slid his hand down, openly grasping and stroking Roz's cock through the fabric, teasing him until he moaned and arched into the touch, a faint pink stain spreading a few drops at a time.

He squeezed firmly, one more time, before releasing his hold. Roz whined, clutching at Zul's arm for more, but his Alpha only gave him a smirk. "Go get your bottle, Roz."

A shove of his larger, powerful legs off the wall had him brushing past Zul, airborne again, flipping easily to reach the box in question. In moments, he was righting himself and gliding back down, clutching a clear tube fitted with a stretchy opening at the top. He pulled his zipper down and palmed his own erection wantonly, panting at Zul, his thumb idly dipping into the stretchy orifice of the bottle.

"No. Not yet." Zul's gaze was intense, his Alpha nature fully on display, hormones practically flooding the cylindrical room around them.

"I -" Roz faltered, his thumb slipping off the top of the bottle, confused as Zul snatched it away and left it to hover weightless at shoulder-height.

"Stop touching yourself. Hands off." Zul's voice hardened, his eyes glittering with *that* look. The one that he knew Roz couldn't help but to obey, and happily.

Roz answered with a rough sound of need in the back of his throat, but he did what he was told. He dropped his ears down and back, bowing his head to show submission as he stopped touching himself. At a prompting glance, he kneeled and settled both of his hands palm-down on top of his thick thighs, just as he'd been taught. His fingers were trembling, big dick hanging lewdly through the opening in his coveralls, untouched but leaking freely. The pearlescent pink drops flowed sluggishly from the tip of his shaft, glistening in the harsh lights.

Zul drew in a deep breath, his voice warm with approval. "Good. That's good."

Zul's eyes were dark as he unzipped and shoved his own coveralls down, stroking himself and looking down with a smirk as Roz struggled to hold himself back. The pink Omega's entire body quivered with restraint, but he took a couple of deep, gasping breaths as he pulled himself back from the edge. Even his ovo-tentacles were trying to behave themselves, laid back against his cockhead so they wouldn't send him over the edge against orders.

Slowing his own strokes, Zul reached out his other hand to tilt Roz's head back so that he could see his face, admiring the blatant need painted across his Omega's features as he panted against his palm.

"That's it." He cooed as he pressed against Roz's jaw, coaxing his mouth open.

Roz's quick, wet breaths faltered into a muffled moan when Zul dipped his thumb inside, stroking teasingly over his tongue, drifting to the inside of his cheek where the flesh was slick and soft. In the harsh light of the hydroponics suite, the only shadows were those in Roz's heavy lidded eyes as he watched, hooked on his

Alpha's thumb, as Zul stroked himself. He let his tethered jaw go slack, letting his dominant mate look at him. *Into* him.

Zul rubbed the pad of his thumb along Roz's tongue again, his Omega giving into the temptation to suck on the only thing given to him. The sensation was sudden and electric, his hand going down to squeeze the knot at the base of his cock. He scolded Roz with a quick 'tsk' - all it took to make Roz's mouth open again, obediently.

Bright blue fluid beaded up at the tip of Zul's dick as it bobbed, rigid, between them. He pulled his dripping thumb away from Roz's tongue and ran it along the ribbed trench of his upper gum line instead, pressing his lip up to admire the double row of Roz's canines, and beyond them, the glistening temptation of his Omega's mouth.

With a barely-suppressed snarl of impatience, Zul shifted his grip to grasp one of Roz's ears, stepping back out of the gravity to hover again. Positioning himself quickly to put his waist at Roz's eye-level, he brusquely fit himself against his Omega's mouth, using his thumb to pull his lips open. He slid in with a grunt of satisfaction, watching Roz's eyes go wide, then hooded, as his cheeks hollowed.

Zul was on a short fuse today, driven by desire for his Omega, his own unexpected attraction to their Beta, and a need to set things right between them all. Not to mention Roz was working him over like he was the last functioning engine on a descent loop, pale blue cock pistoning through those soft pink lips as they both thrust at each other.

"*Fuck* - Roz...you like that? You like tasting me, Omega?" Zul hissed pleasurably through his teeth, murmuring as he held himself back from the edge, thumb stroking the sensitive inside of Roz's ear. "Such a good breeder. We fucked you so hard you made *three* eggs for us. Our *perfect* Omega, so fertile, so handsome, so strong..."

Roz moaned, his fur bristling with pleasure at his Alpha's praise, Zul's hormones sending him into a state of almost delirious satisfaction. Zul pulled back reluctantly, releasing his mate's cheek and ear, snapping his fingers sharply for attention. "*Now*, Omega. Bottle."

Sweeping a tongue across his swollen lips, Roz reached out and handed the bottle to Zul with a shaking hand, watching and panting as Zul used the edge of a rack to pull himself back down. He looped an arm around Roz's shoulders, dropping down to his own knees as he brought the stretchy orifice of the bottle up to Roz's cock.

Zul's voice was low and heated against Roz's ear as he pushed the bottle home, forcing Roz's cock through the tight opening and into the tube. "*There* it is. Now give your Alpha all of it. Show me what a good Omega you are, make me proud. Come *hard* for me now, Roz."

Driven by the potent cocktail of breeding hormones and ritual command, Roz's hips bucked uncontrollably against the bottle, the rest of his body anchored by Zul's firm grip. He moaned and whispered Zul's name over and over as creamy pink fluid burst from the tip of his cock in hot, generous jets. He fucked the mouth of the bottle reflexively, quickly filling the interior and obscuring more than half of his shaft. The fluid swirled in pearlescent eddies as his ovo-tentacles undulated lazily, satisfied at last.

He dropped his head forward, panting hard, twitching involuntarily as Zul gingerly tugged the bottle off of his spent, though still impressive, shaft with a pop. He kept the bottle carefully upright, settling it into a corner of a nearby substrate box before turning back to Roz and embracing him lovingly. As he leaned back, he admired the smear of his own blue precum against the damp pink residue on Roz's belly - he'd always thought the colors his cluster produced looked striking.

Roz's voice was quiet, undeniably happy in the afterglow. "You know, Zul, I once slid into a bottle, to see how it would feel. I never dreamed I'd be *using* one." Zul chuckled, smoothing a hand up and down his Omega's spine. The bottles were only for procreation, and Roz wouldn't have been able to come in one without an Alpha's command, but the admission of experimentation spoke to just how badly he wanted a family. Zul was immensely relieved Roz was getting one now; it was no less than his soft-hearted, headstrong Omega deserved.

Roz reached down to offer his touch on the throbbing, needy blue cock still between them, but Zul stilled his hand with a gentle grip on his wrist. "No, I'll save it for the bottle, she'll need mine soon enough. This was about you. I wanted you to know how much I love you, and Jau and I agreed a long time ago your egg would be fertilized first. You've been such a good mate to us, Roz."

Roz blushed softly, smiling with a giddy laugh. "She'll start her nest once my egg fertilizes. I can't *wait*." His eyes widened. "Ohh. Zul, she's not from Oster, she won't understand the nesting instinct. We'll have to help her with materials, she won't know enough to ask."

Zul nodded. "Jau and I were already prepared for that, don't worry. We've gotten our blankets out and they're in our bed. You'll have to get your mating blanket from storage, we'll sleep with all of them for a night or two, fuck in them a little to get our scents on them properly." He bent Roz's ear to his lips, kissing the sensitive interior until Roz shivered happily.

He hugged Zul tightly, nuzzling his cheek to scent-mark him affectionately. "And I'll harvest some vegetables, we'll all have a good dinner tonight to celebrate. I don't want her eating those awful protein blocks anymore, they aren't good for her *or* the kits."

CHAPTER 8

- CH'IK -

THE CABIN THAT JAU HAD SHOWN HER TO HAD seemed ridiculously opulent by Ch'ik's standards - a bed *and* a table *and* a chair *and* her own private sonic shower - and that was before Jau had briefly returned to give her pillows for the bed. A concerning amount of pillows, really. Did their race need particularly plush sleeping quarters? She typically slept in the *Aeon Hawk's* command chair, so even laying flat was a wild luxury.

Jau had explained that getting the broma pods back to their home planet - Oster - would get her the best price for them, as well as access to better medical tech for the eventual birth. However scarce broma pods were on the black markets she was familiar with, it sounded like Oster was twice as desperate for them. Anything that could *revolutionize the planet's entire social structure*, as Jau had put it, equaled way more credits than she'd pry out of her usual contacts. So yeah, it was all a gamble, but the stasis field would keep the pods safe and she'd at least be comfortable while it played out. No more sleeping in her command chair for a few fraction-cycles - she could definitely live with that.

Ch'ik flopped happily onto her stomach on the bed. Burying her face in one of the soft pillows, she relaxed against it until a deep inhale made her sit up, puzzled. She expected them to smell like the cleansing agent neutralizers used by default, but instead the fabric smelled masculine and metallic, pleasantly so. Sitting cross-legged, Ch'ik curled around it, hugged the pillow close to her as she took another huff. How could some rando Lapann's cologne make her feel so...*peaceful?*

A faint cough by the door port made her look up, feeling foolish for cuddling up with a pillow like this. Zul nodded a greeting, arms folded across his chest, a bottle of something in his hand.

"Jau brought you some pillows, I see." *Why was he looking at her like that?*

"Uh, yeah." She hastily tossed the pillow up against the bunk head like she hadn't been copping a feel on the damn thing. "I...like whatever cleaning solution you guys use, it's really nice."

Zul's ears flicked erect, his fur lightly bristling - in pleasure, judging by the satisfied smile on his face. She hazarded a guess that cleanliness was important to the Lapanns, which was unusual among the spacefarers she usually ran into. Most smugglers were burnout trash piles with command centers like hers - knee-deep in debris and wrappers. Pulsars knew what she'd seen of the *Koton* so far had been immaculate.

He handed her the nozzle-topped bottle with obvious pride and Ch'ik squinted at it. "What the fuck is this?"

She had been hoping for food; she couldn't remember the last time she'd eaten. Wait, she'd had a couple of those water-weak beers back at the bar, did that count? Ch'ik had never been able to get a firm answer on whether or not beer qualified as food, but *those* ones probably didn't. Especially considering she'd been stone-cold sober during that not-so-little 'transaction' on their couch.

"It's nutrients, to help the eggs. You'll need three of them total, but this will help the first fertilize and imprint properly." Zul leaned against the doorframe, the perfect picture of someone trying too desperately to look casual.

"Uh, okay. So I'm...what? Supposed to drink it?" She rotated the bottle, watching the pearly pink liquid inside curl and spin.

Zul coughed in surprise, flushing a deep blue as he stared at the far wall. His body language screamed that he was wildly embarrassed. "Pulsars *No!*"

"Well my species aren't *mind-readers* man! Spit it out!" She gestured with the bottle, watching his eyes track it worriedly, his hands reaching out automatically to prevent her from spilling any.

"*Careful*, please. You're supposed to put the goo..." He cleared his throat, avoiding her gaze. "you know, inside. Where the eggs went."

Her eyes widened as her synapses connected the bottle in her hand, the color of the contents, and Zul's obvious discomfort. "Oh. My. G-Zul, is this *semen*? Did you bring me a pulsars-damned bottle of Roz's cum?" She knew even without his answer, the faint residual warmth of the bottle told her that's precisely what it was.

Well, fuck it. She'd shoved worse up there getting those cut tiramite gems off of Missot 4. She unscrewed the protective cap, rolling her eyes at Zul. "This is weird, for the record. Way more work than it needs to be. Also can you all *please* stop calling it *goo* for fuck's sake."

"Uh. Why?" Zul finally managed to look directly at her, brows raised, though he tugged his ear nervously. She was irritated still, but that was honestly kind of...cute?

"Because it's *weird*, dude. Who even calls it that?" She glanced at the swirling pink liquid again, quietly impressed by the volume.

He blinked, tilting his head. "Well, we do."

Her eyes rolled of their own accord, this time. "Yeah. Fuckin' *obviously* you do. That's the problem. Doesn't exactly - you know - set the mood?" She sighed and set the protective cap on the bedside table, mentally working out how to get that much...*not goo*...into herself without wrecking the linens.

Zul swallowed and turned to leave, mumbling so fast she barely caught the question. "Can I watch?"

She sighed in annoyance, snapping at him. "What, you don't trust me not to chuck it in the recycler? I've already agreed to carry your eggs, might as well make sure they're strong. Not like I'm gonna start half-assing it now."

"No! That's not it at all, I just..." He shook his head vigorously, his hands up in protest.

"You just *what?*" Ch'ik asked, getting even more pissed at his palpable discomfort and shooting him a glare. The embarrassed tilt of his ears was back, but that growing tent in the front of his coveralls? That was new.

"Ohhh." Ch'ik grinned as she waggled the bottle of brightly colored fluid back and forth between her fingers, teasingly. "You're into it. Into it like *that.*"

Zul muttered something that she couldn't quite make out. He scuffed the toe of his boot against the floor at her sound of confusion before he finally repeated himself. "You...said we could participate."

Granted, *this* was not what she had in mind with that invitation, but at least it was a step in the right direction.

"And I meant it. Here -" Ch'ik flipped back onto her bunk with what she hoped was a laissez-faire gracefulness, rather than a boneless collapse. "Watch, then, if you want to."

Ch'ik set aside the squeeze bottle and shucked out of her coveralls and bra, secretly delighted she'd bothered to wear underwear that day. The hungry look on Zul's face after he'd spilled her underwear all over the cargo bay hadn't escaped her, earlier. His reaction to seeing it on her body was even better.

The way that he licked his lips when she leaned back against the wall was proof enough she hadn't been imagining it. Purposefully angling her body towards him, she planted her feet on the mattress and spread her legs.

Zul's hand went so tight on the doorframe that she could have sworn she heard the metal creak. *"Ch'ik."*

That was it. That's what she wanted to hear - that ragged edge of need in the tight-laced Captain's voice.

"Yes, Zul?" With a soft smirk, she traced a finger over the underwear, circled her clit through the worn-thin fabric before she dipped it lower. Slowly, sensually, she pulled the material aside to show him her cunt. It didn't take much to get her aroused on her worst day, but fucking a squirt bottle of someone else's cum as part of a weird, private sex show? New ground, there, but hell if it wasn't doing the trick.

Except it wasn't really the thought of the squirt bottle that was sending warm tingles of anticipation down to her toes, was it? It was the sight of Zul as he stood there, slack-jawed, watching Ch'ik tease herself.

"Come closer, I won't bite. I told you before, I'm perfectly alright with you guys being involved. Fucking Roz was great, but the big pink bastard up and vanished when I was ready for round two. I need some *relief,* Zul."

His eyes widened and his fingers tensed on the doorframe. "We're - we're exiles, Ch'ik. I mean, I can try and find a contract Beta for you, but this far out from Oster, and with our status..." He winced in apology.

She snorted derisively, dipping a finger between her folds, marveling at how wet she was. Pregnancy agreed with her, apparently. "And why would I need a damn

Beta when I've got a cock like *that* hovering in my doorway, Zul?" She stared pointedly at his hand, which had moved to adjust his painfully obvious erection.

His willpower was unraveling as she watched, and she did her best not to be outwardly gleeful about it. He was so damn earnest and tortured about everything - he probably needed a good fuck more than she did. "Ch'ik, it...that isn't done on Oster. Alphas and Omegas only deliver nesting materials and g- uhm, *genetic material*, and the Betas take care of the *relief* part of things."

Flashing him a sultry smile, she dropped her voice to a conspiratorial whisper. "Good thing we're not on Oster then, isn't it? Now why don't you come give me my next...delivery...straight from the source?"

Zul whined as the last of his restraint dissolved, crossing the room in two quick strides. He climbed onto the bed so fast she barely registered his movement, kissing her like she was the only oxygen left in the room, crowding her against the wall. Her fingertips skimmed up his side, and together they unzipped and tugged down his coveralls, Ch'ik using the soles of her feet to push it down his legs. He cursed in a language the translator struggled with, twisting around to yank his boots off impatiently.

Hot damn. Miles of lean blue muscle greeted her as he stripped. She had the distinct feeling the linens under her were going to end up ruined with or without the bottle, which he grabbed from the side table.

"Is - I mean, are you sure this is okay?" He bit his lip as uncertainty ghosted across his features, staring down between her thighs. In response, she hooked her thumbs under the sides of her underwear, arching her hips to shimmy them down.

Ch'ik dangled the garment on the edge of her finger, giving him a teasing wink before dropping the scant handful of lace off the bed. "More than okay. I'm ready for it, Zul - please don't make me beg."

He moved the nozzle down, his shoulders shedding tension as she laid her hand on top of his, guiding him to the right place. She had the distinct feeling none of the boys had navigated *this* particular stretch of space before, if Roz's initial shyness and Zul's hesitation were any indication.

She was surprised to find the nozzle slightly warmer than her body, Zul's eyes locking on her face as he thumbed a button on the base. There was a soft mechanical click and hiss as the internal hydraulics began to slowly press the pearly pink fluid into her. They both watched the cylinder empty, the tip of Zul's tongue tracing his bottom lip as he moved his thumb across her clit experimentally.

She rolled her hips, sliding the nozzle deeper, nodding encouragement. He suddenly shifted onto his hands and knees beside her, and the soft, silky brush of his fur stroked across her stomach, just before the heat of his tongue replaced his thumb. She felt more than heard the sharp intake of breath against her skin as Zul tasted her.

Any doubts she'd had about being his first female partner evaporated. It was clear in every line of his body and movement of his mouth - he was *fascinated*.

What Zul lacked in natural skill, he made up for in absolute worshipful enthusiasm, as well as ability to take direction. Her hand found its way to his head, her fingers massaging the base of his ear and directing his angle when she needed more stimulation. After a moment of hesitation, he began to fuck her with the now-empty bottle, carefully but deliberately, the former contents helping it glide in and out easily.

Ch'ik groaned and arched against his mouth, reaching down to grasp his wrist and slide the bottle out. She gripped his shoulder, pressing Zul onto his back on the bed, a sluggish trail of pink gliding down the inside of her thigh as she straddled his waist. He swiped the trail with two fingers, curling them to press the fat droplet back up inside her, firmly. *Why was that so hot?*

She clenched when he moved his hand up to suck those fingers clean, his eyes burning into hers with need. Unwilling to wait a second longer, she lined him up to her entrance, sinking down on her knees to impale herself on his shaft. It was thick enough that it wouldn't glide home, even with all the extra lubrication, and she had to work herself down in small arches of her hips. She grabbed Zul's hand, for connection as much as to steady herself, dragging it up to her face and licking a long stripe up his palm to catch the last drop of errant fluid.

He growled with approval, his chest thrumming with a low, rhythmic sound that made her feel languid and blissed out as she rode him. The stimulating width of his knot bumped her entrance with each rolling thrust, promising her the stretch she craved so badly. That incredible sensation was practically all she could think about since Roz withdrew. She sank as low as she could, but Zul's knot remained stubbornly outside of where she needed it most.

She whined, her voice high and tight, unfamiliar to her own ears as her nails curled against his chest. "*Please!*"

That steady thrum in his chest grew louder, pulsating under her palms as he gripped her hips, anchoring her down against him and pushing. Her body bowed forward as he slid in fully, his knot locking in and sending her, keening and thrashing, over the edge of orgasm.

He clutched her tightly against his chest, driving into her in short, sharp thrusts as he found his own release, giving a low cry of pleasure against her shoulder. His chest heaved with deep, unsteady breaths against hers, holding her as if he was worried she'd float away.

As the tattoo of his racing heart slowed, he tangled his fingers lightly in her short blonde hair. She hummed, pleased at the sensation, unable to resist squeezing him inside as she'd done to Roz. His hips jerked as he sucked in a breath, glancing up at her in wonder.

"Is that - are *you* doing that? On purpose?" His wide eyes were absolutely adorable.

Ch'ik grinned down, rocking lightly to tease him. "Poor Roz didn't even know I could do that, I think - you're a bit faster on the uptake. You boys haven't bedded a female before, have you?"

Zul shook his head, resting his hands on her hips. His grip felt warm and soothing, and Ch'ik liked that a great deal. She splayed her hands on his muscular chest, holding herself up, peevishly blowing an errant blond strand out of her eyes.

He smoothed his palms up and down her sides, affectionately. "We don't get a lot of education on Oster for - well, *this*. If you had asked me when I was a kit, I'd have told you Betas *couldn't* do what we did for...fun, that it was biologically impossible." His face twisted in delayed regret. "Fuck. The eggs. I hope - I hope that worked the way the bottle would have. Damnit. Jau was supposed to go next, too." He gave a heavy sigh and dropped his head back on the pillow. "I have no idea how I'm going to tell them about this."

Ch'ik frowned, tilting her head. She was a lot of things, many unsavory and some unpronounceable, but one thing she'd never be was the *other woman*. "What's this

- thing - you all have going on? We didn't just fuck with a bonded mate situation, did we? Because I did *not* sign up for that kind of drama."

Zul shook his head, sighing. "No. No, Jau and Roz will be confused, maybe, concerned about the eggs, but not upset over-" he gestured between them, where his knot was locked in tight. "Lapann are fairly open with relationships, we've just been content to keep it to our cluster. Pulsars know we've had offers from tacky people looking to bed something exotic, especially after Jau's matches."

Ch'ik winced inwardly - she'd started out as one of those alien-chasers, though she generally had more tact than the sort Zul was describing. These days, she wasn't so much about galactic dick bingo as much as an old-fashioned mutual good time. She wondered about the 'matches' part - was the smaller Lapann some kind of athlete?

She shifted her weight to get more comfortable and Zul groaned happily, hands squeezing her hips. "Easy, sweetheart, or we'll be here all day."

Ch'ik laughed, bracing herself against his chest to move so she could keep her hips still. "Sorry. I'm not used to being trapped."

Something passed through Zul's expression that looked like regret, but he blinked it away, grabbing her hips more firmly and rolling them over. He smiled softly down at her, on top now, and she stretched her legs with a happy sigh. "Thanks, that's much better. How long until your knot is...uhm, unknotted?"

He leaned down suddenly, kissing her again, whispering against her mouth. "Too soon. I'd love to try satisfying you again, but that might mark two of the eggs as mine. I'm not really sure how all of this works without the bottles." His ears flattened against the back of his head, guilt creasing the edges of his eyes.

One ear flicked, agitated, and he reached down to cup the back of her neck in a strong hand. "But maybe I can make you feel good in other ways, while we wait?"

His hand squeezed once, starting a gentle massage on muscles and tendons that had been locked up for what felt like a dozen fraction-cycles. Her eyes fluttered closed as she sighed happily. "That'd be fine, Zul. Perfect, really."

She heard him give a rough chuckle as he moved his other hand to join the first, resting his weight on his knuckles as his fingers worked slow circles. She lightly dozed, stirring when she felt him move between her legs, his hands giving one last warm squeeze to her shoulders.

Knot loosened, Zul pulled back from her at last, but his shiver of pleasure quickly turned into a look of concern. *Not* the type of expression Ch'ik wanted to see under these circumstances.

"What's wrong?" Ch'ik pushed herself up on her elbows, trying to peer down.

"Uh..." His wide-eyed look did absolutely nothing to calm her down.

"Zul! Focus! What. Is. Wrong." She snapped her fingers at him, anxious for an explanation.

"It's the g-." He stopped, swallowing as he corrected himself. "The cum. The color, it's -"

Ch'ik had realized by now that communication wasn't one of the blue Lapann's strong suits. She was still a little surprised when he gave up trying to explain, swiping a fingertip along her damp inner thigh instead.

In the stark light of her living quarters, a vivid purple glistened on his outstretched fingertips as he stared at it with wide eyed shock.

"Is that not normal?" She raised a brow. What the hell was he freaking out about? Everything *felt* normal on her end. Well, as *normal* as three glowing alien eggs could feel, anyway.

"I-I don't know. I've never done this before. Mine's usually...you know, blue." He gestured at himself with purple fingers, indicating his fur and complexion. Pure panic showed in his eyes as he looked at his hand.

Ch'ik thought about it before deciding that she was *at least* 85% sure it wasn't something to worry about.

Another thought suddenly occurred to her, as she tried and failed to bite back a laugh.

"Like hull paint!" She cackled, crossing her legs with a squeak as she felt another drip run down her inner thigh.

Zul stared at her like she'd grown an exterior heart, absently pressing a cupped hand to her pussy to ensure the *nutrients* he'd recently delivered stayed inside. *Yeah, that really was hot,* she decided.

"What? Think about it. He's pink, you're blue, so when you mix it all together -" Ch'ik waved her hand around her softly glowing midsection "- you get purple, right?"

Zul didn't say anything, but if he didn't know how colors worked then Ch'ik wasn't going to explain it with a kaleidoscope of jizz leaking out of her.

"Listen, what I'm trying to say is that I don't think it's a big deal." She shrugged. "But if you're worried can't you send a message to your home world? Get some sex education recordings beamed back?"

"That - yeah, no." He laughed humorlessly, pain in his eyes before he scrubbed a hand over his face. His eyes shimmered briefly and he sniffed sharply, turning away from her and climbing off the bed silently.

"Zul? Hey, I'm sorry, I didn't mean to-" She hugged the soft blankets to her chest, reaching for him.

He shook his head, his ears plastered tight to the back of his head, his body language radiating anxiety. He walked to her shower area, taking a soft cloth from a cabinet and adjusting the replicator to emit actual water. "It's fine, don't worry about it."

He came back to the bed with the warm, damp cloth and brushed it across her forehead, his gaze softening as he handed it to her. "In case you'd like to clean yourself - I-I didn't want to presume."

Zul slipped his coveralls back on, his ears still strangely drooped. As he moved to get up, he hesitated, then leaned down over her. Ch'ik moved to receive what she thought would be a kiss, only to feel the soft glide of fur across her cheek as Zul rubbed his face against the side of hers.

What the fuck?

Was this like that weird forehead kiss Roz had given her? What the hell was up with this, and why did Zul look guilty? He stared at the faint smear of purple on her thigh like it held the secrets of the universe.

His words came out in a rush. "Try and get some rest. It'd be best for the-" Zul's voice cracked. "-*eggs*. And, um, don't - I mean, let's keep this between us. I shouldn't have done that. Sorry." He nodded stiffly, as if he were a doctor finishing a cursory examination, before hastily ducking out of the room, hitting the door closing panel on his way out.

What the actual *fuck?*

The silence pressed in on her, nothing but the distant hum of the engines reverberating through the room. Ch'ik punched at her pillow to shape it, flopping back heavily as she gusted out an irritated huff. Into the black with all of them. It was a job. Just a job.

And jobs didn't hurt.

CHAPTER 9
- JAU -

It had been almost a fraction-cycle since the night they found Ch'ik at the bar. While Jau enjoyed mealtimes with his newly-expanded, temporary cluster, it was tense. Ever since they'd taken the *Aeon Hawk* aboard, Zul had been actively avoiding Ch'ik. It didn't seem aggressive or angry, but made their erstwhile 4-person crew feel somewhat disjointed. Whenever Jau tried to bring it up with Zul, he dodged the subject, which Jau took to mean he'd likely put his foot in his mouth about something. Classic Zul.

Not that he was much better when it came to awkwardness. Jau was forced to admit to himself that he had it *bad* for Ch'ik. He caught himself holding his breath whenever he watched her lips close around a spoonful of sookrut, or a slice of warm bread. He lived for the way her eyelids fluttered and the nearly sexual noises of enjoyment she made as she ate his food. Something in his chest felt golden and radiant to know he'd provided for her as he provided for all of his cluster.

Ch'ik had used his bottle privately, as expected, though she seemed a little testy when he'd presented it that first evening on the ship. He'd chalked it up to her being irritated at interruptions as she settled in.

Since then, Jau had *the talk* with himself at least twice a day. She was a *Beta*. Of course she wouldn't be interested in him, in any of them. She was only being polite when Roz was laying their eggs in her, even if he thought he felt something in the way she'd grasped his hand as she came that day. He mentally replayed the whole experience as he fucked his bottle to completion that night, and his own fist an embarrassing number of times since then. He wanted to be *sexually* involved with her, and it made no sense - their eggs had been transferred, so he definitely shouldn't be feeling anything for her beyond basic gratitude.

Unfortunately, the fact she'd used his bottle eliminated the palatable excuse of ovulation hormones. Ch'ik would have immediately stopped producing them once the three eggs had been fertilized, at least from what he understood, and Zul had tersely informed them his egg had been fertilized, though out of the order they'd agreed on. That meant that all the inappropriate feelings that flared when Ch'ik glanced his way really were *just him*. All him, and only him.

As the cluster-mate unofficially in charge of laundry, he was also wrestling with another issue, albeit one hard work could more readily solve. For some reason, ever since Ch'ik had come on board, their libidos had gone supernova. There were days when the jumble of coveralls and sheets that he shoved into the sonic cleaner looked like the aftermath of an impromptu hull painting party.

He knew that Roz had taken Ch'ik aside for a quiet conversation about the nesting instinct, and since then she'd occasionally requested used blankets. She'd also asked for a pair of his coveralls specifically once, which made him prouder than it probably should have. As their journey continued and their cluster's sex life picked up, it was becoming more difficult to find unwashed linens and clothing for her that contained their scent but not their seed. Ch'ik had abruptly made her feelings very clear on what they were *not* to call the substance a few days into the journey, and he was puzzled, though happy, to oblige.

When he wasn't tangled in the sheets with his cluster, his mates fell into their old routines. Zul had taken to burying himself in his work again and Roz had been spending a lot of time in the hydroponics suite. The latter worked out fine for Jau, because he'd never cooked so damn much in his life.

All that latent nervous energy had to go *somewhere*, after all, and it didn't feel right to fuck out his sexual tension over Ch'ik with one of his unwitting mates. He consciously kept sex between he, Zul, and Roz as something to enjoy when he wasn't keyed up about Ch'ik, though those times were getting more scarce the longer they travelled. He longed to pour some of his agitation out in a fight, but the *Koton*'s current heading wouldn't bring them close enough to visit the Scrum.

That left Jau without a lot of options. There were only so many cycles that he could spend endlessly working out in the *Koton's* training room. He had offered to work on repairing Ch'ik's ship but she had brushed him off with a curt "No thanks, I can do it myself." As much as he doubted the truth of that statement - the condition of Ch'ik's ship was proof enough that she could not, in fact, do it herself - he assured himself that it was probably for the best. After all, any energy he might manage to burn off working on the *Aeon Hawk* would have been for nothing. He couldn't spend fractions in enclosed quarters that smelled like the delectable Beta without making it worse. Jau was already spending far too many day-cycles walking around half-hard in his coveralls, trying to grip down the knot that swelled at the mere thought of her.

While he was *not* focusing on Ch'ik's soft breasts or the sway of her ass, he cooked. Not only had he pretty much perfected his sookrut to their new Beta's tastes, he was experimenting with a lot of new recipes, too. He had even made his own version of *laht*.

It had been a terrifying proposition; his hands shook as he held the first scant handful of pods Ch'ik retrieved from her ship at his request. They might not have been much to look at, but Jau felt as if he had been given a haul of priceless gems, something far too valuable for some kit from the docks to be allowed to handle. Pulsars knew his own live birth had been due to luck alone - his parental clusters couldn't have afforded even a sliver of laht.

Daunted at the possibilities the dry brown pods held within, he had carefully lined them up on the counter and stared at them for a very long time before gathering up his courage. They could be transformed into his species' most valuable prenatal supplement or, in the wrong hands, they could quickly be rendered into useless garbage. Jau was painfully aware what a huge waste a screw up would be, even with a ship full of the pods at their disposal.

He wasn't trained. He didn't have the right equipment. He was terrified of messing it up. Then, with a small laugh, Jau had realized that feeling completely out of his depth was going to be his default mode for pretty much the foreseeable future.

He didn't know anything about taking care of kits either, but he was going to have to figure it out, wasn't he? Roz could tell him if he was fucking up the parenting thing when the time came, he was the expert of their cluster on that front. The one thing Jau *could* do right now was make sure that those glowing eggs in Ch'ik had every possible chance to thrive.

After an evening's research in the *Koton's* hijacked infonet database, and a few more fractions of diligent preparation, Jau's slow and methodical pace had served him well. There were no words to describe the rush he felt as he stared down at the glossy brown block of *laht* on the counter. Absent the usual ceremonial molds used to make laht back on Oster, he'd had to settle for the smallest loaf pan they had on board. It felt almost sacrilegious. Such a huge chunk of the priceless substance seemed more like a gauche artistic statement than a culinary accomplishment, but it was far from the first time he'd flaunted cultural expectations.

After that, all that remained was getting Ch'ik to actually eat it.

The idea of asking even more from Ch'ik worried them all at first. Zul had even prepared a digital presentation about prenatal health benefits to convince her, given her strong aversion to the *dust* that she had discussed. It turned out to be a tactic that worked wonders for all the wrong reasons. Ch'ik had glared at him for the first two slides, started to fall asleep during the third, then woke herself up with a snort as her head slipped off her propped-up palm. She abruptly declared she'd try it just to get Zul to stop talking.

Thankfully for their future kits, it turned out that Ch'ik was extremely fond of the *laht*, and more than happy to eat it daily. Roz included a piece with the breakfast tray that Jau prepared every morning.

When Roz told him how Ch'ik beamed like the twin suns as she nibbled on it - Jau couldn't resist the urge to tag along and witness her enjoyment firsthand. He told himself he'd only do it once, that it was out of curiosity and nothing else. Zul begged off from joining them for the excursion, emphasizing that they shouldn't bother Ch'ik any more than was necessary.

"It's sweet." Ch'ik murmured when they'd arrived in her quarters that morning.

She had been sprawled on top of the blanket nest with her coveralls partially unzipped and stared at them through hooded eyes - probably still sleepy. Jau had shuffled in the doorway and nodded, even though he had no idea what *laht* tasted like, before hurrying away on some stuttered pretense.

Then he had jerked off alone, sprawled out on the floor of the observation deck, one hand frantic on his cock while the other pinched and twisted cruelly at his chest. His eyes had been fixed out at the crowded starfield, the infinite pinpricks of distant suns burning in the vast void, but all his mind called up was the lush vision of Ch'ik sprawled on her bed.

Afterwards, Jau realized that the *Koton's* environmental controls must not have been calibrated to Ch'ik's liking. She'd been so overheated that she'd had to lie on top of the blankets and hadn't even zipped her coveralls up. Guilt sunk low in his belly at the reprehensible thought that he'd sexualized their Beta's discomfort. As soon as Jau cleaned himself up, he adjusted the ship's temperature to a lower setting - hopefully she'd be more comfortable as they continued on.

CHAPTER 10

- ZUL -

THE DAYS STRETCHED INTO WEEKS, AND TWO fraction-cycles slipped by as the *Koton* spun its way between the stars.

Zul had managed to wave his mates off from spending too much time with Ch'ik or asking questions, cautioning her that they didn't want to discuss the pregnancy, and telling his mates the same thing. Still, Zul lay awake many nights, staring at the ceiling, while Zul and Roz dozed.

He'd broken one of the eggs, he must have - where else would that purple have come from? Sooner or later, when it came time for their kits to enter the world, his mates would find their third damaged - or worse - because of his lack of control. He wanted to cling to Ch'ik's theory about color-mixing, but their cum had never mingled colors before, so it felt like grasping at straws. Every time he tried to think about it, his brain spiraled into panic, so he avoided doing so as much as possible.

Pulsars, why hadn't he used the *bottle*? Academy education on kits was minimal to non-existent, but the process was such a simple one and he'd still managed to fuck it up. He was a *laht*-eating Beta fucker of an Alpha and he didn't deserve Jau or Roz, let alone Ch'ik. He tried to take comfort in the fact there were still *three* small lights in the occasional glimpses of her belly, but with the mortality rate of Osterian birth already so high, even the *laht* might not save a cracked egg.

As light-years spiraled out behind them, he'd been tempted to address his behavior with all of them preemptively. Each time he'd worked up the ears to talk about it at last, his brain flashed images of Ch'ik sliding down on top of him, settling him into silence. He had no idea what to make of the way he felt about her, let alone the potentially broken egg, and like they always taught him at the Academy, mission first. Piloting the ship was one of the few things he knew he could do right.

The course to Oster that Jau had mapped directed the *Koton* through a long stretch of unoccupied space. After a glance at the sensors, Zul felt comfortable enough to set the autopilot on a hold trajectory past Yonce Beta, a picturesque but uninhabited ringed planet. Rubbing out the lingering soreness from the weight of the control rig, Zul joined his cluster and Beta in the dining area, arriving as Jau set dinner down on the table. The thick, savory stew - made with a starchy root Roz had recently harvested - made his stomach growl.

Noticing the tension that still hung in the air, Jau gave him a *look*. He knew that expression - it was the one that let his fellow Alpha know he'd *absolutely had it with this shit*. Even Zul knew that the lack of connection and communication between him and Ch'ik wasn't good for the remaining kits, and it definitely wasn't good for his cluster.

Now it looked like his fellow Alpha was going to be the one to call out the spatial anomaly in the room. Zul's ears dropped, tense and anxious, as Jau set down his spoon and cleared his throat, causing all three heads to swivel his way. "Guys, listen, can we talk about what's going on here? I feel like we need to-"

The shrieking klaxon of an alarm cut him off abruptly. All three sets of sensitive Lapann ears shot up at the sound, and even Ch'ik winced, covering her ears as she looked to them for explanation.

"Hostiles incoming!" Zul jumped to his feet as the meaning of the alarm tone finally penetrated his brain. "Jau, get to the bridge and see if you can -"

Jau was already gone, big leaping bounds that rocketed him from the living quarters to the command bridge, but Roz hung back. In their usual routine of violence and piracy, his role was to run the hull piercing apparatus down in the cargo bay - currently inoperable due to the presence of the *Aeon Hawk*.

Desperate to feel useful, Roz had apparently figured the best use of his strength would be to protect their Beta. Unfortunately, she never seemed to *want* protection. There were days where Zul swore she had a death wish, particularly with her cavalier attitude for "repairing" her own ship. It was a small miracle she'd only fried a few circuits and not her vital organs.

Roz glanced at the door Jau had disappeared through, giving him a pointed look. Zul nodded his assent: his Omega was naturally driven to safeguard their Beta, and that meant isolating her from any projectile fire. Zul set his mug down and gestured towards Roz. "Ch'ik, hurry, Roz will take you to a panic pod in the -"

"*Fuck* that!" Ch'ik shoved a bite of the stew into her mouth and waved the empty spoon at Roz as she shoved away from the table. "What, I can't run a targeter because I'm knocked up? I'm coming with you guys."

She strode out of the room, shouldering roughly past Zul and Roz. After a moment's hesitation and a wordless glance between them, he tugged his Omega's arm as they hurried after her, anxiety palpable, to the bridge.

Jau had already dropped into the control array, sliding the programmed yoke off of the autopilot and onto his own shoulders as he took stock of the situation. Roz hung in the doorway, ears tense and swung forward. Without an assigned spot on the bridge, Zul knew he was doing his best to keep his protective instincts in check.

Looking up, Zul frowned. At first glance the visual field showed nothing other than the ringed purple planet and a vast starfield beyond, but he kept his eyes fixed, waiting. The sensors were all screaming as loudly as his military instincts: there was something there, hidden out of sight under the rings of the planet. There was no way he was going to let it catch him unaware, especially not with their pregnant Beta on board.

Zul dropped into his own command chair, scrolling through the ship control interfaces in hurried preparation. Even as he honed in on his familiar training, his thoughts tangled with worry Ch'ik was angry at him for trying to send her to safety. When he tilted his gaze up to see if she was still pissed, he found her glaring silently at the main visual field.

The unmistakable triangular wedge of an attack ship suddenly cruised into view. A drape of particles flowed off of the ship's iridescent shielding. Detritus from where it had risen up through the rings of the planet cascaded out into empty space. Ice, dust, and chunks of rock that had hovered in orbit for millennia had now formed a plume of debris behind the menacing cruiser. The same ship that, incidentally, had all of its substantial firepower trained on the *Koton*.

Roz's ears were plastered to his head, dark eyes glittering with protective Omega rage. "What the *hell* is that?"

Zul scowled and hissed an Osteran curse, stabbing a button on the research console. "Can't lift the damn registration yet, but with that kind of artillery it's gotta be a merc ship."

Jau stared back over his shoulder at Zul, brow furrowed. "Who the hell did we manage to piss off? We haven't been hitting anyone with those types of connections!"

Before Zul could consider if any of the many furious lifeforms they'd left in their wake would have sicced a mercenary on them, an ear-splitting trill blasted through the bridge. The other ship was attempting to hail the *Koton*; a second later the mercenary's credentials finally popped up in the bottom of the visual field. A long scroll of imperium licenses unrolled under a holo-bust identification image.

Ch'ik groaned out loud as soon as she saw it, and all three Lapann turned to face her. Zul reached across the command console and slapped the comm mute to cut out the piercing ring and the alarm sirens, but the tense, painful silence that followed was by no means an improvement. Roz was practically vibrating at the physical distance between himself and the upset Beta. He rushed over to Ch'ik and took one of her hands in both of his own, eyes big and concerned.

"What's wrong? Are you hurt?" His big pink hands enfolded her own.

"*He's* what's wrong, Roz." Ch'ik tipped her head towards the identification screen, pinched the bridge of her nose with her free hand, and sighed with irritation.

"That's my ex."

CHAPTER 11
- JAU -

Their stunned silence was split by the piercing wail of the hail request as the mercenary ship, bristling with precision weaponry, attempted to contact them again.

"His name is Dr'ec." Ch'ik muttered, hardly audible over the whooping alarms. She pushed her hair back out of her face with a huff, only to have it immediately fall forward again. "And he's a real pain in the ass."

The hail notification had reproduced a holographic bust of the mercenary in question; a visual that left Jau speechless.

Furious eyes with red sclera and white irises glared out, unseeing, from the holographic imprint. Pale face scales, dark around the edges, were set into an elongated saurid skull. The end of his rounded snout was capped with a sharp beak tooth inlaid with black metal engravings; an ugly accessory that looked no better on him than it had the Lurquers. Atop his head, a mohawk of rusty red feathers swept up and back, forming a regal-looking crest. The feathers tapered down into a pelt that covered his neck and shoulders, and a burnished metal whole-arm prosthesis was partly visible on the right. Dr'ec's expression, caught just before the hail attempt, indicated this was not a happy reunion.

Jau blinked, blindly smacking at the console to mute the ringing again. He glanced at the hologram bust before he finally managed to comment.

"Wow. That's - he's - uh, really something."

Ch'ik rolled her eyes, turning to glare out the side window, as if withering side-eye could disarm sonic cannons. "Don't be too impressed. It's fake."

Jau shook his head to clear it, clicking the bust off the view screen. "Huh? What do you mean fake? The ship?"

"His crest." Ch'ik gestured at the top of her own head, the short fluff of blond hair. "It's fake. He wears an imitation one because he's too insecure to admit that he's balding. Those feathers are all synthetic."

"Oh. Uhm, alright. I wasn't looking at his *crest*. I was just thinking that you weren't kidding about fucking your way through the weirdest looking alien species in the quadrant." Jau spun in his control chair, kicking a lever under the counter to activate their battle shielding.

Ch'ik gave a sharp snort of a laugh, as if it had been startled out of her. The sound caused something warm to stir inside of Jau, something soft and at precarious odds with the dangerous situation unfolding around them.

Zul was hunched over in his own command chair, ears perked up in concentration as he ran through the *Koton*'s battle systems, bringing them online and checking for functionality. At her laugh, he turned away from the interface, puzzled. "What's so funny?"

The hail signal rang again. Jau reached out automatically to slap the mute button - again. It silenced the grating chime, but not the new live holo-shot, which showed Dr'ec's face twisted into a snarl. The inside of his saurine maw was bristling with jagged, needle-like teeth, each glistening with a bad aftermarket plating job.

"Rude." Ch'ik finally responded, wrinkling her nose at him without any real malice. "That's my species you're talking about, you know."

"Wait, *What*?" Jau's eyes flicked up and down her body, those luscious curves he shouldn't think about. That he *definitely wasn't* thinking about while his cluster was on the edge of battle. *Fuck.*

Ch'ik gestured idly, crouching in front of an unmanned console and tapping it to life. "Yeah, our males look a lot different. We got some big time sexual dimorphism on Rizen."

Before any of them had a chance to comment, or even fully process that particular bombshell, the tone of the alarms changed. A series of red reticles appeared across the silhouette of the other ship, indicating the guns locked onto the *Koton* had started to charge. The hailing ringtone began to trill again.

"He's just going to keep calling, the persistent fuck." Ch'ik growled and slid her hand down her face. "Might as well pick up and see what he wants." She flicked an annoyed gesture at Zul, nodding. He frowned, clearly unhappy with the progression of events, but acquiesced and opened the comm link.

"CH'IK!" The raptor-like alien's voice was surprisingly high and annoying, belying the fierce expression he'd turned on the holo-imager.

"Shove it, Dr'ec. Stop following me all over the fucking galaxy or I swear to the pulsars I'm going to tell the Imperium where that shipment of tiramite actually ended up."

He hissed, but the sound was forced and caused him to break into a weak cough, instantly ruining the intimidation he'd been going for. "In case you haven't noticed, I'm a *mercenary* you stupid bitch. It's my *job*."

A loud, sharp thump echoed through the bridge - Jau instantly recognized the Lapann aggression reflex. He was shocked: he'd *never* seen their even-tempered Omega stomp. From the look in Roz's eyes, he was about to find a way to jump through the comm and tear the crest off that shrill little piece of ejecta if he insulted their Beta again.

She huffed, rolling her eyes. "Well, genius, last time I checked I didn't have any contracts out on me. So who do I have to thank for the distinct displeasure of your company?"

Dr'ec fell silent, his jaw working as he clenched his teeth, looking off to the side uncomfortably.

Ch'ik scoffed, jabbing a hand through her hair again, making it puff out like a crown of war in the overhead lights. Jau had to squeeze his thighs together in the chair to keep his knot under control. If she was beautiful normally, she was absolutely radiant when she was pissed off. Delectably dangerous.

Ch'ik's voice dropped an octave with cold fury and Jau was forced to turn awkwardly in his chair to hide his erection. "You absolute piece of SHIT! You aren't even here on a *job?* You're stalking me across the quadrant and ambushing my boyfriends for *fun?*"

All three sets of Lapann ears went rigidly upright, the three of them sharing a frantic, wild glance at the title.

Boyfriends? Did she just call them *boyfriends?* Jau shoved the shock to the back of his mind, desperately reminding himself the other ship had enough firepower to smear them across the stars.

Dr'ec's uncomfortable silence was, unfortunately for everyone, short-lived. "You *ghosted* me. I woke up and you weren't on the ship and all your things were gone, and-"

Ch'ik stabbed a finger at the holo-imager, furious. "You *never* listened to me, I told you I was leaving! Why else would I have packed up all of my stuff? I did it right in front of you!"

Dr'ec threw his robotic hand up in the air in a gesture of exasperation. "I thought you meant leaving to go get that Lamerian lingerie I told you to wear! All your stuff was trash! I thought you were taking it out. Well, I guess you *did* after all."

Her eyes widened, the galactic signal for *you done fucked up now, man.* "Oooo, you fucker, I -"

He sneered unkindly. "Finally found a male willing to look past your hideous deformities and you chuck the opportunity out an airlock."

Ch'ik choked with disbelief. "...aaaand this is one of eight *billion* reasons why I left. I *told* you I was sick of your shit ass attitude and the fucking *terrible* sex-"

"You stupid spaceport slut! You're lucky a Rizen male was even willing to- " the loud *thump* of another stomp landed from a different direction, momentarily drowning out the squabble. Jau turned to find Zul's ear flicking like it was a plasma sword ready to eviscerate Dr'ec.

Jau swallowed a groan. He wanted to fuck every person on the bridge *right fucking now*. Pulsars, he could barely concentrate on defense when his cluster insisted on being so hot. He couldn't help he was wired almost as fucking weird as the *Aeon Hawk*. Whether it was pain, fighting, or just the threat of danger - Jau had always been a massive adrenaline junkie, and his cock was hard enough to punch through the shields at the moment.

Was that asshole still *talking?*

"-and that's not even half the credits I lost with that shit you pulled. Hand over the cargo I know you're hauling and maybe I'll let you and your pets live." Dr'ec ran a hand over his crest, bending one of the synthetic feathers at an unnatural angle.

With a growl, Ch'ik reached across Zul, stabbing her finger against the button to disconnect the call, unceremoniously cutting Dr'ec off.

"I'll be right back!" Ch'ik spun around and dashed off the bridge.

Zul raised a brow - Jau knew from experience the *Koton's* captain did not like having his command console fondled. "Wait, what? Where are you going?"

Ch'ik shouted something back over her shoulder before she disappeared out into the corridor, but her words were lost in the howl of alarms as the mercenary ship fired upon them.

"Son of a -" Jau thanked his lucky stars he'd already been immersed in the control array. If they'd had to boot it up, he wouldn't have been able to roll the ship in time to avoid the devastating red streak of energy.

CHAPTER 12

- ZUL -

EVEN WITH JAU'S LIGHTNING-FAST REFLEXES ON
their side, the laser fire came within a whisker's width
of the *Koton's* shields. Zul grit his teeth. The ship could
take one, maybe two, good hits from a weapons system
as advanced as Dr'ec's before the shielding reserves
were exhausted. The *Koton* was an excellent grappler
but there were good reasons that their cluster didn't
fuck with militaries or mercenaries.

Fleeing the encounter would have been the obvious
choice if not for Zul's suspicion that they wouldn't be
able to outrun the mercenary ship. The best thing to do
would be to take evasive maneuvers until they could
figure out something, anything to save their asses.

"Jau, evasi-"

"Already on it!" Jau called back as he spun the Koton down into the thick, obscuring cloud of ice and particulates that composed Yonce-Beta's orbital rings.

Zul turned to Roz, who was looking increasingly fraught with divided concern, giving his Omega the direction he needed. "Follow Ch'ik. Make sure she doesn't fall and snap her neck if I have to reroute power from the lighting systems."

Roz dipped his head in deference to his Alpha even though he was already starting after her. As Roz bounded off the bridge Zul gripped the edge of the console and gave himself a few heartbeats to focus, confident in his mates.

Lapann were not a telepathic species - though pulsars knew that Zul still wouldn't be able to communicate worth a damn even if they were - but they were a true cluster. A well-oiled machine, they all knew their roles when things went sideways. Zul was thankful they didn't mind his tendency to fall back on his Command Academy training, snapping orders as if they were all green cadets instead of a tried-and-tested crew.

Jau spun the ship and plowed through a darker patch in the rings, a grey field composed of some highly ferrous mineral. The dull crystalline cloud muddled the Koton's visual field as the magnetics scrambled the navigational sensors. Jau was calm, but Zul damn near stopped breathing as he watched his mate fly though instinct alone. He rapidly shifted shield support where it was needed, and tried not to focus on the fact that this ship carried everything he had in the universe. That everything he loved in the entire galaxy - including his kits and, just maybe, the Beta carrying them too - was under fire and might be destroyed. He'd unpack that particular revelation when they weren't at death's airlock.

The visual field lit up with lancing beams of red that streaked around them as the mercenary ship fired indiscriminately through the thick cloud. The ship jerked and shuddered as one of the blasts caught the *Koton's* flank in a glancing blow. If Dr'ec could afford to be so careless with his ammunition power, Zul knew their only hope of survival was getting outside of the mercenary ship's firing range.

Ch'ik reappeared on the bridge as suddenly as she had left, a forlorn-looking Roz in tow. Zul glanced over his shoulder for a second and was startled to see that she had rolled her coveralls down and tied the sleeves around her waist, braless beneath the sleeveless white undershirt, her toned arms exposed to the cool ship environment. Her taped-up black canvas duffle bag was slung across her back, the strap cutting across her chest and the softly glowing barely-swell of her belly.

CHAPTER 13

- ROZ -

THE DRAWSTRING AT THE OPENING OF THE DUFFEL had loosened enough to reveal a sliver of the contents, an incomprehensible tangle of cables and wires peeking out from the gap. Ch'ik simply ignored the few questions Roz attempted to ask, brushing off all of his efforts to help with the obviously heavy burden.

This wasn't the time for questions, Roz reminded himself, even though his ears drooped sadly of their own volition. He had to protect Ch'ik, even if she seemed wildly unconcerned with her own well-being. That bag, whatever it contained, was obviously important to her, which meant it needed to be important to him, too. She was already irritated at the situation and he didn't want to make it worse, but his anxiety was almost as loud as the ship's cacophonous din of alerts.

Jau hauled on the steering array with an angry growl as another beam sizzled through the black around them, too close for comfort. Roz grabbed Ch'ik and pulled her down into one of the bridge's padded benches as the *Koton* lurched. Alarms blared as Jau abruptly switched direction, zig-zagging their flight path to minimize targeting opportunities.

Flying nearly blind, Zul worked with him to keep the ship hidden as they dove into the ring of orbiting ice particles. Whipping around a chunk of rock the size of a city, they narrowly avoided a volley of shots from the enemy ship. Ch'ik tugged on a stuck zipper tab, muttering to herself, seemingly oblivious to the mortal danger slicing lances of red light at their ship.

Zul hissed as he redirected their ship's shielding a scant moment before the rock they were using for cover burst apart under a hail of laser fire. Roz's grip went knuckle white on the back of the bench as *Koton* was pelted with the boulder-sized debris. He slung an arm around Ch'ik's shoulders, heart racing at the contact, but he shoved down the joy of touching her again in favor of ensuring his body could protect hers. He knew his cluster and his ship couldn't last much longer in this firefight, and the cold dread of it made his arms feel numb.

Even with the shields, the impacts rocked the bridge. Jau's teeth clicked together audibly as he directed the ship into a serpentine spin through the planet's rings.

The momentum pinned all of them in place for a long, breathless moment, Ch'ik pressing against Roz's side and chest. He tightened his arm around her, letting her scent settle his fraying nerves and galvanize his protective instincts.

When their momentum relented, Ch'ik eased away, though it wasn't hurried - a discovery he promptly stashed in his brain to obsess over later. She patted around the edges of the padded bench, leaning down to peek underneath. " Roz, this thing have a restraint harness hiding anywhere?"

Roz shook his head, giving a worried glance at his cluster-mates at the helm. "No, we don't typically need them. Why?"

"Alright." Ch'ik turned and clasped Roz's face between her palms, looking him directly in the eyes and giving a firm pat to his cheek. "Then I'm gonna need you to hold me down, big guy."

"*What?*" His body sure liked the idea, and he hoped his coveralls wouldn't immediately make that obvious. This was *not* the time.

Ch'ik hauled the big bag up to rest in between her legs and plunged her left arm through the opening at the top of it, all the way down to her elbow. When she pulled her arm free it was swathed in hardware and trailing wires, a messy sleeve of indeterminate technology. Roz didn't know what the hell he was looking at, but some primal part of his brain read it as danger. His Beta was in danger. He didn't like the metallic-solder smell of whatever that *thing* was.

Twisting her wrist in the center of the tangle caused the mess to snap together into a whole-arm gauntlet that stretched from fingertips to shoulder. Electromagnetic cushioning kept the components separated as the machinery began to hum quietly. Tiny lights, recessed in channels along the more substantial parts of the hardware, blinked to life.

Ch'ik stopped long enough to pop a black plastic bite guard into her mouth. Then she twisted again, this time plunging her right hand down into the battered duffel bag. Roz wished for a frantic moment she'd just gotten in the goddamn panic pod when Zul told her to. What the hell was she up to?

"Hey Jau!" Ch'ik called out, yanking the bite guard out again to talk. Roz frowned at the bag opening, watching her withdraw the other half of the inscrutable device. It looked like it could have been a distant relative of Jau's control array, but he couldn't tell what it controlled since it wasn't hooked into anything except itself.

"Yeah?" Jau growled through clenched teeth, barely avoiding another cutting beam of red.

"I need you to get closer to him!" Her eye twitched in discomfort as something hydraulic hissed near her left forearm. Roz growled low, wanting to tear it off her skin and dash it against the bulkhead.

"You want us to board his ship?" Zul sputtered, spinning his chair to face her. "We can't, Ch'ik! We'd have to jettison the *Hawk*."

"No! Just get closer!" Ch'ik's right arm was now also sheathed in coiled cables from elbow to wrist. Roz noticed her give another pained flinch, but before he could reach out and crush whatever was hurting his Beta, Jau pulled another tight turn, making everyone scramble for hand holds.

"How close?" Jau let out a sharp, short sigh of relief as another shot went wide, missing them.

Ch'ik stopped to think about it for a second, then nodded quickly to herself. "Definitely within his firing range." Then she turned the full force of her attention back to Roz.

"Hold. Me. Down." She repeated her earlier order, staring him down with a stern look.

Her eyes flashed with a calculating look before her voice softened to a whisper. "I know I can count on you, can't I, my big, strong Omega?" Roz's brain buzzed with pleasure. Even with death looming over them all, Roz would follow her out an airlock with a tone like that.

Even though he'd been pulled between confusion and concern, both emotions were jettisoned in favor of a deep desire to do whatever she told him to. He ached to pin her again, to put his face in her neck, breathe in her scent, and never, ever stop. But that warm curl in his heart was promptly doused a moment later.

"Roz, I'm going to have a seizure when I slip the math into his system. Hold me down and make sure I don't break anything important."

A seizure?

Ch'ik laid back with a thump on the bench, crossing her arms over her chest. Her skin, pale as starlight, stood out in bands between the machinery. It seemed to glow brighter than the lights on the coils of humming cables, brighter than the new eggs in her belly.

"Is that safe?" Roz frowned, eyes glued to her arms.

She shrugged. "Safe enough."

"But what if -" He plucked at one of the cords looped near her stomach with large pink fingertips, questioning.

"Just don't let me fall off the bench." Ch'ik cut him off, tone hard. "Your precious *eggs* will be fine. If anything gets fried, it'll be my brain, not my body."

"That wasn't what -" He realized where his hand had gone, where she must have thought his concerns originated. Of course he worried about his family, but *her* safety was just as important to him - to all of them.

"Yeah. Sure." Ch'ik slapped a sticky sensor in the center of her forehead and laid back down with her arms along her sides.

Roz huffed with irritation. "Can you *please* stop cutting me off all the time, Ch'ik? I was-"

Ch'ik stared at him, flat and unapologetic, shoving the bite guard back in her mouth. Roz obediently positioned himself to kneel over her. Taking a deep breath, he straddled her hips, hands holding her shoulders down against the springy foam cushion.

"-trying to say. If you have a seizure it's gotta be bad for your brain, and-"

Before Roz could finish, Ch'ik cut him off. Again. Wordlessly, this time, but another interruption nonetheless. As he tried to explain himself, the mechanical hum suddenly became much louder. Her eyes rolled into the back of her head, showing only white as her body went limp underneath his.

Roz dropped his head and braced himself above Ch'ik's prone body, fear flooding his veins. The tangle of equipment wrapped around her arms poked him lightly in the chest as another shift in velocity pinned them both down to the crash couch. He grimaced at the gravity, but held himself up, even though he wanted to crush the whole confusing mess of components into useless little fragments.

Ch'ik had ordered him to hold her down but so far she'd just...laid there. He didn't know what was going on, only that his protective instincts were in overdrive at the sight and feel of her limp body. Her breathing was so shallow that her chest hardly moved, mouth slack and open as if she were - he couldn't even think it.

As if something *really bad* had happened to her.

No. That wouldn't happen. Roz wouldn't let it. That was what he told himself again and again as he closed his eyes and prayed to the pulsars that Zul and Jau got them through this.

CHAPTER 14

- JAU -

"Roz! What's going on?" Zul barked from beside him, attention pulled by their defense. They were both familiar enough with Roz's noises of distress to realize something was going on.

"I don't know! She's -" rustling noises and the faint metallic scrape of machinery, barely audible beneath the annoying persistent velocity indicator, issued from the back of the bridge. "Can we just grapple him already, guys? He won't shoot us if we're attached to his ship, right?"

Zul shared a look with Jau across the command bridge, grinding his teeth with fury at their attackers as he prepared the pedipalps. There wasn't time to figure out what was going on. Everything was moving too fast. There was no plan, no formulated contingency for this situation, but Ch'ik had told them to get closer.

Alright, then. He'd get them closer.

Jau sent the *Koton* careening back into the planet's rings, the mercenary ship right on their fuzzy little tails as he cut the thrusters and dropped their angle. He kept an eye on the proximity system, shivering on the edge of his seat as he waited for the mercenary ship to overtake them.

Dr'ec was a sloppy flier, Jau discovered that much already during the brief chase. Ch'ik's ex relied much too heavily on the quality of his equipment rather than developing actual piloting skills. His reaction time would be just a bit too slow to match Jau's sudden deceleration. All Jau had to do was to think in four dimensions, account for the ice interference with their sensor array, and wait until the exact moment when the ship rocketed past them.

If he'd managed to time everything perfectly, this might actually work. If not, well, they wouldn't have much time to worry about the consequences.

Jau threw everything that the *Koton* had into the upward impulse engines, slamming into the belly of the other ship.

It was closer than he had anticipated. A pained groan of metal split through the screaming sensors as the two ships collided. The force of the impact snapped Jau's face against the control array, whipping him back against the headrest. An arcing spray of blood droplets hung suspended in the air until the gravity drive re-engaged and they splattered to the floor. Jau was too physically stunned to realize that it was *his* blood, from a cut on *his* face, until he heard the familiar hydraulic whine of Zul engaging the grapplers.

The communications module started to bray again as the mercenary ship attempted to hail them, but Zul slammed the mute button. In a minute, Dr'ec would start flying faster, trying to shake them off. It was the same thing most captains did when a grappler like the *Koton* attached itself to their ship like a plasma lamprey. Nevermind that wasn't how momentum worked - panic always took over.

Jau shrugged himself out of the control array and wiped a hand across his bloody face as he stepped back, catching Zul's stare as he lifted his head. They weren't clear of the danger yet, not by a long shot, but nothing got Jau's blood up quite like pain. He was always like that - fighting or flying or fucking, it didn't make a difference - but Zul's expression, that knowing look, warned Jau to keep it in his pants until a more appropriate moment.

Still, he held Zul's eyes when he stuck the bloody digits of one hand into his own mouth while he adjusted his erection with the other. There wasn't much they could do now except sit and wait while Ch'ik did whatever she was doing - if Jau had to deal with his stupid dick being obnoxious then he at least wanted to make sure Zul suffered too. Not Roz, though. Seemed like the big guy had his hands full with their rowdy Beta.

"Roz, what's -" Jau leaned around the console to check on his mate, but stopped short when he saw the tangle of hardware on Ch'ik. "Whoa. Is that a proximity hacker?"

"I don't know? Is it?" Roz shifted, uncomfortable and frantic for an answer.

"Those things are super dangerous." Zul muttered, rubbing at a sore spot in his neck from the whiplash of their sudden attachment. He hadn't recognized the device before, but as Jau identified it everything slipped into place.

"Super illegal too." Jau wiped at the blood on his forehead, stuck his fingers in his mouth to lick the blood off before he noticed the slope of Roz's shoulders. "But, uh, mostly safe."

Zul snorted. "Mostly."

Jau sighed. Could the blue idiot not see their Omega was on the verge of freaking out? No, of course he wouldn't. Sometimes Jau swore they grew Sook with more emotional intelligence than his fellow Alpha. "Zul. Not helping. I'm sure that Ch'ik will be-"

They were all momentarily distracted by the scene on the view screens - Dr'ec had dropped to skim along the surface of a tumbling chunk of rock, as if he were going to try to scrape them off. Jau rolled his eyes. Even an idiot knew that doing so would easily destroy both ships. If Dr'ec was waiting for Jau's confidence to falter, for him to lose the staring contest with an ill-timed blink, then he had another thing coming.

"Oh *shit!*"

The panic in Roz's voice immediately drew their attention. He and Zul watched helplessly as Roz scrambled to restrain Ch'ik. She'd started to spasm underneath him, body arching and going rigid by turns.

She twisted up and arched tight against Roz's bulk, eyes rolled back in her head so that only the whites were visible. A wet gurgling noise filled the bridge as her head thrashed from side to side. Her jaw cracked open, a thick white foam of tiny bubbles boiling between her parted lips, spilled up and out to drip down the side of her face. Her mouth contorted into a pale rictus sneer that made Jau's blood run cold.

"Fuck fuck *fuck.*" Roz's voice had become a whisper of a scream, his ears so tight to his head they were hardly even visible. He used his body to angle hers to the side, ensuring that gravity wouldn't cause her to choke on the foam of her own saliva.

Then, abruptly, the seizure stopped. She dropped down limp to the padded bench, quiet and still as whatever evil had possessed her finally vanished back into the aether.

Ch'ik groaned. Roz cupped her face in both of his hands. Jau had reached out blindly, his hand tangling into Zul's, the two of them squeezing their mutual grip in terror. Jau's heart stuttered in his throat as he watched her eyes, flickering, focusing, and finally, blessedly blinking in consciousness.

"Alright." She sniffed, giving a slight cough, as if she hadn't almost fried her goddamn synapses.

"Alright?" Zul sputtered in disbelief, voicing the stress that had pulled all of them tight enough to shatter.

"Yeah." Ch'ik sat up and rubbed at her face, grimacing as she wiped the foam of spittle off of her cheek. "Got him. Break us off, Zul."

Zul rushed back to the console to disengage the pedipalps. Roz hovered over Ch'ik, gently holding her steady, his anxiety almost visible. She gently waved Roz off, swinging her bare legs off the edge of the bench and sitting up to squint at the visual field. His expression stricken as he shared a look of anguish with Jau, Roz gripped the edge of the bench seat to keep his hands off of Ch'ik. Together, the four of them watched the mercenary ship zip away from the *Koton*, banking up away from the debris field before they could re-engage the grappling gear.

"Hate to break this to you," Zul called out from the command chair as he studied the enemy ship's movements, "but I don't think you did. He's circling back around on us."

Ch'ik shook her head, undaunted by Zul's morose tone. She spit the bite guard out onto the bench and grimaced. "It'll shut him down in a minute or two. That math takes some time to propagate."

"What does that even mean?" Jau forced his eyes off the discarded bite guard, which only led him into dangerous, addictive thoughts of letting Ch'ik absolutely wail on him in a practice ring. *Pulsars* he was fucked up sometimes.

"It doesn't matter." Ch'ik gave a cracking yawn as she twisted her right arm to disengage the hardware that had wrapped around it. Roz held out the bag so that she could let it slide off her hand and coil back down, scowling fiercely at the tangle when Ch'ik was looking elsewhere. "Has he been pinging you still?"

"Yeah. How'd you know?" Jau nodded towards the hail screen with an eyeroll.

"He's always been a pain in the ass. Don't take any more evasive action, just hail him back. I wanna make sure he stays distracted until his system is totally wrecked."

Ch'ik shoved her hair, gone wild with static electricity, off her face.

"We're totally exposed here." Jau reminded her, because whatever plan their crazy little Beta had in mind, he wasn't in the loop. His forehead had stopped bleeding, but he still kept one hand pressed against it, relishing the zings of pain that the applied pressure sent racing across his nerves.

Ch'ik shook her head ruefully. "He won't shoot at us as long as I'm talking to him. He just wants someone to pay attention to his dumbshit whining. Actually, can you guys leave the room for a sec? He's more likely to ramble if he thinks he has my undivided attention."

Roz stubbornly folded his arms across his chest - Jau noticed that he'd zipped the duffel bag tightly closed and dropped it out of Ch'ik's reach. Knowing his Omega, he'd "store" that infernal equipment somewhere she'd never find it, if they made it through this alive.

"Jau and Zul can go into the hallway if they want, but I'm staying here. I'll make sure I'm off-screen." Roz held up a hand, stopping her protests as she opened her mouth to voice them. "I'll be quiet. Sorry, got angry earlier when that piece of space trash was talking that way to you. I can't have you out of my sight right now, Ch'ik. Please, for my own sake."

She nodded with a resigned look. Zul reached over and hit the hail button as Ch'ik positioned herself in front of the imager. Jau grabbed him, tugging him out of the imager view.

Dr'ec's whiny voice blasted the bridge. "Oh, so now you'll talk to me?"

The red feathers of his synthetic crest were slightly askew, but he still had an insufferable look of smug satisfaction on his snouted face.

Zul snapped his fingers towards Jau and flicked his eyes out towards the corridor. Jau couldn't hide the eagerness in his answering nod, the throbbing anticipation in his body. He pressed a few buttons to re-engage the autopilot, following Zul out as the arguing resumed.

"...wow, I almost forgot how terrible you are, asshole."

"*I'm* the terrible one, Ch'ik? You forgot my birthday *ten times.*"

"For fucks sake, this again? Those were *not* real birthdays! You can't recalculate time in every star system-"

Jau went up on his toes to muffle a laugh against Zul's collar as they fumbled against each other in the hall. He may have been smaller than the other Alpha, by far the shortest one in their cluster, but Zul was a nerd. Jau loved him, but it was true. Zul might have been the big strong Alpha when he ordered Roz around - much to Roz's delight, of course - but Zul turned into an entirely different Lapann when Jau got his blood up.

Jau slid one booted foot forward to catch Zul's ankle and hook his legs apart so that their hips could slot together. Once he had his fellow Alpha properly unbalanced, he roughly shoved Zul back against the bulkhead in the corridor. Jau's laugh quickly stuttered into a rough moan as Zul's fingers tripped up along the front of his coveralls, looking for the zipper tab. Jau scraped his front teeth across the mating bite hidden under the neck ruff of Zul's blue fur.

"Ch'ik sounds mad." Zul muttered as he finally got Jau's coveralls unzipped.

Jau panted as he pulled back just far enough to return the favor before he pressed forward again so that they were chest to chest. Knot to knot.

"Yeah. Yeah she does."

"She should..." Zul lost his thought as Jau rubbed their cocks together. "She should, uh, probably calm -"

"She should let us fuck her. In front of him." The answering thought slipped out of him before he could stop it.

A shocked sound tore its way out of Zul's throat, and Jau's ears dropped as a rush of regret and cold fear surged through him.

Oh shit. He had gone too far. He should *not* have said that. What the fuck was he thinking? A burning apology immediately lodged in his throat. He shouldn't be talking about someone else while they were-

Then Zul's cock twitched against Jau's. The taller Alpha made another noise, high and needy, as his hands scrambled against Jau's shoulders, his hips fucking up into the grip Jau had around their cocks. Zul babbled, coming undone with lust, a torrent of words spilling out in a heated, conspiratorial whisper. "Yeah, yeah, oh *fuck*. Yeah we should, we should screw her right - unh - right in front of the screen while he watches -"

Oh. *Oh, fuck* was right.

Zul was as turned on as he was at the idea of fucking Ch'ik. Jau's blood was on fire. His brain went spiraling off into a cascade of previously-forbidden possibilities, savoring the new realization he wasn't alone in his fantasies.

Then, it was Zul who pulled back. Jau saw the same worry in Zul's eyes that was tugging at his own chest. He surged up to claim Zul's mouth with his own, anxious to silence it in both of them. The kiss was more filthy than comforting, but that was its own reassurance - if they were indulging in a fantasy so taboo they could barely voice it, then at least they were in it together.

Ch'ik's voice filtered into the hallway, sharp and irritated. "You don't get to recalculate planetary alignment to get a new birthday for every new star system you visit!"

Again that grating whine. "Well I should! Especially since you blew my arm off!"

Alright, well. *That* wasn't exactly the type of violence that Jau was into from, like, a personal perspective. But he was horny enough to ignore it. Especially when Zul was panting against him, cock was already leaking blue beads of fluid that smeared across them both. Jau reached his free hand down and hooked it under Zul's knee, hiking his mate's leg up around his hip so he could fuck against him better. Jau pointedly looked down as he swiped his thumb across his mate's leaking tip, tilting his head up to give Zul a sharp-edged grin.

"That really gets you wet huh? Thinking about stripping Ch'ik down and fucking her right there on the control panel. Getting this fat knot in her. Making her scream our names while-" Jau relinquished his grip on their dicks to spit in his palm, slathering it across their knots as his fingers curled again. "-while that mercenary piece of shit watches and jerks off in his fuckin' jumpsuit because *he can't have what's ours.*"

"Oh!" Zul gasped as Jau treated him to a particularly vicious twist of his palm that pressed the slick heads of their cocks together. "Oh, fuck. Yeah, Jau. *Yeah.* He could see..."

Jau leaned in to nip at his mating bite scar on Zul. "What? What are you gonna show him, Z? Are you gonna stretch her open while she sucks me off and -"

And wasn't *that* a thought. Ch'ik's smart, soft mouth licking at him - not the type of thing that a Beta would *ever* do back home. It was a ridiculous idea, so outlandish it was laughable, but Jau could envision it, clear as the twin suns. That visual, combined with the throbbing pain from his forehead cut and the feel of Zul's shaft on his, drove him feral with want.

Zul cupped Jau's shoulder for balance, stroking his thumb slowly and deliberately across his own mating bite on Jau's neck. The tender gesture brought Jau briefly out of their frenzy, confused, but the taller Alpha continued, wrenching a breathless, broken moan out of him.

"We would - he could see the eggs, Jau. He would have to look at Ch'ik and see them in her, know that *we* did it. That we knocked her up, that Roz put our kits in her and, and -"

It was too much for words, and their frenzied mating dissolved into frantic thrusting, pleasure-seeking with an energy they hadn't kindled since they'd first formed a cluster. Jau mercilessly fucked against the taller Alpha, driving him aggressively back against the wall as if he could knot him without penetration. Zul let him shove and push, lost in his own pleasure, fucking up into Jau's grip and using his own hand to make it even tighter. Jau's lean body went whipcord-tight, trembling as his movements grew rapturously instinctual.

Zul broke first, choking Jau's name, spurting up into their twin grip in hot gushes that sprayed into their belly and chest fur. Jau, unable to resist the slick glide of his mate's cum, quickly doubled it, his hips kicking sharply against Zul as he chased his own release.

Panting, he leaned up to mouth against Zul's collarbone as they pressed their bodies together, riding out the last of the aftershocks with a tight roll of his hips that made Zul's tail twitch. They weren't tied together, but it was just nice to stay pressed against each other, to wordlessly breathe in the scent of his mate. Jau's higher brain functions were still overwhelmed at the forbidden fantasy that they somehow, unknowingly, shared.

Through his post-coital buzz, the argument blasting across the bridge seemed tinny, and far away. Still, the furious voices shifted through the edges of his awareness as Zul cheek-marked against the mating bite on Jau's neck affectionately.

"...and you still haven't apologized!" The saurian sounded like a petulant child. What had Ch'ik ever seen in that guy?

"I'm not going to! I told you not to touch my stuff!"

"What kind of crazy bitch puts *vaporization mines* in her underwear drawer?"

"What kind of *dickhead* doesn't listen when some crazy bitch tells him to leave her stuff alone?"

"Hold on. What the fuck? Something's wrong with my ship -"

As the comm on the bridge went finally, mercifully silent, Jau gave a last little lick to the mating bite scar he'd made so many cycles ago, leaning back to give Zul a lazy smile. Zul's attention, however, was drawn down to their cum-streaked fur. His mate's ears were dropped back in contemplation.

"Z?" Jau rolled his hips playfully, drawing an appreciative groan from an overstimulated Zul. "What's up?"

"Our colors didn't mix either." He murmured, distracted now, drowsy and fucked out enough that he wasn't paying attention to his choice of words.

"Uh, obviously?" Jau wondered if he'd literally screwed his mate's brains out. "Wait. What do you mean *either*? When have they ever-" His question was cut off by a flurry of voices from the bridge.

"Ch'ik? Are your arms okay? Do you need -"

"Fuckin' - quit it! I know how to stand up on my own." Ch'ik was spitting mad, from the sounds of it, and damned if that didn't make Jau's dick twitch with appreciation all over again.

"I know! I know you do, I'm trying to *help!*" Roz's composure had finally cracked. "Stop biting my ears off!"

"Stop treating me like I can't do shit!" A loud slam of indeterminate origin.

Zul and Jau stood frozen against the wall, cocks out and fur wet with ribbons of colorful semen, as Ch'ik stormed past them. They hadn't even had time to reach for the zippers on their coveralls before she disappeared in the direction of the cargo bay.

CHAPTER 15
- CH'IK -

CH'IK SHOVED AN ARM THROUGH THE TOP OF HER own coveralls, zipping them back up. Stomping her way down to the corridors of the *Koton*, she ground her jaw as she silently seethed. Why was this stupid ship always so *cold*?

At least the sleeves of her jumpsuit covered up the tiny scabbed dots down her arms, the contact points where the proximity hacker had linked into her muscle fibers. Damn things always itched terribly, but this time they seemed worse than ever. She had to fight to keep from tearing at the ones still exposed on her wrists and the backs of her hands as the anger surged through her.

This would have been the perfect time to blow off some steam through a good old fashioned fuck, but *that* wasn't an option either.

The fact was, none of the Lapann were interested in her. Not the way that she had hoped, anyways. They doted on her, sure, but every time she'd tried to find some other way to pass the time with them, her shipmates had either politely deferred or ignored her entirely. Roz constantly treating her as if she were made of glass definitely didn't help.

They clearly valued her only for her ability as an incubator. Which was fine, that was the deal. That was the *whole fucking deal* that she had agreed to. The problem was, she'd expected they'd find her appealing enough to fuck every now and then, not just to constantly coddle and treat like an incompetent piece of planetary ejecta.

Ch'ik slammed her way into the cargo bay, or, she would have if the doors weren't all automatic, with air cushioned tracks that made it impossible for them to actually slam. It was wildly unsatisfying, and it made her even more determined to do something, anything to make herself feel useful. Any elation that she'd felt at the successful hack and fucking over her shitty ex was long since boiled away by her simmering rage. Seeing the familiar silhouette of the *Aeon Hawk* brought some peace to her soul as she realized she could work on repairing her ship. At least she was good at *that*.

There was a toolbox bolted to the wall of the cargo bay but Ch'ik ignored it. She didn't want to give the hard-headed, idiot Lapann the satisfaction of knowing that she'd had to borrow anything from them. She didn't remember where she'd stashed her own mishmashed set of tools, not for sure. She had a sneaking suspicion that they were somewhere under the crates of Broma pods in the *Aeon Hawk's* hold.

Fine. It was fine. She'd work on electrical stuff, then; she didn't need tools for that. If Ch'ik had to splice anything together then she could strip the insulation coating off the wire with her teeth. Worked like a charm before, right? She'd only gotten singed the one time, and it hadn't even paralyzed her. Much.

She *would* get her ship back to prime condition. That way, she could drop through the cargo bay doors as soon as these eggs were out of her. The Lapanns would get what they wanted, she'd get away from this freezing cold ship and to a market that'd bury her in credits for these broma pods. *Then* this whole experience could be an amusing anecdote to tell at a bar as she picked up lifeforms who *were* interested in fucking her.

The zipper of Ch'ik's coveralls was the loudest noise in the cargo bay as she slid it back down far enough to see the slight swell of her belly. She stared down at herself for a long time, at the gentle glow of the eggs within her diffused by the thin white fabric of her shirt.

Ch'ik had never thought of herself as the type of lifeform that did a lot of good in the universe. She did what she had to do to survive. This thing that she was doing, these eggs inside her body, felt like a good thing, but that didn't make her reasons for agreeing to incubate them any less selfish. It didn't mean that she wouldn't go back to her old life as soon as these tiny lives could exist outside of her, but until then, she'd do her best for them.

Fuck it. Time to get to work.

Ch'ik got down onto the floor and shimmied under her ship, looking for the panel that housed the bulk of the wires for the peripheral electric panel. It looked like the dent at the corner of it had wrecked the latching mechanism - it didn't slide open like it normally did when she kicked it - but she was crafty. The damage wasn't going to stop her: she could just force the panel with a pry bar and some elbow grease.

Ch'ik hated to be reliant on anyone for anything. She took care of herself, always had. Opening mechanisms were for the weak.

Self satisfaction sizzled through her brain when she finally loosened the panel enough to reveal the guts of her ship's electrical system. Okay, so maybe the dent was a *little* worse than she'd thought. The reinforced hull had nearly sheared through all the bundles of wires in its path as it crumpled.

There was a lot of rewiring work to be done, although Ch'ik decided not to bother with the power lines that ran to her docking signals; she never used those anyway. Still, it looked like her teeth would be getting a workout.

Losing herself in the work for a while, she focused on her goal, making sure she didn't splice the wrong color of wires together again. The calm of familiar busywork had started to overtake the fury in her chest when she heard a set of heavy footsteps approaching.

Beneath the ship, obscured as her vision was, Ch'ik couldn't see much beyond a thin horizontal slice of boot soles. She'd known from the moment she heard him enter the bay, however, that Roz had come to find her. Resentment swelled at the way that information had slid into her brain: immediately and uninvited. His tread was all too familiar: it was the same one she heard at the end of each sleep cycle, a sound that filled her with excitement and anticipation. After a fraction-cycle of false hopes, it eventually gave way to glum resignation. She finally accepted that Roz was never going to do anything beyond standing in the corridor to watch her eat breakfast.

It wasn't Roz's fault, really. After all, Ch'ik was the only dumbass on the *Koton* who'd let her imagination get ahead of the terms of their deal. She wasn't mad at him, not really. She was mad at herself.

The boot soles shifted in her periphery as Roz kneeled and then sat on the flat floor of the cargo bay, legs crossed, and Ch'ik waited through long drawn out moments of silence until finally he spoke up, his voice soft and heartbreakingly sad.

"Ch'ik - we are, I mean, the *Lapann* are a tripartite reproductive species."

Ch'ik snorted into the tangle of wires. The glow of her belly was a convenient work light, at least. "Uh, yeah. I noticed."

"Without an Alpha, the eggs I produce don't mature. They won't glow."

"Alright, great, cool." She hissed softly, shaking out her hand as a zap of power bit her fingertip.

"It's almost impossible for an Omega to find a Beta, but even pairing up with an Alpha is, well, it's a dream."

He didn't sound like he was bragging. He sounded like he was fighting back tears, but Ch'ik's temper was still running hotter than the live wire she'd just jerked her hand away from. She slammed the electric panel shut, angry he'd intruded on her alone time. Her voice snapped out, sarcastic and furious. "And you got two, wow, I'm so happy for you."

"Ch'ik. Please. Please don't, I'm trying to -" Roz's voice choked off. Ch'ik finally wiggled out from under her ship. He was slumped next to the *Hawk*, red-rimmed eyes telling her he'd clearly been crying. Her resolve caved like a rotten broma pod at the sight of the miserable Omega.

She sighed, sitting up in front of him, cross-legged. "Fine. I'm sorry. What are you trying to tell me, Roz? I'm listening."

Roz took a deep breath as he tried to center himself.

"I was always a runt." He forced the confession out, like it was physically painful.

"What, you mean until you hit a growth spurt?" It was hard for her to imagine the pink hulk of a male in front of her had ever been less than impressive in size.

"Huh? No, I mean, I still am." Roz scratched at the base of his ear as Ch'ik stared at him in disbelief. "Omegas on Oster are usually a lot bigger. I'm not a good specimen at all. Jau says that's probably why I'm so overprotective, because I've been trying to make up for it my whole life."

Ch'ik wanted to argue, to reassure him, but the way he'd treated her - like a damned child - lodged in her chest with palpable resentment. She let the silence stretch uncomfortably until Roz continued.

"I knew, with my size, a cluster wasn't likely. When I was younger I wanted *so badly* to find an Alpha to want me back. To love me enough to want a cluster and a family with me and..." Roz's shoulders tightened as he swallowed, his voice coming rough.

"There was a cluster of five on the farm I worked on. Two Betas, three Alphas, kits all over the place. They owned a lot of land, hired me on for harvest season, and it was so..." His eyes squeezed shut, tears wetting the fur at the edges of his eyes, dewing on long eyelashes.

"They'd let me hold the baby, the smallest kit, after I finished up in the fields each day. They encouraged me to chase around with the big kits in the yard, too. They never mentioned their Omega, so I didn't ask. I didn't want to seem presumptuous, you know? I knew that it'd - I mean, figured that it had been painful, whatever it was that had happened to him."

He scrubbed a hand across his eyes and didn't open them again this time. Pain dripped out of his mouth with every word that he spoke.

"I just hoped that they'd be able to love me, too. I was younger then. Naive, I guess. Stupid. I-" He exhaled a long, shuddering breath, composing himself.

"I thought that I showed them how *good* I was, then maybe they'd ask me to stay. I tried so, so hard to show that I could be good, Ch'ik. Then when the harvest was done and they asked me to go and talk about something, I really thought they might want me. I was overjoyed, I thought I'd finally found where I was supposed to be."

"It turned out they'd never had an Omega. Not as a permanent part of their cluster, anyways. If someone appealing came through with the harvest then they'd ask him to stay through his next season, with the agreement that he'd move on afterwards. Take a payment for services rendered and never be seen again. That was what they called it. *Services rendered.*"

He coughed, but Ch'ik could tell from the way his throat bobbed that he was fighting tears again. "And that's not a bad thing, I *know* it's not. It happens all the time, it's normal, it's - it's a beautiful thing, to help life come into the world. I was stupid to feel the way I did, I know that. Who would be so selfish that they wouldn't help? Omegas don't get sentimental over business arrangements any more than Betas do."

Ch'ik could tell that those last words weren't Roz's own. Sure, they came out of his mouth, but his clenched jaw told her that he was echoing the cruel words of others in his past. She felt discomfort burrow into her stomach: this whole time, she hadn't really considered how the *Lapanns* felt about all this. She'd been assuming they were happy she was involved, and that everything else was fine.

Clearly, everything else was *not* fine.

"I was selfish. I couldn't lay an egg and leave it behind... not for any number of credits. Not even for the perfect cluster, one that could afford as much *laht* as they needed to make sure the kits would be healthy. I wanted a family, not just a business arrangement."

He turned bright, clear eyes on her, practically vibrating with passion and sincerity.

"I *want* a family. I *am* selfish. I want to protect you. I want you to stay, Ch'ik. Pulsars help me, I want you to stay with us, but I know that's not my choice to make. You're doing a wonderful thing for us, even if you're happy to leave after the kits are born, but I wish *so much* that you wouldn't go."

Ch'ik went to him then, her hard little space-smuggler heart broken by his raw truths. She hugged him as close as she could, given the fact that she couldn't fit her arms around him and the bump of her stomach got in the way. Roz's big body curled around her as he let out a single low sob against her shoulder.

"I'm sorry." She whispered, put a hand on the side of his neck where the white garrotte scar showed through his fur and held him there, her heart unexpectedly open and tender. Ch'ik had never been one for apologies but she had, maybe, been a bit of a bitch to him back on the bridge. It wasn't his fault that Dr'ec always brought out the worst in her. "I'm sorry I was so mean to you earlier."

Roz sniffed and she felt his nose wiggle against her neck, his words watery. "It's okay."

"No, it's not." Ch'ik sighed. "Listen, Roz, I'm not good at relationships. That's why I don't have them. But..."

Ch'ik trailed off as she realized where her traitorous words were going to lead her. But nothing. This was a temporary, mutually beneficial relationship. A *business arrangement*, despite Roz's own distaste for the idea. She was doing these guys a solid in exchange for a ride. And maybe she had hoped to have some fun along the way, sure, but that wasn't happening. Even if it would have, even if she could have got the Lapann on board with fucking her brains out the way she wanted, none of it would have changed the fact that 'long term' wasn't something that worked for girls like her.

She switched gears, needing to do *something* to comfort the distraught Omega in her arms. "...but you're worthy of love, Roz. You really are. Those idiots don't know what they missed out on. You're going to be a great parent, too."

He still shook slightly, his breath coming in snuffling gasps. She frowned, wishing she could go back in time and stab the Lapanns that had cracked his heart open. Lacking a chrono device, she settled for climbing into his lap, pressing her back to his chest. She'd loved their brief moments of contact before she'd fired up the proximity hacker, and wanted more of it. They could be selfish together, right now, she decided.

She pulled Roz's arms around her, under her own arms, and tugged the top of her coveralls off, placing his palms on her glowing belly below her bra. Ch'ik closed her eyes, tilting her head back onto his shoulder, and truly relaxed for the first time in fraction-cycles.

And they both sat there in the cargo bay, his big pink hand gently rubbing soft, slow circles on her stomach, until things felt a little more right with the universe.

CHAPTER 16

- CH'IK -

ALMOST THREE FRACTION-CYCLES HAD PASSED now, since that first night Ch'ik had boarded the *Koton*.

Things had been better on the ship since she and Roz had their heart-to-heart; things were more cordial, less strained all around. That didn't mean that Ch'ik was thrilled when Jau called a crew meeting.

She'd been sleeping like shit as the pregnancy progressed, so early-morning gatherings weren't high on her to-do list. When she did manage a few fractions of shuteye, her dreams were surreal kaleidoscopes that didn't leave her feeling rested in the least. To make things even more difficult, her belly had rounded out just far enough that zipping up her coveralls had become uncomfortable.

It wouldn't have been that bad if the Lapann hadn't kept their ship temperature set so damn low - she swore it hadn't felt this chilly when she first came on board. Now, Ch'ik hated leaving the cozy confines of her nest any more than strictly necessary.

But Jau said that it was urgent, and that he couldn't just broadcast it over the ship's intercom system. Ch'ik hauled her exhausted body out of her living quarters, wandering slowly down to the command bridge.

The Lapann were already there, Roz sitting on the crash bench, Zul and Jau in their respective command chairs. At least the bridge was warmer. Conversation abruptly screeched to a halt as she shrugged off and tied the sleeves of her coveralls around her waist, leaving her torso in only a thin white t-shirt. When she looked back up, two and a half sets of eyes lingered on her body. She squirmed, self-conscious at the examination, even though she was sure her deformity was covered.

Jau cleared his throat, the first to shake off their strange stupor. "Alright, I've got good news and bad news." His ears twitched up as he leaned forward with his forearms on his thighs, hands hanging between his knees. "Which do you want first?"

"Bad news." Ch'ik and Zul chorused, even as Roz brightly chimed in, "Good news."

"Uh." Jau gave his Omega a fond look. "Well, the good news is that I can fix it. The bad news -"

"Wait, what? What's broken?" Zul's ears snapped up, squinting suspiciously at Jau.

"The *bad news*," Jau repeated as he raised an eyebrow at Zul's impatience, "is that the stasis equipment is fucked."

"Fuck." Ch'ik's stomach flipped, at least as much as it could while full of eggs. She could lose the entire cargo hold of broma pods if they didn't get that fixed.

"Yeah. That's what I said." Jau sighed, rubbing his forehead with the heel of his hand, body language stressed.

"Jau?" Roz's gentle voice prompted him to explain further.

He shook his head, sliding a hand over his ears and looking back to the three of them. "Sorry. Didn't get a lot of sleep. I was doing a run through of all the onboard systems for maintenance, and I noticed that the stasis field power source has been draining ridiculously fast the last few days. It must have been damaged internally in the fight with Dr'ec last fraction-cycle, but I guess it had been hanging on until now."

"But you said you can fix it, right? So what's the issue?" Ch'ik had crossed her arms over her chest, defensive even though she had no need to be. She didn't like it when they stared at her like she was a freak, and now she couldn't help but picture her entire haul rotting away. The thought of losing the broma pods after all of her effort, everything that she had done - was *currently doing*, Ch'ik corrected herself as she put one hand on her glowing midsection - was unbearable to her.

"Well, that's the *extra* bad news." Jau said.

"You didn't say there was *extra* bad news." Zul groused, rubbing at his eyes. It looked like none of them were getting enough sleep.

"That's because there's, like, *three* extra bad newses. I *could* fix it if we had the parts, but we don't. Thankfully, I know where we can find them, but it's all black market stuff. We also don't have enough credits on hand to make that kind of buy." He paused, wincing before tilting his gaze to Ch'ik. "And...I know how we could get the credits, but..."

"But we aren't going to like it." Roz finished with a tired note of acceptance. Meanwhile, Zul's right ear had picked up the repetitive tic that she'd begun to recognize as a tell for his unease.

"Aren't going to like *what*?" They all seemed to know what Jau was referring to, but Ch'ik was left out of the loop, annoyed by the exclusion.

"We aren't too far from the Scrum. It'll solve all of our problems in one fell swoop." Jau smiled, a cheerful, puzzling contrast to his mates' obvious apprehension.

"The *Scrum*? Sounds like a genital disorder." Ch'ik frowned, starting to side with Zul and Roz based on the name alone.

"Yep!" Jau declared brightly. "The good ol' wretched hive. Number one source for black market goods, questionable morals, and all manners of villainy."

Well, that didn't sound any worse than the backwater skids where she refueled the *Hawk*. "Alright. So like a secret cool guy pirate hangout?"

"Mmhm." Why the hell was Jau practically vibrating in his seat?

"Sounds fake." Ch'ik snorted and tightened her arms over her chest, baiting him a little for more information. Why the fuck was he so psyched about this?

"Oh, it's real." He tapped the navigational screen with a fingertip, where a course was charted already. "*And* it's close enough that we'll get there before the stasis equipment is toast."

"So, I assume this *Scrum* will have power sources for sale. But where are the credits going to come from?" She squinted at the course, which seemed to lead out to the middle of nowhere.

Jau looked positively gleeful. "*That's* the easy part, Ch'ik. We're gonna get a short term loan and multiply it by betting on yours truly at the fights."

Jau's plan was met with a chorus of groans from the other two Lapann.

When Ch'ik turned away from the screen, Roz had begun to pluck at the edge of one long scarred ear, anxious, a frown etched into his face. "No one is going to book you in a fight."

Zul dropped his head into his waiting palms, muttering through his fingers. "And *no one* is going to give us a loan."

Jau's tone turned wheedling. "Oovooa might give us an advance, Z."

Roz huffed a rueful laugh.

Jau wrinkled his nose defensively. "A *small* one. *Maybe.* If Zul turns on the charm." He turned to her, explaining "Our fence, Oovooa. She has a bit of a soft spot for Zul. Personally I don't get it, but -"

"*Wow.*" Zul threw him a hard look, offended.

"I'm just *kidding* Z, you know I love you. And good thing our fence does too, 'cause *you're* gonna get those extra credits and bet on me down at the pit."

In a rare moment of largesse, Ch'ik piped up. "If you're that confident that you'll win it back, you can put the *Aeon Hawk* up as collateral."

The three Lapann shared a look that Ch'ik couldn't translate, but it reminded her of concern.

"What? We're all in this together, right?" Unease coiled in her belly. They'd seemed so confident in Jau's fighting skills a second ago - was there a chance he could lose?

"Right." Roz cleared his throat. "It's just, well, The *Aeon Hawk* is..."

Zul cut him off with a gesture. "We all know how attached you are to your ship, Ch'ik. We would never ask that of you. *Right*, guys?" The other two nodded eagerly.

"Oh! Speaking of being in this together -" Jau dug around in his coveralls and withdrew one of those clear plastic jizz bottles that they all seemed so obsessed with. Ch'ik bristled slightly - she had to make peace with their lack of sexual interest in her, but she sure as shit wasn't shoving any more of those damn bottles in herself. The eggs were already fertilized, damnit. That's what they'd told her.

She suddenly realized that Jau wasn't addressing her at all. His single eye stared at Zul instead, a slash of a smirk on his face, and Ch'ik realized she was definitely missing something.

Wait, did *Zul* have to get a bottle shoved in *him*? How was *that* going to help the eggs? Man, she was lost.

Jau swung the bottle back and forth between his fingertips, a mocking singsong lilt to his voice. "Oh Zuuul? Do you have something you want to share with the class?"

Ch'ik turned and watched as Zul blushed a deep shade of purple, dark splotches blooming across his face and neck, making him look like he'd been stricken by a terrible fur-based disease. He dropped his head into his folded arms on the console in front of him, hiding his face.

Jau turned and grinned at her, raising a brow. "Lovely Ch'ik, oh Beta of my kits, did you and Zul perhaps... engage in a bit of taboo designation mixing?"

She spun, glaring at the back of Zul's head. "You didn't tell your mates we *fucked?*"

His voice came out muffled as he refused to look up. "I *said* that I had contributed my genetic material."

She stomped over and swatted lightly at his shoulder, admonishing. "But you didn't tell them *how?*"

Zul just burrowed his head into his arms, his ears flattened in silent embarrassment. "I was so scared I'd hurt one of the eggs, I was terrified. I felt like a kit caught stealing sook."

Roz stood and wandered over, splaying a wide hand on Zul's back. "Why didn't you tell us? You know we wouldn't have been upset."

Zul sighed, the dark flush of color lightening, even though he still wouldn't lift his head. "I know, I just... I was scared, and it would have been...I don't know, awkward."

Jau broke into a good-natured laugh, joining them with a squeeze to Zul's shoulder. "Z, buddy, everything you do is fucking awkward." He snickered and dodged as Zul jabbed an elbow in his direction.

Roz smiled at Ch'ik. "Jau and I just found that-" he nodded towards the bottle, still in Jau's hand, "-when we were getting the ship cleaned up after that run-in with your ex. Lapanns only keep one bottle with them until they mate, and since you're fully fertilized, we realized it had to have happened...another way." Roz's gentle amusement was much kinder than Jau's blatant glee at Zul's discomfort.

Ch'ik straightened, unashamed of what she and Zul had done together. "Yeah, and so what? We both liked it. At least I can say *I* did, even with the whole-" She waved a hand in the vague direction of her genitals, "-color-mixing purple cum situation."

Jau gasped conspiratorially. "Is *that* why you were mumbling about color mixing when you came all over me? You were doing a *science experiment*? You *nerd!*" He poked Zul's side with a snort.

Zul groaned, the hectic colors of mortification flushing his neck almost solid purple. "It's not *like* that, Jau - I thought the color meant I'd - that I'd *broken* one of the eggs or something! I freaked out! I've been trying to stay away from her ever since, hoping that if I broke an egg that at least it was mine, that I didn't hurt my cluster's kits..." His voice twisted with emotion and guilt.

Roz and Jau shared a long look with one another, Jau gently squeezing the back of Zul's neck, affectionately. "Is that why you've been waving us off every time we tried to talk about her? Why you've been telling us to stay away?"

Ch'ik frowned, crossing over to the console and hoisting herself up to sit on an edge with a little help from Jau. She tapped the edge of Zul's leg with her ankle to get him to look up.

Ch'ik sighed with exasperation. "Zul, listen to me. Jau and I rigged one of the cargo scanners yesterday with a very narrow field-focus to check the eggs. There's three in there, Zul, and they're all doing just fine. You didn't hurt anything, and if you'd bothered to *talk* to me, I could have told you that."

A sudden thought occurred to her.

"Also, you're an *asshole!*" Sure, she was pissed, but her tone had a giddy edge to it that belied her anger. She was mad at Zul for essentially cock-blocking her for fraction-cycles, but an undercurrent of excitement rose in her blood. As the pieces clicked into place, she realized that miscommunication, not disinterest, was likely responsible for her goddamn dry spell. "If you didn't tell them that we fucked...then I'm guessing these two have no idea I'm into it, right?"

Charged silence descended on the bridge. Jau's mouth hung slack with shock, but the heat in his eye made Ch'ik squirm with pleasure. It was Roz who finally managed to ask the question, hesitant and sweet.

"You'd really want that? With *us?*" He was puzzled, as if she'd just admitted she was sexually interested in the control panel. If she'd had to go another fraction-cycle without relief beyond her own hand, hell, she might have been.

"Fuckin' *pulsars*, yes, I do, I don't know how else to make it clear! I'd let you *all* fuck me right here, right now." She stabbed a finger at the control panel under her ass, the only flat surface in the room, for which she only held a platonic interest. For now. "I'm so pent up I feel like I'm going to explode!"

"But..." Zul raised his head. His ears dropped back with a shame she didn't understand until he added, "Betas don't *like* that. I already lost control and subjected you to my deviancy once, and I nearly hurt one of my kits in the process. I couldn't possibly-"

Ch'ik hissed in frustration. "You blue idiot - what, did you think I was faking it when I came all over your cock?" Jau's ears went erect at her declaration and his expression grew hungry. She was too caught up in her own thoughts to address *that* at the moment, and her voice rose an octave. "And do I look like I give a zero-G fuck what *Betas* are *supposed* to be? I'm not even Lapann! I *told you*, I'm from Rizen."

Jau gently touched his own nose, though his intensity didn't dim a fraction. When he spoke, his voice held a raw, sensual edge. "We scented you from outside that bar, Ch'ik. When Roz is in season, he produces pheromones that other males can't usually detect. When a compatible female is exposed to them, she releases a signal scent that draws in fertile males and stimulates our protective instincts; that's what lays the groundwork for our clusters. We all caught it from you, which means you must have latent Lapann DNA."

She splayed a hand over her own stomach, staring sightlessly at the far wall. "I...I can't see how I could be Lapann. I mean, I was a camp spawn, I never knew my parents, but it's not like I'm rocking ears like yours or something."

Roz shrugged. "However it happened, you're our miracle. We know your scent, and you're able to carry our eggs. You're a Beta."

Ch'ik laughed, but there was a shaky edge of hysteria in it that she needed to get under control, stat. "But I look *nothing* like you guys!"

"Well..." Jau offered. "Betas always have some white fur," he pointed at her hair, the white-blonde shock that she had so often shoved out of her eyes and desperately needed to buzz off again.

Zul's eyes automatically dropped below her waist before he caught himself, blushing again.

She bit back a grin, knowing exactly where his mind had gone. *Perv.* "Plenty of life forms are blonde, that doesn't prove anything."

Zul tugged at his ear nervously. "She's right, guys. She doesn't have the third nipple, it's probably just a fortunate genetic fluke she can carry."

A sound of choked emotion spilled out; Ch'ik couldn't hold it back. Her hands flew to her mouth as she pulled in a shaking breath between her fingers. The Lapann immediately clustered around her, radiating worry and overlapping questions of concern until she waved them back, gulping air.

"Do you remember-" Ch'ik swallowed hard, genuine tears pricking at the corners of her eyes for the first time in... she couldn't remember how long. "-do you remember when Dr'ec said that I'm hideously deformed?"

They all nodded, a synchronous dip of their heads. Roz kicked at the floor for some reason, but Ch'ik was too overwhelmed by her epiphany to worry about his apparent restless leg syndrome.

Ch'ik pulled the back of her thin white shirt up above her head, twisting her torso to put her back to them. "- this is what he was talking about."

As soon as Ch'ik turned she heard three quick intakes of breath and she knew that they had seen it - that small brown circle in the middle of her back. Slightly to the left of her spine, up between her shoulder blades, the feature that had been the source of so much ridicule when Ch'ik had been growing up in the orphan camps.

"Is that...?" She looked over her shoulder to find Roz's eyes gone wide.

"My third nipple." Ch'ik confirmed, hanging her head a bit. "The crueler kids at the camp always used to say my parents abandoned me because I was deformed; Rizen females are only supposed to have two, one on each breast. I, um - well, when I *get to know* a partner, I usually lay on my back or face them. I've gotten a lot of flak for this over the cycles, so it's easier to just...you know, keep it to myself."

For a moment none of them said anything, the air between heavy with revelation. That same air was also incredibly cold, and all three of Ch'ik's nipples - exposed as they were, now - had started to harden. Ch'ik shivered as she pulled her thin shirt back down around her neck. She'd had just about as much self-redefining emotional revelations that she could handle for the day, and her threshold for physical discomfort was eroding the further the pregnancy progressed.

She chafed her arms with her palms, trying not to shiver. "Can one of you please turn the temperature up? I'm fuckin' *freezing*."

Jau scrambled to the control panel, almost tripping over his own feet as he hurried to obey her command.

"Alright." She said finally, after she had gathered her thoughts and the bridge felt less like a freezer. "If I'm part...Lapann...it doesn't really change anything. Not to be indelicate about it, but I still want to fuck all of you hard enough to dent a ship's hull, so -"

Ch'ik had never known a starship crew that ate as well as the Lapann, but Roz and Zul still descended on her like they were starving. Putting her shirt back on turned out to have been a wasted effort. She laughed as Roz's big hands grasped at the bottom edge of her shirt, immediately pulling the garment back over her head. He tossed it carelessly over his shoulder to a far corner of the bridge, his expression equal parts rapturous and ravenous. Zul slid onto the console beside her, his lips finding her neck like he'd been waiting cycles to taste her again.

Finally.

"Wait." Jau's voice was low and rough as he stared at Ch'ik, watching his mates converge on her.

"Both of you have gotten to experience our sweet Beta already." He stared directly at her, one-eyed gaze burning with demand. "I'm next."

Ch'ik moaned at the promise in those words, rolled her hips up against Roz's wide thigh as she felt her cunt throb in anticipation. She reached out to Jau, eager to pull him into the huddle. "Then what are you waiting for? Get over here!"

All of her lustful anticipation derailed as Jau shook his head.

"No."

Ch'ik glared at him over Roz's shoulder, furious. "No? The fuck do you mean, *no*? Didn't we just have some big heart to heart-" she waved her hand in a vague circle of the room, "-about how bad I want it? Fucks sake!"

Jau closed the distance between them faster than she'd thought possible. If his smoldering gaze wasn't already setting Ch'ik's libido on fire, then the way that he stalked over and loomed into her space would have. Better still, he reached out and traced a finger across her lips. Her eyes flicked down to Jau's hips, lingering on the painfully obvious bulge restrained within his coveralls. She smirked as she darted her tongue out to lick at the tip of his proffered digit.

Zul had leaned back to watch, openly palming himself through his own garment. Roz's grip clutched at her thigh as he moved back slightly, giving his smaller Alpha room.

Ch'ik silently gloated as Jau traced his fingertip down from her mouth: she knew he wouldn't be able to resist, now that they'd finally gotten on the same page. Smug in her triumph, she pushed her body into his touch as Jau ran his hand down along the column of her neck, between her breasts, over the soft swell of her belly. With agonizing slowness, he shoved her coveralls aside as his hand drifted lower and lower. Then he reached the edge of the soft white curls between her legs, the place where she needed him most.

But it was there that he stopped short, so tantalizingly close, and ducked his head to whisper in her ear. "I. Said. No."

Now, she had never been a delayed gratification type of gal. Nothing was guaranteed from one day to the next - not even life itself - and thus there was no reason to put off pleasure. Ordinarily, a male teasing her like this would infuriate her enough to write him off as a partner, but this time was different. Ch'ik felt like a ship's tether about to snap from the delicious tension, and instead of snarling at Jau for literally cock-blocking her, the situation made her writhe with glee. A fraction of a second later it occurred to her.

Oh. Right. That was because he made it *super hot*.

Instead of unleashing the demands she wanted to, Ch'ik squirmed, desperate for sensation. She turned hooded, pleading eyes up to him, trying a different tack.

"Please, Jau?"

Jau gripped her jaw in a palm, fingertips under her chin forcing her to look into the penetrating blue of his good eye. He gave a rueful shake of his head and a sinister smile.

"I don't fuck before a fight, Ch'ik. So I'm not fucking you, and *they aren't either.*" The declaration was as much a statement of fact as it was a thinly-veiled warning to his mates.

"Time is of the essence, and we don't want to lose the pods. But after I win..." Jau's eye gleamed with dark promise as he ran his thumb slowly along her lower lip.

"Zul." He snapped sharply over his shoulder, pointing at the helm, his intense gaze never wavering. "Lock in our course for the Scrum."

CHAPTER 17
- ROZ -

EVEN THOUGH HIS LITTLE POWER-FLEX ON THE bridge had left them all with knots that wouldn't quit, Jau was downright cheerful after Zul had locked their course in. Roz always felt torn over his mate's excitement when it came to the Scrum.

Intellectually, he knew that his smaller Alpha was the fiercest, most skilled fighter he'd ever met. He also knew something his mate's opponents never did, because he and Zul were careful to keep it secret: Jau had a serious *thing* for pain. Thankfully it wasn't all-consuming - Roz himself much preferred the softer side of love and connection, and Zul veered more towards passion in the moment. That meant some of Jau's particular tastes were best satisfied in the pit.

After their meeting and unexpected discoveries about Ch'ik, Roz and Jau were headed to the cargo bay once more. Jau was the most knowledgeable in their cluster when it came to the inner workings of starships, thanks to a kithood on the docks learning at old timer's elbows. Roz was passable - when it came right down to it, there wasn't a vast starfield of difference between some of the more advanced farm equipment and ships. He'd offered to help stabilize the stasis field: he knew he wouldn't be able to talk Jau out of his plan, but he at least wanted to spend time with him before the pull of the Scrum stole his attention away.

Once they'd made it safely up the rickety ramp into the *Hawk*, Jau tugged him close in an embrace. "Are you alright with this, Roz? I know you seemed just as eager as we did, but I also know how agreeable you are."

As a runt, Roz had been pushed down the seen-but-not-heard route since kithood. He'd heard from his parents, his siblings, and even other kits growing up that he was a mistake. All life was beautiful but even so, Roz was lucky to be alive, worthless, and a thousand other wounding words. By the time Zul's rigid military upbringing and dysfunctional family life crossed trajectories with his own, Roz was well and truly cowed - submissive to a fault. He'd been so happy just to be noticed that he'd have done anything for the dashing blue Alpha that gave him the time of day.

When they first got together, Zul wasn't completely clueless about mating. Roz had already been through a few cycles on his own and understood, at least in theory, how everything fit together with a partner. Unfortunately for him, Zul's knowledge had come largely courtesy of Academy locker room talk and his shithead of a cousin, Marr. Zul had fumbled through their early encounters laying on heavy degradation, pushing through awkwardness with vehemence, calling Roz things like a *knot-hungry slut* in the heat of the moment. Roz absolutely hated it, but he had been desperately afraid of scaring off the only Alpha that had ever been interested in him.

Besides, Zul was an Alpha and seemed to know what he was talking about.

Zul had *not* known what he was talking about.

When Jau came into their lives a few fraction-cycles later, he'd courted Roz properly, with thoughtful gifts and sweet romantic gestures that had made Roz's tail quiver. Jau's treatment made Roz feel like the biggest brute of an Omega on Oster, rather than a runt that was lucky to have even one Alpha.

After Jau had courted Roz, the first time all three of them had fallen into bed together, Zul had started his usual degradation routine. Immediately clocking the discomfort and sadness on Roz's face, Jau had delivered a stinging slap upside Zul's head, bringing everything to a screeching halt for an impromptu meeting.

After a very long night of talking, a few tears, and relief on everyone's parts, they'd become a cluster of three.

Zul kept the firm hand Roz had grown to enjoy, but happily nixed the awkwardly-performed cruelty they apparently both hated. Sex got a *lot* better after that, and Roz's heart did too. He'd always love Jau for voicing what he couldn't, among countless other reasons.

Roz sighed and nuzzled against his Alpha's neck, breathing in Jau's comforting scent, undeniably masculine with a metallic edge.

"I've been-" He gave up trying to bend down to his shorter Alpha, minimizing the eternal height difference problem they'd had to get creative with. Roz settled down onto his knees so Jau could hold him close the way he liked, his cheek against the smaller Alpha's chest. "I've been thinking about her ever since, Jau. I didn't know if it was Beta hormones, or *me*, or what, but it's been driving me crazy."

Jau let one of Roz's long ears slide through his fingers. "Me too. This is crazy, but it feels right, somehow. Maybe it's because we're exiles, maybe it's because those pods behind us could eliminate one of Oster's worst problems, or maybe it's just - " He lifted Roz's velvety ear tip to his lips, pressing a soft kiss to his fur. "That we're all falling for that rowdy Beta on our bridge."

Roz leaned heavily into his Alpha's hand, enjoying the comfort of his touch. "We should tell her about Zul's family though, shouldn't we? I mean, we're headed back to Oster and she doesn't know why we were exiled in the first place."

Guilt passed over Jau's face. "You're right, but let's wait until after we're done at the Scrum. We don't want to scare her off. If we can't get this stasis field fixed, it'll all be a moot point anyway - Oster itself would have their ears if Zul's family tried to stop us."

Roz nodded. He didn't like keeping secrets from their Beta, but as long as Jau agreed they could tell her soon, he could wait. "You know we'll have to be the ones to tell her - Z's about as good at opening up as Ch'ik is at ship repair." He huffed at a spark that shot out of the wall.

"*Thank* you." Jau laughed, a deep, beautiful sound that made Roz's fur bristle happily. "She'd probably shank me if I said it to her face, but yeesh. This thing's a pulsars-damned disaster." He tugged the makeshift hold's door open, where the gray-green glow of the stasis field flickered erratically in a room-wide dome over the broma pods.

The two of them sighed with exasperation, Jau ducking out of the ship for a moment to get their tools. Halfway through the task, it became clear that, unsurprisingly, the main problem was the *Aeon Hawk* itself: even with Jau's initial modifications, the ramshackle electrical system couldn't handle a stasis field drain. The two of them set to hauling crates off the ship into their own cargo hold, patching the stasis field into the *Koton's* considerably more reliable electrical system. Shoring up what they could from the field generator, Jau seemed satisfied it would hold until the Scrum.

Roz offered to take over cleanup duty, extracting a kiss from Jau to pay for his Alpha's early escape. He'd also made it worth his own while, turning it into an extended makeout session that sent Jau out of the *Hawk* with an impressive erection pushing at his coveralls.

Once his ears registered the hiss of the cargo bay's door in Jau's wake, Roz lifted the internal tray off the tool box. Alone now, he set about his *other* reason for staying back, carefully wrapping four broma pods in rags and tucking them beneath some lighter tools.

Ch'ik's chaotic boxes of cargo weren't labeled or accounted for on a manifest; there were so many overflowing containers she'd just told Jau to "take what he wanted" when the Alpha had made her *laht*. He and Jau hadn't inventoried the crates as they'd moved them off the *Hawk*, either, so Roz took comfort in the fact that his small theft would likely go entirely unnoticed.

He had his own plans for the Scrum, and now he had everything he needed to bring them to fruition.

CHAPTER 18

- CH'IK -

Ch'ik was glad this *Scrum* place was apparently only a day outside their course. If she thought sexual frustration on a ship of uninterested partners was bad, knowing they wanted her was worse.

She'd been all ready to take care of herself that evening - as she had almost every damn night since she boarded - but Jau had caught her arm in the hallway and backed her into a wall, slowly. He'd kissed her neck and asked if she'd be a good girl for him, if she'd wait to let his hands be the next ones to touch her. Something in her brain had damn near short-circuited at that.

It wasn't a demand, exactly, but her body was certainly eager to stand at attention and salute. Hell, she'd waited this long, and all this newfound tension was turning out to be surprisingly fun. Ch'ik's previous bunk buddies had all been fairly transactional, so this

185

was an interesting veer off the usual path. She'd nodded, and he'd leaned in and rewarded her with a kiss that made her glad the bulkhead was holding her up.

After a fitful sleep, where at least she was no longer freezing, Roz had brought her breakfast and sat with her as she ate her *laht*. It was like someone had popped a stasis field around the three of them on the ship, and Ch'ik was delighted to find the Lapann no longer skittish to be physically close to her. As she finished breakfast, a gentle chime sounded as the *Koton* started the descent loop to the Scrum. Roz offered her his hand, which she took, as they walked to the bridge together.

What Zul pointed out to Ch'ik on the visual field was neither the largest or the smallest object on the radar. It was, as far as Ch'ik could tell, just another lumpy bit of planetary ejecta that had been caught in the orbital field of a regular old asteroid belt. She suspected that the Lapann's destination was nothing more than a particularly misshapen asteroid, which was something of a letdown after all the hype. An unimpressed expression stayed on her face - at least, it did up until the moment when they finally got a visual of the infamous Scrum.

Her jaw dropped as she first laid eyes on the outlaw station; as much as Ch'ik liked to consider herself a fairly experienced spacefarer, she was still shocked and awed by the sight of their destination. It wasn't an asteroid at all, but rather a mind-boggling conglomeration of ships that had all been fused together. Her eyes flicked back and forth over the mass of vessels as she tried and failed to catalog the components.

It was almost too much to take in - there were ships of every size, make, model and origin she'd seen in her travels, and even more models that she hadn't. Half of an Imperium carrier, squared off and utilitarian, protruded from the side of the curved hull of a luxury cruise liner. A sleek black saucer bisected an elderly-looking frigate, in turn connected to a mining barge by a mass of tiny comet-hopper shuttles. An endless fleet of ships, all bonded together like a cluster of fruit, or a particularly virulent colony of metallic mold.

"Wait until you see the landing zone." Jau's voice was warm with amusement as he directed the *Koton* in a wide arc around the side of the conglomeration of ships, past a neat row of booster rockets.

They skimmed over a long smooth expanse that must have been the hull of something huge, once, now deeply subsumed in the conjoined mass of ships. And there, at the far end of the incongruously flat field, was a tree. Well, the bottom half of a tree, anyway.

Part of its gnarled trunk protruded from the side of a superyacht cruiser, gnarled brown bark that transitioned down into the wide lateral spread of a root system that dwarfed the *Koton*. Roz moved to stand beside Ch'ik, and it was a testament to just how awestruck Ch'ik was that she didn't shrug off his protective hand when he rested it on her shoulder. Puzzled, she tried to parse which part of the dizzying mass served as a docking bay - nothing she'd seen passed as one so far.

Jau piloted them toward the center and turned the nose of the ship towards the tip of one of the massive roots. She gasped softly when an octagonal orifice suddenly twisted open in the wooden surface.

"What the f..." Ch'ik watched in awe as they descended through the long and winding root and up into the trunk of the tree. Rough exterior wood gave way to smooth grain that spiraled out as the channel expanded out into a multi-story interior dock, massive in scope. As they exited the hidden entryway, rows and rows of bays, built in stacked rings, rose along the inside of the trunk's hollow interior.

Packed with all manner of ships, most of the atmospheric membranes were already occupied. The few available spots attached to the habitable side of the station were apparently the wrong size or configuration for the *Koton*, as Jau passed them by without comment. Ch'ik continued to ogle as Jau searched for a docking spot.

The first handful of levels held grapplers galore, shuttles, and plenty of nondescript haulers that could have been smuggling anything from minerals to lifeforms. She looked with envy at a stealth ship so sleek that the edges of it were impossible to perceive, docked neatly beside an amorphous blob of purple gelatin with constantly-undulating edges. The sheer scope of the docked ships made her head spin, the chaotic array somehow even more overwhelming than the cobbled-together mass of the station itself.

"How the fuck... how did I not know this place existed?" Ch'ik wondered aloud as she took in a ring of neatly parked blockade runners with identical paint jobs.

"It's, ah - invite only." Zul chuckled, tapping at a screen and busying himself with their docking routines.

"All these guys got an invite?" Ch'ik gestured at the seemingly endless rows of other ships "And I didn't?"

"Well. How many long-term friendships have you forged with other outlaws?" Jau asked conversationally, smoothly guiding the Koton into a docking bay and securing the ship tether.

"I - I mean, I spent some time with a few..."

Zul smirked, raising a brow. *Smarmy fuck.* "Building trust or working off steam?"

She wrinkled her nose at him, annoyed. "...alright, fuck you. Point taken. I'm apparently not as badass as you guys."

"The colony exists on the mercies of secrecy - unspoken honor among thieves, even if some of us are more tarnished than others." Zul shrugged. "The *Koton* has falsified credentials, so we're able to dock anywhere as long as no Imperium border cruisers get a bug up their ass to do a sweep. But there are plenty of crews that operate without the landing privileges that we do. The Scrum is their only option. There's basically no other hidden colony this developed in the quadrant, so it's in everyone's best interests not to let the location leak."

"Wait." Ch'ik cut in, mind still reeling as she followed them down the ship's ramp. "Colony?"

None of the Lapann answered, but they didn't need to - she had looked up.

The size of the place was obvious as the *Koton* approached it, but until she was *in it*, her brain wasn't quite ready to comprehend the interior of the Scrum. The conglomeration of ships had been completely scraped out inside; the conjoined hulls outside were the only remnants of the original crafts. The huge empty hollow within had been filled with levels upon levels of sprawling architecture, a wild hive of a megastructure far too large to behold in its entirety. From the vantage point of the dock - clearly a major hub of activity - Ch'ik looked on in amazement. The tower blocks lurched off into a dense maze of buildings that spread out and rose up to dizzying heights.

The interior city had no natural sources of light, a scattering of bioluminescent visitors notwithstanding. There was no lack of illumination here, however. The neon holographs that shone from every building facade smeared into ambient incandescence, bright as a planetary sunset.

Limned in artificial glow, the distant jumble of the city was fashioned of strange, dark silhouettes. Structures of all shapes and sizes had been built at odd angles, thrusting up into empty central spaces and occasionally merging in bizarre intersections. The junctures were a sure sign of an otherwise-invisible mess of irregular gravity fields.

"I thought you called this place a station. This is no *station*, Jau." Ch'ik waved her hands in indication at the sheer scale of their surroundings.

Jau rubbed at his ears, a tic that Ch'ik had come to associate with the Lapann wanting to duck a subject. "Yeaaahhh, I probably did. It's easy to forget how big it's gotten over the cycles."

"Pfft. You're half the reason for the expansion." Zul muttered, only to be met with a jab from Jau's elbow.

At Ch'ik's confused look, Jau sighed, shoving a hand through his hair.

"That big fighting ring I told you about? They run high stakes matches here, once a cycle. The losers have to surrender their ships to get permanently welded onto the Scrum." Jau nodded towards the nearest wall, a smooth but irregular plane of welds and bolts that continued into another.

Roz rolled his eyes. "We're just lucky you've never lost."

"It's not luck. I'm just that good." Jau cracked his knuckles with a grin.

"Wait. So if the loser's ship gets added to the Scrum, then what does the winner get?" Ch'ik looked at the walls with a renewed expression of wonder.

"... bragging rights?" Jau gave her a lopsided smirk.

"Wow. You'd put your whole livelihood on the line - your *ship* - just to beat another lifeform?"

Jau nodded, looking chagrined but not exactly ashamed.

"Yeah." Roz added, arms crossed disapprovingly over his wide chest. "That's exactly it. It's just a stupid ear-measuring contest."

"Wow. Alright. That couldn't have made you too popular." Ch'ik muttered, still a little sore about Zul's earlier comment about her lack of friends.

"It definitely has not." Zul confirmed, side-eyeing a grinning Jau. He stopped and turned to Ch'ik, lightly setting a hand on each of her shoulders. She was startled at the familiarity of the contact. Even though they'd been intimate, he'd been giving her the brush off for so long it felt disorienting now.

"Ch'ik, there's no way we can talk you into waiting here, is there?" His thumb brushed the side of her neck, setting her emotions off-balance again.

"It would be much safer for you back on the ship." Roz seemed increasingly agitated the further they got from the *Koton*, as if there were snipers with plasma rifles lurking in every neon-lit window.

"Sorry fellas but I'm definitely coming with you. I told you before, I'm not a sideline kind of gal." Ch'ik said as she gave Roz a hard look, pleased to see his ears drop.

Zul nodded and gave her shoulders a last comforting squeeze, turning around and resuming their route.

"Just make sure you stay close," Roz cautioned, ear flicking at a nearby sound. "We need to keep our eyes open here. This isn't regulated space."

"No kidding." She stared out at a skinny twist of scaffolding that bent between gravity fields at a nauseatingly acute angle. "Galactic building codes don't seem to have high priority."

The Lapann formed a tight triangle formation around her as they made their way through the dense crowd at the docks. Her translator implant sputtered and stalled at the sheer variety of language in the air around them, politely pausing its attempts to parse the volume of chatter. Every once in a while it managed to pick up a basic noun in a familiar language - fuel, gun, foot, energy drink - and the words became discordant interjections in what was otherwise incomprehensible background babble. Those rare translations flicked into Ch'ik's brain just often enough to put her on edge, even as the teeming throng of lifeforms thinned out as they moved down into the wild tangle of the city.

A few minutes later, the very idea of direction ceased to have any meaning. Ch'ik had the distinct impression of moving downwards even as they trekked *up* a steep staircase that took them past a tentacle-only brothel and into a darker level of the city. The lifeforms that they passed stared at their strange group with blatant interest, openly gawking at Ch'ik and the Lapann as they moved deeper into the maze of buildings.

They made their way through a series of damp alleyways where coils of lightwire had been strung through empty spaces between the narrow twisting lanes. The atmosphere recyclers must have struggled to strip the condensation from the air for so much liquid to accumulate. Ch'ik glanced down for a moment as their boots splashed through a series of shallow puddles and saw the rainbow sheen of chemical contaminants flicker and break as the surface tension was disturbed by their passing. Sinuous reflections of the overhead lightwire fractured into smaller writhing worms of light that wriggled right out of Ch'ik's perception as her attention was drawn to another moving flicker.

The lights in her body had moved. *The eggs.*

All three of the eggs had shifted, ever so slightly. The realization stopped Ch'ik dead in her tracks, her boot soles mired in disgusting condensation as she stared down at her stomach. She hadn't felt anything at all, wouldn't have trusted her own eyes if she hadn't become so obsessively attuned to the eggs' location over the past fraction-cycle.

Then there was a big wall of warm weight at her back as Roz stopped just short of bumping into her. Jau and Zul fell back as well, all on alert with their ears perked up to listen for any sign of danger.

Roz's hand splayed comfortingly at the small of her back. "Ch'ik? Are you okay?"

"Yeah." Her heart hammered in her throat, despite her conscious efforts to calm down. The lie came too easily off her tongue, a lifetime of cons and weaseled promises always at the ready. "Yeah, I'm fine, sorry. Let's go."

The overwhelming strength of her initial reaction surprised Ch'ik - it wasn't like she hadn't stared endlessly at the glowing orbs. It wasn't like she hadn't been there when Roz laid the eggs into her body. But all the knotting and fertilization and physical changes as her body grew had just become real: a new level of context for what she was doing with herself. She wasn't really sure what to do with all the emotions her deal was, unexpectedly, dredging up.

Ch'ik couldn't have said how much longer they walked. Time and travel had become distant concerns. Her physical self trudged deep into the bowels of the city but her mind soared through some far away sky, flipped and twirled with the evidence that the tiny glowing things in her body were alive.

"We're here." Zul announced in a wary tone.

Startled out of her reverie, Ch'ik looked up to see that Zul was standing with his hand on the edge of a grimy concrete wall. It had been festooned with bundles of cables, each running vertically up the side, vanishing into the darkness beyond the softly glowing lightwire. A circular door of polished metal beckoned, so shiny and clean that Ch'ik could have mistaken it for a mirror if not for the handle. A flickering red holograph arched overhead, spelling out OOVOOA - FENCE in bold lettering.

Roz and Jau had huddled together, muttering a heated conversation. Whatever they'd been arguing about, it looked like Roz had either lost or given up.

Jau nodded to Zul and squeezed her arm gently. "Ch'ik, you're going to hang here with Zul while Roz and I go see about setting up a fight. No one fucks with Oovooa, so you'll be safer here than where we're going. We'll be back soon though, okay?"

She glanced at Roz, who seemed anguished at leaving her side. She did her best to give him a reassuring smile.

"Be safe then, guys. Kick ass if anyone fucks with you, okay?" That got a timid smile out of the big Omega as they turned to leave, which settled Ch'ik's heart.

"Fair warning, Ch'ik. Oovooa can be - uhm - different." Zul said, his expression carefully neutral as he pounded on the door with the side of his fist.

The red holograph blinked out, shifting into a green greeting that tracked around the circumference of the door. The hatch opened with a hiss, swinging inward into a room filled with harsh light. Ch'ik had to squint her eyes against the brightness as she ducked into what appeared to be a tiny tea room.

A low, round table, covered with a frilly lace cloth, dominated the center of the space. On the walls, shelves upon shelves of little ceramic figurines rested, staring uncomfortably at her *en masse*. On closer examination, they all depicted interplanetary fauna engaged in unlikely activities - at least, Ch'ik didn't think that Kymber killing beasts usually cuddled in baskets or played with balls of string. Two overstuffed couches covered in garish flower print cloth completed the aesthetic, each laden with decorative pillows. The seating was angled towards an open spot in the room, where a massive pressure suit crouched in the center of a woven pink rug.

Of all the oddities in here, the pressure suit was one thing that Ch'ik was familiar with. She had encountered a couple during that hectic summer on the prison planet, and recognized it as a top-tier AAD - an atmospheric adaptation device. They were designed for life forms that had evolved under extreme pressure conditions, like gas giants or water worlds. The suits, while admittedly ungainly, kept them from being crushed or decompressing in low-pascal environments.

This one was a basic bipedal setup with four arms that ended in blunt three-fingered gloves. Most of the suit was a dull dark bronze, but shiny metal bands emphasized the seals at the articulated joints and around the neck of the helmet. The flattened dome atop the pressure suit was reinforced with bolts and bands of metal that stabilized the clear viewport in the center.

The viewport, a circle of reinforced glass that looked to be about as thick as Ch'ik's wrist, arched over a vast single eye. Round and red, it was speckled with copper flecks that became denser around the I-shaped pupil at the center.

Ch'ik blinked. The eye did not. Zul cleared his throat and stepped forward.

"Thanks for agreeing to meet with me. Oovooa, this is my, um. My..." He cleared his throat, panic sneaking into his expression.

Ch'ik rolled her eyes as Zul faltered. Jau was right - Zul really was a nerd.

Oovooa's eye was - she thought, anyway - still staring at her. Taking the initiative, Ch'ik stepped forward and extended a hand in greeting. "Ch'ik Wazo. Nice to meet you."

Oovooa lumbered over with a disconcerting twist of limbs and reached one heavy glove forward to shake Ch'ik's hand. Her pressure suit was much larger than any of the ones that Ch'ik had encountered on the prison planet but her grip was well-calibrated. Firm yet gentle, Ch'ik's small hand all but disappeared in her grasp. The handshake lasted a beat too long, an awkward stretch of silence made more awkward still by the utter silence in the small, insulated room.

Ch'ik pulled her hand back, but when the pressure suit glove stayed suspended without any sort of reaction she realized that Oovooa was distracted. That vast eye was fixed on her belly, staring with unnerving concentration.

The glow of the eggs was still visible through the unzipped front of her coveralls. They hadn't moved since the last time that Ch'ik had checked, but the viewport of the helmet and the shimmering eye within stayed trained on her midsection for long, disturbing moments. Ch'ik snuck a glance at Zul, who remained still, expression unbothered - evidently this was normal to him. Alright then, she'd wait it out too.

Finally, Oovooa pivoted the suit's helmet back towards Ch'ik's face.

"**What is that light in your stomach! Is it food!**" As the words filtered through the speech port on the pressure suit, they were strung together like questions. The fence's tone, however, was one of chipper exclamation.

It took Ch'ik a moment to answer, baffled by the contrast. "Uh, no. They're babies."

"**Ok! Did it taste good!**" A slight tilt of the pressure suit helmet, the eye rolling a little.

"Oovooa, that's not -" Zul started, cringing back when the pressure suit helmet rotated towards him with an uncanny speed.

"**I am not talking to you! I am talking to her!**"

The tone of the speaker had not changed at all but it felt like the temperature in the tea room dipped lower than the *Koton*'s had in the first fraction-cycles of the trip. Ch'ik saw Zul's eyes go wide before he ducked his head in silent apology, shoulders trembling as Oovooa turned back to Ch'ik. Zul's reaction told her all that she needed to know about the threat Oovooa represented. She didn't need to know the specifics of *what* was in that pressure suit to understand the lifeform in front of her was dangerous.

Something thick, wet, and indiscernible moved inside the viewport of the helmet, disconcertingly obscuring the eye for a moment. Ooovooa ventured the question - or statement - again. "**How did it taste!**"

"How did what taste?" Ch'ik had dropped a hand to her stomach reflexively, her skin prickling with unease.

"**The babies!**" The pressure suit arm waved, awkwardly, in the general direction of her stomach.

"...what?" Ch'ik asked again, wondering if the taxing volume of languages in the Scrum had cracked her translator. There was no way Ooovooa was saying what Ch'ik thought she was saying.

"**Did the babies taste good! When you ate it!**" The helmet awkwardly tilted to the other side, as if the lifeform was trying to poorly imitate the casual poses of bipedal conversation.

Alright, so maybe she was saying what Ch'ik had thought she was saying. A wave of disgust washed through her at the thought.

"No! I don't eat babies. Why would you say that?"

"Oovooa, can we just talk about the -" Zul tried to cut in but Ooovooa just waved him off with one heavy three fingered glove.

Despite Ch'ik's reaction, Oovooa didn't seem at all concerned or offended, pressing on. "**Because it is in your stomach!**"

"'That's - that's where the babies grow." Ch'ik splayed her hand wider, as if it could protect the kits in her from the strange, hungry creature.

"**Oh! Ok! It is alive!**" A jerky up and down motion accompanied the exclamation. *Was that supposed to be a nod?*

Ch'ik couldn't tell if it was a question or a statement. She just kept one protective hand on her stomach. The moment of awkward silence stretched until, finally, Zul spoke up.

"So, Oovooa, about that advance on our next payment..."

Again that wet sloshing across the viewport. "**When the babies is done growing, what does it do! Does it chew its way out**!"

"Uh, no. I don't think so?" Ch'ik had been trying not to think about that part, honestly.

The shoulders of the pressure suit rolled in what Ch'ik suspected was supposed to be a shrug.

"**You will let me know, yes! Come back and tell me if it chews out through your abdominal wall!**" Oovooa reached out a heavy gloved hand to pat Ch'ik's arm. "**If it does not chew its way out you can still tell me! And let me see it! I have never seen a babies before!**"

"...alright?" Ch'ik ventured, hesitantly.

"**Ok! Good!**" Oovooa twisted the torso of her pressure suit back towards Zul. "**You are not my favorite any more!**"

Zul's blue cheeks seemed to pale at the news, his ears dropping with dejection. "I'm not?"

"**No! Your Ch'ik is my new favorite. Do you understand!**"

Ch'ik shot a smirk at Zul as he stuttered out a reply. "Oh, uh. Alright. Yes, I guess. I understand."

"**Okay!**" Oovooa returned to her spot on the pretty pink rug, tapping a hidden sensor in the side of the table. An overwhelmingly complex holodisplay of scrolling numbers and actuarial charts flickered to life. "**Now we can discuss your tiresome business!**"

CHAPTER 19

- JAU -

It wasn't customary for Lapann Alphas to fight for sport. Omegas might - to prove their strength and try to attract mates - but Alphas had evolved to be smaller and faster. They used these traits to hunt and provide for the cluster, while their Omegas stood guard over the home and kits. Jau had, however, taken up the hobby at the shipyards in his previous life. Any reservations that his cluster mates may have harbored for his unusually violent hobby had disappeared long ago. They hadn't had the luxury of adhering to the classic designation stereotypes after all, not when Jau already had the skills and money was tight.

Roz had fought a few times, early in their exile, but betting odds always shifted to favor him. Their cluster made exponentially more profit, however, when Jau stepped into the ring. The presumed disadvantages of his missing eye and smaller size meant that he was usually underestimated by bookies and opponents alike. He found it sweet that, despite his obvious prowess for defense, his protective Omega still insisted on standing watch in the corridor. Jau cheek-marked his mate before ducking into the promoter's familiar, cluttered office.

The air inside was thick with haze, the cool clouds of vapor that were omnipresent around Rama. Anyone looking for the beleaguered fight organizer at an event needed only to follow that fruit-scented fog, hard at work obscuring Rama's complex crown of bifurcating horns. In the enclosed space of the office the effect was too much - cloying, overwhelming - but Jau just twitched his nose and attempted to suppress his disdain. Had he sensed the Lapann's discomfort, Rama would have doubled down on his constant vaping, if for no other reason than to deter Jau from bothering him.

"Hey, Rama!" Jau grinned cheerily, twitching an ear.

"I thought I told you to stay away from me." Rama didn't look up from his desk display, but shook his head mournfully at Jau's voice.

"Rama. *Buddy.*" Jau clicked his tongue, admonishing. He ducked as one of his ears brushed the myriad strands of tiny, tinkling bells that laced the low ceiling. It was one of the many reasons Roz preferred to wait in the corridor - the poor guy would have ended up tangled as soon as he stepped through the door.

"What did I tell you last time, you Lapann menace? Nobody here is going to fight you anymore. Healing vats are too expensive since the blockade went up." Rama finally looked up from his desktop to level Jau with a glare and a deep sigh of regret.

There was a good reason that Jau went to Rama to set fights, even if it was a less than noble one. When options were limited Rama would book whatever fight he could, regardless if the same match would have been barred in a more regulated (or even slightly more ethical) port of call. Refusing to book a fight - no matter how dangerous or ill-advised - would have been tantamount to sacrilege for Rama. The tiny bells along the ceiling were actually a tribute to some obscure god of violence, and Rama's fighting ring was his perpetual act of devotion.

At least, that's what the promoter had told him once after they'd knocked back a bit too much mushroom liquor at one of the station's many seedy bars. Jau suspected that the profits didn't hurt, but he'd tactfully kept that to himself. Good thing too - it would have bitten him on the tail right about now.

"Nobody here is going to fight me *unless* -" The pods wouldn't spoil; Jau would get the money for the fuel cells, Rama would set a fight for him. Jau repeated it like a mantra. *He just needed a nudge, that was all.*

"*No*. No 'unless'." Rama took an exasperated hit of his vape.

"- *unless* I go up a weight division?" Jau supplied, encouragingly.

"*No*. No one's available." The fine branching curls of Rama's horns cut trails through the thick clouds of his office as the grumpy promoter shook his head, tossing his hands into the air. "Believe me, I wish there were! There's literally no one."

"Wait, really?" Jau settled back on his heels, frowning. This was unexpected.

"Yes, really, you got rocks in those ridiculous ears of yours? All my regulars are...indisposed." Rama puffed out another thick, hazy cloud as he continued to glare peevishly. "T.J. got arrested on a job, Yu Aoi went back to her home planet, and Kin-Daza-Daza encased themselves in some kind of impenetrable glowing cocoon three fraction cycles ago. In *my* storage closet!"

Jau couldn't help but snicker as Rama turned and shouted that last bit over his shoulder towards the back of his office. When he leaned around the corner, to look, he realized Rama wasn't kidding. A stack of crates stood in front of a closed door, gentle white light glowing through the door frame.

Rama turned back and narrowed his golden eyes. "It's *not* funny, Jau. I can't get to my shit in there with that fucking thing in the way."

"Can they even hear you in there?" Jau bit back a smirk at the mental image of his old drinking buddy evolving on top of Rama's credit-receipt cases.

"I don't know." Rama hissed testily. "And I don't care. All this crap is killing me! My whole operation is in shambles...do you know I've got a guy for the non-symmetrical heavyweights div now? But I haven't even been able to book him a fight since -"

Jau's ears perked up before he could stop them, setting off a chain reaction of jingling bells. "Pulsars, Rama! Why didn't you lead with that? I can help you."

"That's not a good idea."

"Well, *I* think it is." Jau leaned closer, planting his palms on the desk.

"That's not your morphological distribution *or* your weight class, idiot." Rama snapped. His horns scattered wisps of smoke as he shook his head in exasperation but it was replaced moments later by another chunky cloud as Rama continued his furious vaping.

Jau pointed to his single eye. "Non-symmetrical."

"That's not what non-symmetrical means and you know it." He sighed heavily, his voice softening. "You're a pain in my ass, Jau, but I've known you a long time. I don't want you to get slaughtered out there, kid."

Jau fought the urge to roll onto the balls of his feet and bounce his weight in excitement. "I bet everyone else would though, wouldn't they Rama? Lots of people on this station that I've humbled in the ring, coming out to watch... betting against me..." He made a prompting gesture, a rotating hand that invited Rama to share in imagining the possibilities.

Rama stayed silent for a long time, but Jau had seen the familiar calculating look in his eyes. He knew he had landed the suggestion. Rama finally blew a cloud of vapor out of his flared nostrils and gave a reluctant grunt of assent.

"The guy's name is Frizbee. He's new, came on right after the last time you were here. Five arms, real big. Bigger than that hulking pink cluster-mate of yours in the hallway. Hits like a rogue asteroid. I'm telling you this so that when you die out there, your ghost can't say that I didn't warn you."

"As if I would haunt you. My ghost has better things to do." Jau rolled his eyes, smirking.

"You'd swing by to hang out with Kin-Daza-Daza." Rama pointed out as he took a long pull on his vape.

Jau mulled it over. "Yeah. I might, actually. Kin-Daza-Daza's cool. Pretty sure they still owe me a celebratory round from our last fight, too."

"Hmph. I'll tell them you said so if they ever-" Rama yelled angrily over his shoulder, "-*get out of my pulsars-damned storage closet!*"

He waved a hand in dismissal as he turned his attention back to his desk display. "Go back to your cluster, Jau.

I'll send you a ping with the fight details later today."

Jau grinned and reached up to run his fingertips along the strand of bells, setting off a wave of joyful chiming that buoyed him as he stepped back out into the corridor.

Roz was still standing next to the door, arms crossed over his chest, ears cocked and at attention for any sign of trouble. "Well?"

Jau knew his Omega had been hoping Rama would wave him off, that they'd find some way of racking up the necessary credits without punches being thrown. He tried to look resigned, but inside, he was borderline giddy at the idea of being back in the ring.

"He said yes. There's a really easy fight, real glass jaw of a guy, he's going to set me up for spectacle's sake." Jau shrugged.

Roz huffed and rolled his eyes - he knew his mate better than that. As he got ready to launch into a lecture, Jau rolled up onto the balls of his feet and gave him a lingering kiss instead.

"Don't worry about it, Roz. I'll be fine, you know I will be. Let me provide for my cluster, keep us flush with credits for when the kits arrive."

Roz sighed wearily, running his hand over his scalp to pull his ears back. "I don't like it, Jau, you know I don't, but I trust you. Please be careful."

CHAPTER 20

- ZUL -

THEY ARRIVED AT THE FIGHT VENUE - THEIR cluster cutting through the crowd like a plasma knife through flesh. As they made their way to the locker room, Jau stripped down to a pair of tight black shorts and tossed his coveralls to Zul. Ever the fastidious one of their cluster, the blue Alpha folded the garment in half and rolled it up into a neat cylinder, tucking it under his arm as Jau limbered up in the empty pit ring.

Zul took a long moment to appreciate his mate. They'd worked off plenty of steam in the bunk, both together and with Roz, over the last fraction-cycle, but this was different. In the bright lights of the pit, Jau's defined muscles, silky yellow fur, and wiry form made his mouth water. Like Roz, he didn't like it when Jau got injured, but watching him prep and fight was still pure visual foreplay.

"You want me to take it to a certain round?" Jau pitched his voice so it only reached his cluster, startling Zul out of his ogling.

Zul shook his head, murmuring in return. "The odds are high enough against you, we don't need to get fancy with it this time around."

"Oh yeah? What am I sitting at?" Jau stretched his neck to either side, rolling his shoulders.

"Uh..." Ch'ik squinted at the proximity readout on her wrist comm, flicking through a few screens. "Boards say you're sitting at ten to one."

Jau whistled long and low as he lifted his arms above his head. He flipped his right palm up the station ceiling, clasped the wrist with his other hand and leaned to the left, pulling his right arm to feel the stretch along his ribs. "Wow. Alright."

"That's... not good?" Ch'ik asked.

Zul chuckled. "No, it's great. It means we're gonna make a bunch of money. The only thing it's bad for is his ego."

"Ten to one means the bookmaker thinks I'm gonna get my ass whipped out there." Jau explained with a wrinkle of his nose. "Very insulting."

Roz looked at the far side of the empty ring, where Jau's opponent would eventually enter, his jaw tight. "Jau. You're getting into a fistfight with a guy that's got five arms. That's three more fists than you. It's not surprising they-"

"So? It doesn't matter how many punches he can throw if I'm better." Jau cut him off as he fixed a one-eyed glare on their Omega. "They should have more faith in me."

"I know that, I do, it's just-" Roz soothed.

Zul cut back in, annoyed. "We don't want them to believe in you, Jau! We get paid out better if the odds are stacked against you! If you insist on this madness, it ought to at least be worth your while. Your ego will survive."

"Hmpf." Jau spread his feet and leaned over and put his palms flat on the floor, looking between his legs at his upside down shipmates. "I guess."

Zul sank down into a nearby chair, rubbing his temples and trying very hard not to stare at Jau's ass. His fight shorts, modified in the back to let the short, downy length of his tail protrude, left very little to the imagination, and Zul had been wrestling with his knot since Ch'ik's declaration on the bridge. Sleeping next to his mates under Jau's pre-fight celibacy edict had been torture.

Jau unceremoniously straddled Zul's lap, facing him and holding up a roll of fabric tape. Zul grunted, unable to resist burying his face against his mate's neck as his own knot swelled at the proximity. "You bastard. You know what those shorts do to me."

"What?" Jau feigned innocence, his blue eye sparkling mischievously. "Just needed some help taping up my hands, Z. If you don't want to, I can always ask R-"

Zul grumbled, grabbing Jau's hand with the tape in it, using his teeth to free the end of the roll. "Still a bastard. You're lucky I love you. Save some of this knot for me, huh?"

Jau rolled his hips, slowly and deliberately, with a grin. "Always, Z. Love you too." He flexed his fingers as Zul finished wrapping the tape, nodding with satisfaction before sliding out of his lap.

Ch'ik was leaning up against Roz, bodies molded to one another, Roz's arms draped over her shoulders. Satisfaction coursed through him at the sight of his Omega and his Beta together - Zul had made a conscious decision to leave Osterian conventions in their wake last night. Overcoming an upbringing of "proper" cluster orientations made him feel like a war was going on in his head, but there was no denying what Ch'ik made them all feel. The Lapann trio had talked long into the night, and agreed: nothing that felt like this could possibly be *wrong*, no matter what the Academy and the council preached.

"Go find seats, Roz. I gotta finish warming up." Jau curled a taped hand behind Roz's neck, pulling him down for a lingering kiss over Ch'ik's shoulder. He leaned back, raising a brow at Ch'ik in question. Their Beta grinned and closed the gap without hesitation, giving Jau a good luck kiss that emphasized she'd meant what she said on the bridge.

Jau swept his tongue tip along his lower lip, flicking his tail at Zul as he walked towards the ring.

"I'll see you all soon."

CHAPTER 21

- ROZ -

Roz was always grateful for his size when the cluster needed to navigate crowds. He might have been of middling size back on Oster, but his bulk demanded respect almost anywhere else off-world. He kept Ch'ik behind him, and Zul fell automatically in line behind her, driven by just as much instinct to protect their pregnant Beta. The Scrum wasn't the kind of place she needed to be wandering alone.

The pit showed signs of popularity and cycles of wear: while the vast layers of stands that wrapped the center ring far below were structurally stable, the paint had seen much better days. Here and there, dents and cracks showed in the metallic planks that comprised seating. The view down to the fighting ring was vertigo-inducing from the top levels, practically stuck in another atmosphere to accommodate the sheer mass of spectators. Thankfully, as guests of one of the fighters, their cluster got to sit in one of the first three rows by the ring itself.

Fencing, tiramite-plated and thick, arched over the ring in an incomplete dome of criss-crossing bars. In most matches, it served only to delineate the fighting area, though it could be laser-charged for more intense pair-ups - never lethal, but damn near sometimes. The current pairing inside the dome appeared to be some sort of rodent-derived species, zipping around the sides of the fencing in a violent, tail-whipping chase. The small creatures were largely ignored amid the murmur of the crowd, all impatiently waiting for the roster to hit the main event.

Jau's handsome fighting profile holo was already front and center in the massive hovering display, just beside a holo of a sneering, lumpy blue alien with five concerningly-muscled arms, all flexed. A glance at the scrolling information below revealed that the odds had shifted 12 to 1 against Jau. Roz reached across Ch'ik to tap Zul's leg, nodding up at the display. Zul held up his wrist comm, showing he'd gotten their bet in at 11-to-1. Roz grinned - Oovooa had fronted them more credits than he expected, and that was a welcome bit of news.

Roz squeezed his Alpha's leg lightly, raising his voice to be heard over the din. "Zul, going to grab a drink, I'll be back soon, okay? Are you and Ch'ik going to be alright?"

Ch'ik looked at him curiously, and he felt a frisson of guilt in his stomach. He'd been glued to her side as often as she allowed since the firefight with Dr'ec, so leaving her unprotected to get himself a drink likely seemed odd. He ignored the sensation, reminding himself he *was* still protecting her.

Zul nodded, draping an arm over Ch'ik's shoulder, respect flickering through his eyes at Roz as he pressed a kiss to the top of her head. His Academy-trained Alpha might have been dense in some of the finer points of emotional connection and communication, but he wasn't stupid. He might not have known exactly what Roz was up to, but he didn't need to be reassured it was important.

Roz's pilfered broma pods, wrapped carefully and tucked in an inner pocket of his coveralls, weighed heavily at him despite their negligible mass. Despite being an unrepentant pirate, he had an unspoken rule not to steal from individuals. Con-glom liners and Imperium ships, sure - they could cover it. But not single craft operators like Ch'ik, even if she was a smuggler. This was for her, though, and he could make peace with that in his dubious ethical playbook.

The only issue with his crowd-parting size was the fact that a large, pink Lapann stuck out like a loose piece of radiation shielding in the general crowd here. Al'ghi, as wise as he was borderless, had taken that into account when he picked their meeting spot. As Roz came face-to-face with what appeared to be a solid metal wall, a tentative touch of his palm went straight through the high-end holo overlay. He smirked, following it through into what turned out to be a wide alleyway.

The opaque mass of floating jelly in front of him became a shifting palette of dark purples, hovering over the puddles of shimmering condensation.

Roz nodded with a wry grin. "Saw your ship on the way in, surprised it's held up so well after that last loop."

The jelly coalesced, shivering into a slightly-taller column.

Roz shook his head emphatically. "No, no, I don't mean it like that, come on. I'm not looking to bring up what happened on Trixllo. I actually have a job for you, if you're interested."

The blob flattened out, the small protruding edge at the top of the mass tilting to one side, sliding halfway down.

"So I heard. But guys like us? You know we're never really *out* of the game. Don't get me wrong, I'm probably going to be scaling back pretty soon myself, but that's half the reason I need this done." Roz snorted ruefully.

The purples shifted chaotically to paler tones, the center of the blob expanding outwards slightly.

He shrugged. "Okay, 'Ghi, I was just trying to give you first dibs on it. I'll take my broma pods elsewhere. It's a shame, though, no one else is half as good as you are."

The blob peevishly flattened into a disc near the ground. That's when Roz knew he had him.

"Yeah, interested all of a sudden now, aren't you? Yes, they're real, you should know me better than that. I might be a pirate, but I'm not a pulsars-damned liar." He shoved a hand in his hidden pocket and retrieved the cloth bundle, unwrapping it carefully. In his giant palm, the pods looked a lot smaller than they actually were. After Ch'ik had initially explained her "contraband," Roz had sat up a few nights on the infonet. His research had quickly turned up the *dust* she talked about, as well as its wildly inflated value on the black market.

The cool gel-like pressure of 'Ghi pressed on his fingertips, angling his palm down slightly. Roz had never been sure where his old friend's eyes were, exactly, but understood he was perceiving the pods somehow. A wriggling tentacle of gel undulated off to the side.

"Nevermind where I got them. What matters is that there's a merc out there that insulted my Beta and tried to kill my cluster. He needs to understand who he's fucking with. I'd send that message personally, but I'm on a time-sensitive job myself. Can't stand the thought of this piece of trash sucking any more air without consequences, so I came to you."

Another gel-tentacle snaked along the ground, oozing against the side of Roz's boot.

He huffed a sigh of exasperation. "Of *course* I came to you first. But like I said, I'm sure I can find some other assassin to take the job..." A single soft pink brow arched in question.

Another flat disc of irritation in response, complete with a few short waving tentacles.

Roz grinned brightly. "Well, if you insist."

The blob heaved itself upwards to hover in front of Roz's chest, an indentation opening in the center like the mouth of a cave. He shoved the bundle of pods directly into the dent, head snapping up at a soft gasp from the unobscured far end of the alley. A pair of botanical species, stick-like and lanky, blushed a deep green and scuttled past the alleyway. From what his translator caught, they weren't sure if they were witnessing an assassination deal or an act of public copulation, but knew better than to interrupt, either way.

Watching until their scandalized audience had vanished from view, Roz lowered his ears and set his jaw, thinking about the vile things that waste of atmosphere had called the Beta of his kits. "Don't vaporize him. Give him a solid Trixllo Handshake for me instead. I'll ping you with the details."

They both turned abruptly and exited on different sides of the alley - they were a pair of professionals, and they understood the need for discretion from here on out. Roz promptly kicked the entire encounter to a dusty corner of his mind, content that his Beta and his cluster would be avenged. If Dr'ec somehow survived Al'ghi's tender mercies, well, Roz would be happy to deliver a Trixllo Handshake of his own.

A raucous cheer erupted in the distance and Roz's ear twitched up - *damn*, this had taken longer than he anticipated. He'd have to hustle back; it wouldn't be Jau's turn yet, but from the increased volume of the crowd, it sounded like the roster was creeping close.

When he reached the stands, he took a long moment to orient himself. He'd been sure he left Zul and Ch'ik *right here*. A deep inhale confirmed their scents, only just beginning to fade. His heartbeat thudded with alarm, making it hard to pick up individual voices and sounds. The sheer *size* of the crowd at the Scrum pit made a visual search nearly impossible, and panic started to set in as his instincts kicked into overdrive. Jau would shortly be on the wrong end of five fists. His other Alpha and their Beta were nowhere to be found. And, even though he'd just handled the problem, there was still an angry merc on their tails.

Movement tugged Roz's gaze to the bot sweepers, curving in a synchronized dance to clean the blood off the ring floor, but it was a figure beyond the dome fence that snagged his attention. Rama, nearly obscured in his ever-present vape cloud, caught Roz's eye. Each of his antlers had been tipped with gold foil for the event, and the bright overhead lights glistened and sparkled across the almost infinite, fractal-like points. Though Roz disliked Rama for his ostentation and his willingness to throw Jau into danger, he was filled with sudden gratitude for the fight promoter when Rama smiled reassuringly and tipped his many-antlered head towards the concession area.

Nearly knocking over the pair of wary botanicals he'd spotted earlier in his haste, Roz shouldered his way to the concession area. In a quadrant full of dull-hued species, one advantage his cluster had was their highly-visible pastel coloration. It wasn't an enviable trait when they were trying for stealth on foot, but right now, Roz didn't give a shit. The sight of Zul's blue ears, Academy-straight and snapped up as he stayed alert for their Beta, sent relief rushing through Roz.

Ch'ik held a tray laden with the best of the worst snacks the Scrum had to offer, each item more nutritionally regrettable than the last. Roz squeezed his own fingers into his palm, willing himself not to speak out of turn. The kits would be fine; Ch'ik ate well enough on the ship, he reminded himself, and what she did with her body was her own choice.

"There you are!" She waved and smiled brightly, handing the tray to Zul. Roz gathered her against his chest and nuzzled the top of her head, his heartbeat still thudding with worry. He took deep lungfuls of her scent, willing his Omega instincts to stand down.

Ch'ik laughed against his fur and eased back, taking a long sip off of a cup full of milky green liquid. "Sheesh, missed you too, big guy. Did you get your drink yet?"

Roz blinked, confused for a moment before he remembered his cover story. "Oh, uh, no. Couldn't find anything I liked."

She thrust the green cup towards Roz as Zul smirked at him over her shoulder. "Here, you can have some of mine! I dunno what this is, but as soon as I smelled it I had to have some. Can you believe Zul tried to talk me out of it?"

Roz's stomach dropped, his complexion threatening to turn the same color as the vile beverage.

He didn't know what the perpetually-oozing sources of the liquid were officially called, but Scrum parlance dubbed them "titbeasts" and her drink "titbeast juice." Roz could hear them now, the wet flipper slaps against the floors of the stockade at the edge of the concession area. The way that the creatures lowed and rumbled as they extruded the juice was the stuff of nightmares.

His cluster had only sampled the stuff once, and only then because taking a shot was traditional hazing for the Scrum's pit fighters. Roz had puked for three sleep cycles, and Jau hadn't managed much better when his time had come. Bafflingly, titbeast juice was very popular across the quadrant - a startling number of lifeforms had developed a taste for the vile liquid. He'd just never thought the Beta carrying their kits would be remotely interested in slurping down the wretched stuff.

Roz shook his head hastily, both disgusted and impressed that Ch'ik was downing it happily. She shrugged and took another long sip of the chunky beverage as they made their way back to the stands. Roz gave Zul a wide-eyed look behind Ch'ik's back, which he returned - he didn't understand her taste for it either. Maybe it was a gestation thing.

As they settled back into their seats, Ch'ik cuddled into Roz's side, almost as if she could sense his agitation. Whether it was conscious or their designations pulling at each other, he was happy to accept it, breathing in her burnt-sugar scent until his nerves settled completely. Zul slid an arm around her waist, the back of his knuckles brushing Roz's side affectionately. He was glad for the comfort as the doors on either side of the pit slid open and silence fell across the arena.

He swallowed hard at the sheer size of Jau's opponent. The multi-armed menace was named Frizbee, according to the display above, and the alien in question was as solid as a slab of titbeast butter and twice as ugly. Roz watched from the edge of his seat as Frizbee whipped the towel off his trunk-thick neck, flinging it around a corner post. Turning his head, his three shining white compound eyes fixed on the small yellow Alpha, who grinned fiercely in response.

Roz liked to think that he had come to terms with it over the cycles, but deep down he still felt guilty for regularly letting one of his cherished Alphas jump directly into harm's way. Jau loved fighting, *really* loved it, in a way that neither he nor Zul could fully relate to. Roz only fought to protect his cluster; the idea of doing it for fun still made him feel like his translator was on the fritz. It helped that Jau never lost, at least, but Roz still spent every fight dead silent in the midst of a cheering crowd, feeling like his heart had been cut out and tossed, helpless, into the middle of the ring.

Roz muttered an Osterian prayer under his breath as Zul's grip tightened on Ch'ik's hip.

CHAPTER 22
- JAU -

THEY MET IN THE CENTER OF THE RING.

Frizbee reached out to shake hands with both of his left arms *and wow, wasn't that a real dick-swinging move.* Jau, not to be outdone, obliged. Sure, it was awkward to twist his right wrist around in order to shake each of the craggy hands in one of his own, but Jau made it work.

A chuckle rippled through the crowd at his calm response. Appearance and intimidation went hand-in-hand in the pit, and he wasn't about to let this half-assed lopsided muscle spider show him up before the first punch even sailed. The background noise of the crowd receded into a murmur of anticipation until, finally, the bell rang.

Jau couldn't read the facial expressions of whatever species his opponent was, but the alien's sloppy fighting stance showed he expected an easy victory. That wasn't to say he wasn't intimidating: Frizbee looked like he could have handled himself against an opponent of his own size and speed. The big guy would have even had an easy advantage over a fighter Jau's size if he'd have just taken it seriously. As he warily circled his rival, Jau guessed that Frizbee heard the unbalanced odds on the match and let it get to his head. He'd seen it a million times in other fighters, and it made their inevitable expressions of defeat that much sweeter.

Those who had never fought against Jau before never really understood just how tough he was. How hard he could hit. How much punishment he'd gladly take.

Jau stayed light on his feet, watching through the protective barricade of his hands as he and Frizbee circled one another in the ring. When he feinted close enough to tempt Frizbee into taking a shot at him, his multi-armed opponent threw punches one-sided, a row of fists in clumsy, staggered, succession. He swung fast but moved with a heavy lumbering gait as he tracked Jau around the ring.

There was always the faint possibility that Frizbee was hiding some ingrown biological protection or wet tech, but if everything was as it appeared then this wasn't a fair fight.

Not at all.

Jau drove forward with a flurry of punches that Frizbee deflected on the solid wall of his three right arms. He immediately took the bait, swinging on Jau with his two left fists. There was no way to avoid the blows, or maybe Jau just didn't want to, because he didn't bother to dart or deflect. All of Jau's pent-up energy sizzled to the surface of his brain; he knew from experience that there was no better way to release it than through the searing song of pain.

Frisbee's upper left connected with Jau's nose, heavy fist like a steel hammer. Hot blood immediately gushed across Jau's upper lip and into his mouth, dripping down the fur of his chin and along the line of his jaw. Before Jau could even dart his tongue out at the delicious metallic tang, Frisbee's staggered lower left swung in. The second merciless blow split Jau's face so deeply that the blood flooded his sinuses and sent his brain into a dizzy spin of guilty pleasure.

Frizbee may have drawn first blood, but blood was nothing. Jau had forced himself well within Frizbee's guard. Too close to hit. Jau's opponent seemed to realize his mistake belatedly as he tried to reel backwards, but it was far too late for Frizbee to save himself.

In that moment the crowd sucked in a breath as a single entity, tense with anticipation, but time didn't slow down. Jau had never experienced the rumored fighter's dilation of perception. That would have become hesitation in the pit, and he never allowed himself the luxury. Here, there was only his own certainty, a well-earned confidence refined through cycles of ecstatic violence.

Jau's body was a tightly-coiled spring. His mind was a meat grinder. His soul was a light and ever expanding thing, free of any doubt. The path to victory was laid out clearly before him: not only for this fight, but for all things.

He would beat Frizbee. Then, he'd repair the stasis field with their winnings. Then, they would get the pods back to Oster. And *then* Ch'ik would stay with them, forever and ever, until the quiet ends of all of their days.

Jau stepped forward and ducked to dodge the next blow. He planted his feet and popped back up with a grin on his face and blood on his teeth.

A quick right jab, a hard left hook. Then it was over.

Frizbee dropped to his knees on the grimy canvas mat, wobbled briefly, then slumped forward - unconscious - to faceplant in the center of the ring.

The crowd exploded with noise.

Cheers of joy and shouts of outrage in equal measure, mixed together into one indistinguishable wave of sound that crashed over Jau as he scanned the crowd until he saw them. His cluster, smug and proud. His

Beta, staring at him with her soft mouth slightly parted and her eyes wide and dark. It would have been the right time to wink at Ch'ik, to flash a suggestive - if bloodied - smirk, but something about her gaze burrowed into him, deep and hot. Jau had to look away before his knot started to swell up.

It would be so obvious, in the tight little fight shorts. Every being in the audience would look at him and *know* how bad he - he, a *Lapann Alpha* - wanted to claim the *Beta* of his kits.

His teeth ached, and it had nothing to do with the blood that stained them.

CHAPTER 23

- CH'IK -

ZUL AND ROZ'S SHOULDERS HAD SAGGED VISIBLY with relief when Jau laid out their opponent with that last incredible punch. Across the ring, a shiny-antlered figure emerged from a dramatic fog and raised a hand to their group, tilting his head towards a row of buildings nearby.

Zul leaned in and brushed his cheek against Ch'ik's in that strange, slow movement the Lapann frequently repeated with one another. A moment later, Roz tugged her closer and did the same thing on the other side - she was going to have to ask them at some point what the hell that was about.

"Ch'ik, in a minute or two, Jau's going to come up from the ring. Roz and I are going to go collect his winnings from Rama and get the stasis components we need."

Zul's gaze was soft and doting, a gentle smile pulling at his mouth.

Roz gave a light chuckle. "What Zul isn't saying is that Jau gets a little...worked up...after a fight. He's probably barely going to dunk his head in the healing vat, and only then because Rama basically makes him. Usually he takes out all that excess energy with us, but..." He grinned at her, bumping his hip against hers. "What I'm saying is that you may want to stretch first. Have fun."

She blinked. *Oh.*

Ch'ik had assumed that Jau would need time to heal, that his delightful prior threat was one that would give her free rein to fuck Roz and Zul in the interim. What if she *hurt* Jau? That wouldn't be good - she'd have to be gentle, careful of his injuries, even though she was truthfully eager for some rough-and-tumble.

Jau appeared at the end of the aisle, blood still staining the edge of his jaw. His face was essentially healed, but an angry red slash in his lower lip curiously remained. Why wouldn't he take the time to get that healed too? The vats worked quickly enough, and access to them was an expensive luxury.

Zul and Roz each wordlessly gave her shoulders a squeeze, getting up in tandem and walking towards the buildings beyond the ring. Ch'ik was left sitting alone in the stands as the pale yellow Lapann, blood-spattered and half-feral, stalked towards her with a manic grin. Discomfort and concern quickly melted into heat that pooled in her core, remembering his promise.

He silently offered his hand, the blood-tinged fur of his knuckles reminding her of the last time he'd done this, back in the bar. This time, there was no hesitation as she curled her fingers around his and rose with a knowing smile.

They moved away from the pit, beyond the stands and back into the tangle of the colony. Ch'ik had no frame of reference for time in the Scrum; there were no suns to rise or sky to darken. Everything sort of smeared together, an endless neon-edged unreality that wasn't getting any easier to parse. The surreal setting fell into the background of her consciousness as Jau dragged her through the teeming crowds, steadfastly ignoring the multiple people calling out to greet or congratulate him.

When they reached the docks everything was just as busy as it had been when the *Koton* landed. Jau didn't seem aware of the attention his appearance was drawing - pupils blown black and wide as saucers with adrenaline, the fur of his face and chest still caked in blood. The interest of the occasional bystander wasn't lost on Ch'ik. They might not have known the specifics, but she knew that *they* knew that Jau was dragging her back to a ship to make her his second conquest. The grip on her hand, the determined set of his shoulders, the angle of his ears - it declared his intentions with every step.

Yeah, Ch'ik was going to get fucked, *and she didn't care who knew it.* Let them all stare, none of them would have dared to intervene. More importantly, none of them could have what was *hers* to claim.

They made it back to the ship, at least. Together, they stumbled up the ramp and made it no farther than was necessary to not draw a crowd.

Jau's hands were greedy on her right away, sliding in through the open zipper of her coveralls to skim along her sides, her ribs and hips, the glowing curve of her belly. He had shoved his face into the soft spot between Ch'ik's shoulder and neck and the light scratch of his fur on that sensitive curve made her feel like she was going to vibrate out of her skin. He pressed a series of nipping kisses up the column of her neck, and for the briefest moment she felt the unyielding surface of his teeth before he shuddered, powerfully, and resumed the softer press of his lips.

His voice was reverent, trance-like as he smeared his own tacky blood across her skin with a groan. "I wanna suck your cock until you scream my name -"

Alright, well, they'd deal with *that* later.

Maybe if she was in her right mind Ch'ik would have stopped him and given a quick rundown on the difference between a clit and a cock but, then again, maybe not. She wasn't a fuckin' narc. That shit didn't really matter: he'd seen her naked with Roz's knot in her, and that meant he knew the basics of how everything *fit together*, as Roz put it. Hell, Ch'ik counted herself lucky that she'd manage to stop all of them from referring to their jizz as 'goo' - Jau calling her clit a cock was minor in comparison. Maybe a little hot, even.

"Yeah, yeah *fuck*, get your mouth on me -" She panted, leaning heavily against a bulkhead.

Ch'ik shrugged out of her coveralls, a practiced roll of her shoulders that freed them from the garment. Jau helped her yank off her boots without stopping what he was doing, which was *definitely* hot. If she'd have known how this night was going to go, she would have worn something nicer - maybe one of those lacy numbers that made Zul's brain go offline.

Thankfully Jau didn't seem to care. He shoved his face against the front of her plain white underwear and inhaled deeply, scenting her. His tongue darted out and gave a quick, teasing to lick at the fabric over her clit and Ch'ik's tenuous control snapped. She ran her hand through the shock of hair between his ears and gripped, blonde strands winding through her fingers as she rolled her hips wantonly and pressed against his face.

He groaned happily in response, but most of the noise was lost in the damp fabric. It would be stained, Ch'ik realized distantly, noticing the odd pink smear against the white. Blood, Jau's blood, the cut on his lip that she had reopened by rutting against his mouth. The part of her brain that was still capable of higher functioning urged her to pull back and apologize, to tell him that she'd be happy to wait until he'd visited the medical bay, but that part of her brain was small. Very small, and shrinking by the moment. Then she rolled her cunt against his bleeding mouth again and Jau made what was, quite possibly, the hottest noise that Ch'ik had ever heard.

The last remaining bastion of sense in her brain winked out of existence.

Panting, she pulled her underwear to the side and was immediately rewarded by Jau's seeking tongue. He licked in between her folds, up to her clit, and lingered there with broad strokes of his tongue that threatened to buckle her knees. He settled heavily on his own knees, snaking an arm around her waist to keep her body pressed against his mouth.

The nails of her free hand scraped against the metal of the ship's wall behind her and she whimpered, shocked he'd pushed her body so quickly towards a peak. There was something deeply satisfying, primal even, about having a blood-smeared fight victor on his knees for her, devoted to her pleasure. She leaned into that sensation of power as she rode his mouth to completion, his name a joyful shriek on her lips, her grip on his hair almost certainly hard enough to sting.

He cradled her hips, stilling his tongue and simply keeping his mouth pressed tightly against her as her body settled. He might not have known what to call her anatomy, but damned if he didn't understand the more important aspects of how it worked.

"Fuck. Jau." She panted, and let her head fall back against the wall, endorphins flooding her so deeply she imagined this is what dust felt like. Unlatching her fingers from his hair with a mental cringe, hoping she hadn't hurt him, she combed them through softly instead.

He ran his tongue up one last time, making her twitch, sitting back on his haunches with a blissful, hungry expression. Guilt cut through her pleasant haze as she spotted the line of fresh, dark crimson staining the fur below his lip.

"Oh, shit, I'm so sorry Jau. Your lip-"

He was breathing heavily, and it wasn't with the effort he'd just expended. From the look of the erection her new lover was sporting, he'd be lucky if his coveralls weren't punctured clean through in a minute. He roughly shoved the fabric off his shoulder, tugging impatiently at the zipper, his voice a deep growl.

"Don't be sorry, Ch'ik. Use me. *Hurt* me. *Please.*"

She stared at him in fascination as he stripped down, throwing the messy bundle of cloth and boots into the front room of the ship behind them, sinking back down to his knees in front of her like a supplicant. She held her breath, playing cautiously with the new possibility the Alpha had literally laid at her feet.

Using the wall to hold herself steady, she carefully lifted a foot and pressed the naked sole against his furred chest, relishing the softness. She locked eyes with him and gave a single, small nod, shoving without warning and sending him sprawling onto his back. At the contact, his cock jumped, leaking copious amounts of golden precum all over his shaft as he looked up at her in a lustful stupor.

Ch'ik moved to stand over him, one foot to either side of his waist, and he automatically lifted his hands up to steady her. She braced her palms on his, careful of her stomach, and lowered herself down to her knees over him. Unwilling to wait, she reached between her legs and found his shaft, hard as tiramite and pulsing, notching him against her entrance and sinking down with a breathless sigh.

Looking down at him through the soft curtain of her hair, a warmth expanded in her chest at the adoration in his expression. She cupped his cheek in an uncharacteristic surge of tenderness, catching herself and tempering it by sweeping the pad of her thumb across his split lip. He went almost rigid underneath her, his eyes rolling back with a strangled, ecstatic noise as he drove upwards, shoving his knot against her.

Craving the delicious stretch she'd enjoyed with his mates already, she pressed her thumb harder against the wound. Jau's body answered her with a deep shudder of pleasure, and the breath whooshed out of her lungs as he pressed up, almost mindlessly, forcing his knot into her in two sharp thrusts.

Her palms smacked against his chest to steady herself in the sudden onslaught of movement, fingernails curling on instinct to keep herself stable and seated on him. He gave a sob of pleasure so profound it made her skin prickle with satisfaction. A quick study, she dug her nails in deeper to hear it again, clenching around the fist-sized girth of his knot at the same time. He was only slightly smaller *there* than Roz or Zul, but his shorter frame fit against hers so well, it was as if they were created for one another.

She'd already gotten the orgasm she wanted, and Jau had fought so well for her - for all of them. Ch'ik was happy to give him everything he needed, now, taking her own pleasure from the savage beauty of his expression. She rode him slowly for a few minutes, digging her nails into his chest on the downstrokes, waiting until he sounded wild with need. Leaning down to kiss him, she closed her teeth around his abused lip, tugging it until he drove up again with a

J.L. LOGOSZ & VERA VALENTINE

sharp cry, flooding her with warmth inside her core as he came.

In the tense, erotic haze of their coupling, an alien urge seized her. She tilted her head back, her mouth feeling crowded and achy, curling her lips as she dove back to Jau, to that beautiful expanse of skin between his neck and shoulder. Every fiber of her being honed in on that softly-furred stretch of him, already marked with two faint crescent moons. Just shy of her goal, her head stopped, held in place. She growled in frustration, jerking back to see a wide-eyed Jau, one fist lightly clutching her hair.

"Ch'ik? What-? Were you?"

She sat up further, a gentle touch on his fingers to release her hair.

"I - I don't know. I wanted to *bite* you for some reason, not for like..."

She blushed, slightly, surprised she was still capable of doing so. "You know, for fun. Sorry, I don't know what the hell came over me."

The intensity of Jau's expression made her pulse pound in her ears. Reaching up to cup her cheek, she startled at the sudden intrusion of his thumb between her lips. Her confusion only doubled when he fisted her hair again with his other hand, holding her head in place as he gently thumbed her upper lip up and gasped.

246

"*Fuck!* Pulsars, Ch'ik. You've - you've got, I mean - your teeth are sharpening. This is *impossible*. Betas don't bite." His expression softened at her obvious confusion. "You were trying to give me a mating bite. We don't know if that's hormones or instincts taking the helm, but I need you to know that's the only reason I stopped you. The *only* reason." His voice was strained with longing that made her tighten around him.

He groaned, dropping his hands to her hips and carefully rolling their bodies to put himself over her. She hissed slightly at the cold metal of the deck on her bare back, forgetting it completely as Jau leaned down to kiss her again. He began slow, short thrusts, moving his knot inside her in a way that made her toes curl. His chest vibrated with something deep and reverberating. It wasn't quite a growl, but something in her found it alluring enough that all of her nipples pebbled - two against his furred chest, one against the firm metal of the deck.

He ran his cheek slowly along her temple, a possessive rumble in his voice. "When we bite each other, it's going to be because you want it, Ch'ik, and it's going to be all of us. Do you understand?"

She nodded, only half-comprehending as her body eagerly responded to his once more.

CHAPTER 24

- ZUL -

FIVE FRACTION-CYCLES HAD PASSED NOW SINCE they'd met Ch'ik, and life aboard the *Koton* had gotten exponentially better in those 140 days. Finally able to shrug off the crushing guilt that his lustful impulses might have hurt one of their eggs, Zul and Ch'ik had fallen into bed several times together. He'd been learning more about how to use his mouth on her, about what she liked and what was off the experimentation list. The latter had resulted in a small ear bruise when he misinterpreted her reactions - a lesson learned. While the cluster all enjoyed under-tail play, Ch'ik did *not*.

Their Beta had been spending more time in her nest, and they'd had to pick up more blankets at a port as she added to the cozy cradle of fabric. The loose circle, rich with their scents, rose a few inches from the surface of her bunk. It formed a cozy hollow she slept in, usually alone, but occasionally with he or Jau - and at least a few thrilling times, with both of them.

Roz was simply too big to fit comfortably in the nest with her, so he and Ch'ik often stole naps together in the cluster's bed, among other recreational pastimes. Jau, trooper that he was, had started doing laundry twice as often.

Ch'ik also emerged from her room more willingly as time went on - at first because she begrudgingly needed help with things like her boots, difficult to reach now with her growing belly. Though initially driven by simple boredom, she'd taken an interest in learning how to cook with Jau, and the finer points of gardening with Roz. Zul had personally tried to teach her about helm controls of the larger ship, but she nodded off every time he started in on explanations. Instead, they'd taken to occasionally cuddling up in her nest and watching old episodes of Night Beats together.

Jau's winnings had taken care of everything they needed and then some. Not only had they gotten new stasis equipment that could handle some turbulence, he'd gone out of his way to provide for the crew as well. Before they'd left the Scrum, Zul had snuck out and gotten the most impressive collection of cooking spices he could find at the market, as well as updated navi maps for Jau.

It took a little searching through the dank botanical quarter of the station, but he'd found a beautiful collection of hydroponic seed-starters for Roz, as well as some tiramite-tipped cutter cones for the *Koton*'s piercing mechanism. Roz was too cluster-minded to ask for something for himself, but Zul specifically chose items that benefited the entire ship to head off his protests.

And for the beautiful Beta of his kits, the best maternity coveralls credits could buy. As much as they all loved ogling her necessity-driven open zipper look, he knew it couldn't be comfortable. Three tiny blankets also made their way into his purchases - while they cost far more credits than mere slips of fabric ought to, just the sight of them made his fur bristle happily. *Three.* He hadn't fucked up, after all.

He stashed his gifts in an unused cabinet of the cargo bay, waiting until they'd hit a particularly boring stretch of the journey to surprise his cluster-mates. Jau promptly plopped into his command chair, dipping a fingertip in a few of the spice jars to taste them, practically giddy over some sort of rare red powder. Roz grinned over his new seeds beside Jau, the two of them chatting animatedly at the dishes they could create once they could be harvested. Ch'ik strolled back onto the bridge, dressed in the new coveralls, smiling brightly.

"Wow, this is *so* much better - I can breathe! I mean, not that I've been wearing a lot of clothes recently." She winked at Jau, who popped a spice-tipped finger out of his mouth to adjust the crotch of his coveralls, leering.

She snorted a laugh, shaking her hair out of her eyes - it had been getting long, thanks in part to eating well and a regular infusion of both nutrients and *laht*. "Now if I could just get this pulsars-damned hair out of my eyes all the time, I'd be great. Ugh."

Ch'ik puttered around on the bridge for a while, not doing anything in particular other than repeatedly shoving her hair back out of her eyes and staring at them.

Zul couldn't tell if she wanted something or if this was just some previously unknown facet of the Beta nesting mechanism. He thought about asking, but before he could Ch'ik sneezed as a strand tickled her nose, loudly declaring, "That's *it*, I'm shaving it off. I don't care anymore."

Zul tapped a button on the console, finalizing the new navi map download. "Okay."

Ch'ik looked at him with a tilt of her head. "That's it? Okay?"

Her confused tone made him swivel his chair to face her. "Sure, it's your hair, Ch'ik. Why would I care if you cut it?"

She gave a fond look. "It's just - well, I'm just not used to a guy - guys - not having a loud opinion about stuff like that."

Zul managed to stop his ear from flicking with irritation, but just barely. They'd picked up enough chatter during their visits to the Scrum to gather that not all species considered males and females to be on equal footing. That shit didn't fly with him. If Ch'ik wanted to be comfortable, he would make sure she was comfortable, period. "Do you have clippers?"

She wrinkled her nose pessimistically. "I...think? They're buried somewhere in the *Hawk* though, and probably rusted."

Nope. He didn't like the idea of rusted clippers anywhere near their Beta. "I have a clean set in our quarters - you want me to help you do it? I haven't really used them since the Academy, but I still remember how."

It had been many cycles since the Academy, but he still recalled the faint tickling buzz that came with shaving his Captain's rank into his fur.

She laughed softly, voice teasing and warm. "Still waters run deep. Who knew that military stick up your ass would come in handy?"

He rolled his eyes, checking the download as he rose, stretching. "I *don't* have a stick up my ass."

Just before Zul got to the doorway, Jau grabbed him from behind, playfully bouncing his own hips into Zul's ass. The smaller Alpha went up on his toes to nuzzle his mating bite, sending a shiver of pleasure down Zul's spine. "Want one?"

Zul laughed, sliding a hand behind him to grip Jau's cock through his coveralls. "Tonight? I have a haircut to give right now, and apparently you've got a one-track mind."

Jau nipped his mark teasingly and grinned. "Alright, I *suppose* I can wait. Think you can clean me up too? I've been getting shaggy since the Scrum."

Roz offered to take a turn at the helm so Zul could show off his latent Academy skills. A few minutes later, Ch'ik was sitting in a chair dragged into the front room of the ship, a tarp underneath her, as Zul stood and turned on the clippers. "You're sure about this? You just want me to take it all the way down?"

"*Please*. It'll be such a relief. I just don't wanna deal with it for another two fraction-cycles. Maybe I'll grow it back out once the kits are here, but you can always trim it again then." She huffed out a breath, straggly blonde strands dancing in the air in front of her.

Zul and Jau glanced at each other over her head. Their trio had initiated several late night discussions, now that their collective attraction to Ch'ik was no longer a secret. They all wanted her to stay, but had agreed as a cluster not to pressure her into it. Even so, it was hard not to get their hopes up every time she let something idle like that slip. The faintest indication she'd be sticking around after the birth made his heart thud happily in his chest.

He swallowed, focusing on the task at hand, flicking on the clippers and gently brushing her hair up her scalp. The first pass of the clippers sent a handful of silky blonde strands tumbling to the tarp with a soft whisper. Her shoulders visibly relaxed at the sound. "Thank you for doing this, Zul."

"My pleasure, Ch'ik. If it makes you happy, it makes us happy." He smiled as the clipper carved out another path, sending more blonde hair to the floor.

Jau watched eagerly, grinning as he bent down to nuzzle the nape of her neck, whispering. "I personally think it makes you look even hotter."

Zul tsked, trying to nudge his mate away with a hip. "Let her be - she's gotta hold still or I'm gonna fuck this up."

Jau changed tactics, standing to nip at his mating bite on Zul's neck, instead. Zul was forced to hold the clippers aside as the pleasant sensation slithered down his spine. He swallowed a soft moan as Jau's heated growl purred in his ears. "Nah, Z. You know exactly what you're doing."

"Come here, you horny pain in the ass. Let him finish and I'll brush you out." Ch'ik clicked her tongue and pointed at the ground between her legs.

Jau snickered and plopped down between Ch'ik's legs, sitting on the floor and resting gingerly back against her rounded stomach. She grabbed the nearby brush and started smoothing out his tousled blonde locks as Zul removed what was left of hers.

She scrubbed a hand over her freshly-shaved scalp when Zul was done, tapping Jau's shoulder to trade places with him. "Oh man, this is great Zul. You got it so even! It's such a chop job when I try to do it myself." She grinned at her own reflection in a bulkhead, running her fingertips over the faint, downy stubble.

"What about you, Jau? You want me to take it down too?" Zul finger-combed his mate's shorter locks.

"Mm. Nah, Ch'ik needs something to grab, after all." He tilted his head back and grinned at Zul as Ch'ik laughed. "Let's do it shorter in the front and on the sides, but leave it long in the back."

It only took a few minutes for Zul to clean up the shaggy ends of Jau's hair, shaving the sides down after he'd had Jau weigh in on the look halfway through. Even he was impressed at how handsome his fellow Alpha turned out after the haircut, and Jau was incredibly pleased to have more peripheral visibility. Ever the fighter, his mate.

Zul used the same polished bulkhead as a mirror, trimming himself up. He'd work on Roz later in the evening, once they'd set the autopilot up for the night. Ch'ik reclaimed the chair, and Jau had tugged her bare feet into his lap, massaging them gently. As Zul dusted off, he turned to find Jau enthusiastically explaining the finer points of pit fighting to Ch'ik's stomach as she watched, bemused.

Pulsars, was he in love.

CHAPTER 25

- CH'IK -

Like a switch had been flipped, the lights in her belly seemed to shift more often now, getting a bit brighter every fraction-cycle. What felt like nothing at first gradually became movement she could feel, the eggs rising and sinking inside her. She had to concentrate to feel it, really - they were just faint twitches, a tickle here and there, but every one of the Lapann reassured her they were doing alright.

The day after her haircut, she sat on the crash bench on the bridge. She'd dragged a few pillows from her room over the last fraction cycle, making it a sort of back-up nest. The longer she was pregnant, the more she wanted to be in the presence of at least one of the guys, as often as possible. She'd been watching Jau examine their course when a strange, repetitive jerking lightly twinged her belly. She unzipped her coveralls in a small panic, splaying a hand across the softly-glowing dome of her stomach. Somewhere along the way she'd started feeling *very* protective of the growing lives inside her.

At her soft noise of puzzled distress, Roz immediately crossed the bridge and laid his hand over hers. He shook his head, raising a brow in question. She explained what she was feeling, pulling down her coveralls to get a better look at her stomach. As Roz watched, one of the lights shivered in a strange, jerky rhythm. Naked joy spread across his face, soothing her nerves as much as his touch and scent did.

"Hiccups." Roz explained in quiet awe. His eyes welled with emotion and his little pink nose twitched with delight. "One of our kits has the hiccups, Ch'ik." She let out a sigh of relief as he called for Zul and Jau to come and see, before their kit had a chance to steady itself.

As they crowded around her stomach and took turns rubbing it, a flashing yellow light caught her eye. "Hey, Zul, what's that alarm for?"

"Hm?" He looked up, eyes creased with happiness and pride in his kits. Both emotions instantly washed out of his expression as he turned to see where she pointed. "Oh fuck! Jau! The pulsar-damned blockade's *manned!*"

Jau rocketed to his feet and dashed to the nav array, frantically swiping through screens. "When the hell did *that* happen? Shit!"

Roz frowned as he explained their panic, holding tight to Ch'ik's hand. "Our forged documents get through bots and automation just fine, but they're going to fall apart under manual examination - they're old. This part of the blockade hasn't been manned since we left Oster. It's always been our go-to for getting in and out of the quadrant because there's never been manual examinations."

Sure enough, outside the view screen, Imperium cruisers congregated around the gateways in the shimmering blockade. Long lines of ships were backed up in a haphazard scramble nearly as thick as the docking situation back at the Scrum. She clocked mainly ice haulers and personal pleasure craft as they waited to be checked and ushered through.

"There's no way. This checkpoint is *never* manned." Jau muttered to himself, ears laid back flat in irritation as he dropped into the control array and guided them into one of the staggered queues. "There must be something going on, I don't -"

Ch'ik's stomach sank, the joy brought on by the kit's hiccups abruptly cut off at the dread that coursed through her. "Why are we going through a blockade in the first place? We need to go another way! They can't board and find the pods - they'll confiscate them and toss us all in prison. I am *not* giving birth in prison."

Zul's jaw clenched, glaring at the Imperium cruisers and the handful of ships ahead of them in line. "We can't, Ch'ik. They'd tail us, it'd be too obvious we were trying to circumvent the blockade at this point."

She cursed, awkwardly hauling herself up off the bench with a helping hand from Roz. "Alright, new plan then. I'm going to get us someone *else's* registration. Where's my proximity hacker?" A sharp thud sounded behind her.

She turned to find Roz's ears dropped back, his arms crossed on his chest. "*No.* I don't want you to use that damned thing, Ch'ik! That was the scariest moment of my life, I thought - nevermind what I thought. It *hurts* you!"

Ch'ik was shocked the quiet Omega was putting his foot down - both literally and metaphorically. That was very un-Roz-like behavior, but she had no patience for it at the moment. "Dr'ec had a shit-ton of security on his ship - he can't fly worth a damn but he turned that thing into a fucking fortress. You think these old-as-hell freighters are gonna be locked down like that? This isn't going to be like last time Roz, I'm not going to have a seizure. Please, trust me."

Roz shook his head slowly, eyes creased as he tried not to tear up. She laid a hand gently on his arm, running her thumb along his soft pink fur. "It's going to be okay, really it is. I wouldn't do *anything* that put the kits in danger, alright? I promise."

Roz pulled her up against his chest, tucking her head under his chin. She felt a cold drop of moisture along her hairline before he released her with a sharp sniffle. "Alright. Alright. But I don't want *you* in danger either, Ch'ik. If you start seizing, I'm going to reduce that thing to fistfuls of metal scraps, you understand me?"

She smiled and cupped his cheek. "It's gonna be fine, big guy - help me get set up?"

Reluctance oozed out of every movement, but he hauled her beat-to-shit duffel bag out of a cabinet she didn't remember stashing it in. Shoving an arm in and twisting her wrist, she pulled it back out encased in the machinery. "Now, I'm only stealing this time, not disabling, so I'm not going to seize up like last time. Just hold me steady, Roz."

With her free hand, she dug around the bag until she found the bite guard. Blowing dust and pastel fur off of it, she shrugged before moving to pop the still-grimy half-moon in her mouth.

Roz grimaced, grabbing it from her. "Pulsars, Ch'ik. Give me a second." He muttered, sticking it under the sonic cleaner panel with a chastising look as he handed it back over.

She gave him a sheepish grin and slid it into her mouth. "'Fank 'ou."

She climbed up in his lap again, putting her back to his chest like they had in the cargo bay. He really made a very comfortable seat, no matter what they happened to be doing. She grinned, flashing the bite guard as she relaxed into his fur. The faster operation didn't require both gauntlets, thankfully, because she wasn't relishing the idea of itchy dot-scabs on *both* arms.

She hugged the circle of Roz's arms as she tumbled into the strange void that meshed body, mind, and tech. Aiming for one of the furthest ships in the digital queue that was still physically close enough to access, she started hunting for unprotected registrations. Picking a far-off line on the list would give the *Koton* plenty of time to put parsecs behind them and vanish into open space. With most of the usual protections blown wide open in preparation for examination at the blockade, it was child's play - no one was expecting a proximity hacker *here*.

Ch'ik didn't know what the fuck a leprechaun was, or why it was fortunate, but the *Lucky Leprechaun* had the distinction of being *unlucky* today as she quickly copied the registration, deleting theirs in her wake. By the time the unfortunate freighter proved who they were via secondary means, the *Koton* would be long gone. After a quick glance at the pilfered ship's manifest, she dropped back out of the hacker, tugging it off her arm.

Roz frowned at the tiny red dots as she rubbed them absently. *Cost of doing dubious business, big guy.* "Alright fellas, we're good to go. Jau, can you rig a holo-overlay on the cargo hold? Some kind of shiny yellow metal, pressed into trading discs. Looks like they were carrying a *lot*."

Jau nodded, flipping through screens as Zul glared through the front window at the waiting Imperium officers in the distance.

CHAPTER 26

- JAU -

ALTHOUGH IT WAS A TENSE FEW MINUTES, CH'IK'S stolen registration got them through the checkpoint; it looked believable enough that the officers hadn't even examined his holo-overlay in the cargo hold. He was confident it would have fooled them, but very grateful they didn't have to put that confidence to the test.

Once they were clear, Ch'ik dumped the hacker back into her bag and stomped over to their command chairs, poking Jau in the chest with a finger. "Alright, fess up. Why the fuck are you guys sneaking through a blockade? I thought we were just fucking off and killing time while we waited for these babies to be born."

Jau shrugged out of the control array, running his fingers through his newly shorn hair. It was going to take all of his willpower not to get turned on by Ch'ik's explosion of anger - just that finger poke to the chest was enough to make him start to stir in his coveralls - but even Jau knew that this was *not* the time. "There's a good explanation. I promise."

"There had fuckin' *better* be. I've been exiled from plenty of places, you generally just gotta keep quiet if you sneak back. Who the hell did you guys piss off?"

Zul sighed heavily. "Family."

"Oh." Ch'ik seemed as if she had been caught a bit flat-footed by the reveal, but Jau couldn't tell if she was surprised, confused, or both. He'd gathered that Ch'ik had been raised in some kind of foundling center, so it was likely that family hadn't even occurred to her as the source of potential strife.

"I come from a highly successful agricorp cluster back on Oster, but we - Jau, Roz, and I - were exiled because of my uncle." His ears were swung forward in shame, sliding a guilty look at his own cluster-mates.

Roz crossed the bridge, wrapping an arm around Zul's shoulders and kissing his cheek. "And we told you back when it happened that we were perfectly okay with tossing our lot in with yours, Zul. There's no place Jau and I would rather be than with you."

Their heads bowed beside each other as they took turns cheek-marking one another - a practice they'd since explained was a sign of trust and affection. Zul smiled softly at their Omega, sharing the same look briefly with Jau before turning back to Ch'ik.

"After I graduated from the Academy my uncle hired us to transport a shipment of *laht* cross-planet. When I was getting the paperwork together I noticed something... odd. I went digging, because by then the three of us were a cluster, and we knew we wanted kits. My cousin might have been generous with *laht* at parties when we were just overgrown kits ourselves, but as we grew up, my uncle got him into line. Even with the family connection he never would have sold me the *laht* at a discount. It would have been impossible for me to get any for Roz." He squeezed the Omega's hand on his shoulder gently.

"It's not that we can't reproduce without the *laht,* but there are problems. Lots of lost kits, endless heartbreak." Roz shoved a hand across his face as he sniffled. "A cluster will try and try and try until they get lucky, but those losses hurt. The emotional scarring can run so deep that by the time a healthy kit arrives, the cluster is wounded. Sometimes too deeply to recover." Zul shifted to wrap an arm around Roz's side, squeezing him gently.

Jau tugged Ch'ik down into his lap, nuzzling her neck as he explained further. "Zul didn't know much about crops, but Roz did. Some paperwork got filed along with the generic shipment manifests by mistake, and Zul and Roz managed to unravel a nasty little secret. *Laht* is rare because broma is so difficult to grow, but it's also being tightly controlled by a single cluster to make it all but unobtainable. Zul's family cluster."

Zul grimaced. "My *uncle's* scheming, shitty family cluster, please. *You* are my family now, not them. My uncle's side of the family had evidently been genetically manipulating the broma plants on our planet for generations, and actively driving the scarcity to keep themselves flush on credits. I knew something wasn't right with them - they were the ones that raised me, and I all but ran away to the Academy to escape them in the first place."

Ch'ik rested back against Jau, who massaged her hips and lower back with strong hands as they talked. She raised a brow at Zul. "So you're telling me you come from a family of scheming baddies with generations of genetic machinations behind them?"

He nodded. "Unfortunately. I'm sorry I didn't tell you sooner - I didn't want you to rethink the pregnancy, but that was incredibly selfish of me. You had a right to know whose kits you're carrying, and the danger we're going to face getting back to Oster."

She barked a laugh. "*Wow*. I mean, I don't think you have anything in common with them, if that makes you feel any better. You *really* don't seem the type. I think the kits will be just fine, if maybe prone to being emotionally stunted."

Roz bit his lip to keep from smirking, laughter dancing in his eyes, which had since stopped tearing up. Ch'ik much preferred that happy look on him.

Zul huffed. "*Anyway*. I confronted my uncle about it and not even a day later, the *laht* had vanished from our ship. Our exile was already on the info-net, and we had every Osterian law enforcement agency on our tails trying to haul us in for questioning. *Laht* theft would have landed us all in prison, away from each other, and we'd exchanged bonds by then - we decided that wasn't an option for us. We've been on the run ever since."

Roz stroked one of Zul's ears through his fingertips. "They'd taken the evidence, too, and no one was going to believe a bunch of exiles. We couldn't let it stand, even if we couldn't take them down with us, so we lifted our entire hydroponics bay from his uncle's orbital estate on our way off-world. Wish I could have seen his face when he walked into a room full of bare walls and sparking wires." He grinned proudly.

"So-" Ch'ik began, hesitantly. "We're gonna be in a world of shit if they find out we're back on Oster before we can get the pods into the hands of the masses?"

They all nodded.

"But," she continued, narrowing her eyes, "selling the pods to the masses, even above market rate, also means royally fucking over your terrible family?"

Another round of nods.

"Well, hell. I'm all for sticking it to the assholes of the galaxy as long as I get my payday too. I'm down. Gotta make sure the universe is safer for o- your kits, right?"

She looked uncomfortable as she hastily corrected herself.

Jau grimaced. They all really needed to talk about what was going to happen once the kits arrived. The problem was, Ch'ik could give Zul a run for his credits with the way she dodged Jau's attempts to broach the subject. She could joke about Z being emotionally stunted all she liked, but *it takes one to know one*, Jau thought grumpily.

Ch'ik zipped her coveralls back up, pressing a hand over her stomach to steady it as she struggled to get to her feet from Jau's lap. Zul rose from his chair and extended a hand to her, which she hesitated to take.

"I don't like asking for help," she mumbled, trying unsuccessfully to get herself up again. Even with Jau's hands bracketing her hips in support, her growing stomach made it a difficult task.

"Then don't." Zul said kindly, holding his hand out towards her again. "Just take it."

It was a simple act, putting her hand in Zul's palm, but in that moment, something as substantial as gravity had begun tugging the four of them even closer together.

CHAPTER 27
- CH'IK -

CH'IK CRACKED A YAWN, PEEKING AROUND THE doorway to the observation deck. Roz had told her on the comm to come by, interrupting one of her increasingly-frequent naps. The kits demanded a great deal of energy from her, and while the guys were great at providing both nutrition and recreation, she'd done her body no favors in the cycles prior.

In the center of the observation deck, Roz had made an enormous nest. Ch'ik wasn't sure where he'd scrounged up all of the materials for it, but she wasn't going to complain. It looked wonderfully soft and big enough for all four of them: Ch'ik couldn't wait to snuggle up in the middle of it to take the weight off her aching hips.

She sank to her knees on a convenient pillow, tipping forward awkwardly onto all fours with a sigh. "Explain to me again why I had to haul my huge ass down here?"

Ch'ik pretended to gripe, but her false grumpiness evaporated when Jau crawled over and rubbed his face playfully against her butt. She grinned as she swatted at him and flopped onto her side. "Menace."

Jau pulled back from where he had been nuzzling his way to the backs of her thighs. "You better stop that, or I'm definitely not going to stop *this*."

"We'll have plenty of time for that later." Roz rumbled, sliding behind her and tugging her back up between his legs. He'd embraced his role of 'sturdy chair' happily as she moved through the fifth fraction-cycle of the pregnancy. "Jau, go get the snacks so you don't miss it."

"Miss *what*?" Ch'ik asked, perplexed, as Jau hopped up and sauntered off.

"I'm almost done calibrating the ship's telescope. You'll see soon." Zul's voice drifted over from the control panel. "Just have to pair the signal with this pulsars-damned remote, so I can -"

The observation dome above their heads flickered and jumped through a progression of shots as the view shifted and zoomed in from the wide, black, starfield that was visible to the naked eye. A small tweak sent the view tumbling to a distant nebula. Jau rejoined them with a tray of snacks that he balanced precariously on the edge of the nest, but Ch'ik hardly registered the smug look that he shot her as he passed over a bowl of sook sticks. All of her focus was directed at the screen as the image finally enhanced and resolved.

Thick columns of cosmic dust and gas towered at the edge of the nebula, hundreds of light-years tall. Ch'ik watched, awed to an uncharacteristic silence as Zul zoomed in again. A column's edge became an entire jagged mountain range of brilliant light, all but consuming the screens of the observation deck.

The dense formation of gasses smeared out into the darker center of the column where Zul had aimed the imager, but the upper peaks of the mountains streaked up into brilliant yellows and golds against a rich, velvet black that took Ch'ik's breath away. Wispy clouds of purple and blue shrouded the soft valleys between the dusty spires, while vast falls of bright white ionized gas flowed along the rock-like ridges.

Deep cobalt veils of gas and dust hovered around the towering peaks, illuminated by starlight from distant galaxies.

Although the ship's telescope made it appear as a distant peak, Ch'ik knew it wasn't actually a landscape they watched. They were newborn stars cradled within a stellar nursery - and with a chuckle, she realized she was one galactic mother watching another.

"Holy shit." She damn sure wasn't a poet, but a view like that demanded *something*.

"Yeah." Zul said as he flopped down into the nest alongside them. He balanced the telescope's remote controller on Roz's thigh and took one of the bowls of puffed corn from the snack tray. He gently nudged Ch'ik and pointed to the highest of the pseudo-mountaintops as he tossed a piece of corn in his mouth. "Wait until you see the wildlife."

He'd pointed to a beautiful umber pinnacle, twisted up like taffy and topped by two tempestuous streamers of charged particles that jetted in opposite directions. The pair sprayed scorching radiation out into the bluish-black space beyond the clouds, both violent and captivating. Zul took the controller back from Roz's wide thigh and twiddled with the controls, reorienting and zooming the telescope in further.

The pinnacle shifted to a radiation-swept peak that became the full focus of the observation screen. The impossibly slow swirl of the gas plumes was interrupted by patches of unusual black emptiness darting in and out of the distant carnelian eddies.

Ch'ik drew in a sharp, awed breath as she stared at those swimming shapes. They were like holes in the fabric of the cosmos, moving as if they were alive in that radiation-drenched vacuum.

"Void whales." Jau whispered to Ch'ik conspiratorially, grinning as he bit down on a sook stick.

"I see two and, uh - a tiny third one, maybe? Next to that dust disc." Roz pointed and Ch'ik turned her gaze just in time to see a smaller slip of nothingness, larger than a planet, peel away to dive down through an oblique orange spray of light. It flicked the empty fin on its tail and swam back up, only to disappear along the bulky blackness of one of the larger void whales.

Ch'ik stared at the display and watched in shocked silence as, thousands of light-years away, the stellar creatures lunged through jets of incandescent gas. She held her breath as one breached up out of the dusty streams of raw energy shed by the still-forming stars.

"Here, taste this." Jau pressed a chilled bowl into her distracted hands, clearly far more used to the stunning sight of the beautiful, impossible animals. "I tried something new with the teroid melon. Tell me what you think."

Not wanting to miss anything, Ch'ik didn't look down as she popped one of the frozen orbs into her mouth. It melted into a cool, smooth jelly as she chewed - bright and refreshing, with just a hint of tangy bite. She swallowed, ready to give Jau her seal of approval as she watched the largest of the void whales circle around the tip of the stardust pinnacle. But as the cool bite slid down her throat, something moved inside her, eliciting a shocked squeak.

"Oh!" Ch'ik looked down at her midsection, majestic void whales forgotten.

"What's going on?" Jau leaned over her as he tracked her gaze, confused. "What happened?"

Ch'ik tried to think of how to explain it, when she felt it again. A tiny, unexpected jab to her insides that startled a vague exclamation out of her mouth. "Wha?"

All of the Lapann had sat up and they crowded around her as Jau explained. "You got a giant smile on your face all of a sudden."

"Oh." Ch'ik said again, and only then did she realize a grin had curved her mouth. "Oh! Yeah, come here. Give me your hands."

Ch'ik slid the zipper of her coveralls down and took their hands, one at a time, positioning them carefully on her stomach. None of them spoke as she pressed them to the tight swell of her midsection, looking at each other with wondering expressions as their huge hands nearly engulfed her pregnant belly. Faint light gleamed between their fingers on the darkened observation deck as Ch'ik reached for the chilled bowl.

"Alright. Hopefully this will work a second time." She said as she popped two more of the cold green orbs into her mouth, chewing and swallowing them. "Okay, now wait for -"

Before Ch'ik could finish her sentence, the kits within her erupted in a flurry of strong little kicks. The grin on her face was so wide it made her cheeks ache. Understanding dawned immediately on the Lapann's faces - Zul just looked shocked, but Jau and Roz both had to wipe away tears with their free hands a moment later. By the time the kits had settled down and stopped kicking they were all visibly moved.

Just a job, she told herself again. Ch'ik had needed to remind of that more and more frequently as the fraction-cycles had passed, and she scolded herself again as she held their hands to her body. *Just a job*.

It wasn't as convincing, this time.

Jau gently ran his thumb along the curve of her belly, his voice quiet. "Ch'ik, listen. I know you and Roz have talked about this a few fraction-cycles ago, and we're all kind of in this comfortable *routine* about everything, but we really want you to consider staying with us."

The kits kicked again in response to her sudden surge of adrenaline. She wasn't one for *plans*. That was a four-letter word in her world, a shackle that fit just as tight as Imperium cuffs.

Zul started to talk, choked on his own saliva, and promptly had a coughing fit, starting again in a strained voice. "Ch'ik - you may be the Beta of our kits, but you're so much more than that. To us. To me, I mean."

Jau rolled his eyes. "To *us*. To all of us. We want you to stay. What do *you* want?" Roz nodded eagerly, smoothing his palm over her stomach.

Ch'ik bit at her lip as she looked down at the glowing swell of her stomach. She wanted to be overjoyed by the blatant statement. It was everything she'd ever wanted, in some deep corner of her heart, but in that moment all she felt was slow dread seeping into her brain.

"Oh please, guys. I'm a mess. A *hot* mess, don't get me wrong, but you'll be just fine with the kits. There's three of you, after all, you can take turns feeding them and everything." Her eyes stung despite her determination to choke back everything swelling in her chest. "You don't want me."

Roz's face crumpled as he snatched up her hand, holding it to his chest. "Ch'ik, this has nothing to do with the kits. You're amazing. Hellbent and determined to electrocute yourself with shoddy wiring, but incredible. You're so smart, stubborn, and beautiful, I can't imagine life without you at this point. None of us can." His words came in a rush, shoulders dropping with the relief of renewed confession. He cradled her palm up against his mouth, kissing it tenderly.

She shook her head, adamant. "No, you don't get it, Roz. Trouble follows me, I just mess up everything I touch. That's why I got the *Hawk* in the first place. If you don't stay in one place for too long, you can't fuck things up too badly. The fraction-cycles I've spent here...this has been the longest I've spent off my own ship since the orphan camps, and there's a reason for that."

Zul gently squeezed her thigh, looking to Jau helplessly for assistance. Jau frowned softly, leaning closer to kiss her shoulder. "Don't worry about what you think *we* want right now, Ch'ik. We asked you what *you* want."

She dodged the question, still too tangled up in her own brain to admit it out loud. "What if someone uses this-" she gestured at her stomach, "-against us, or something? What if Dr'ec comes back and hurts the kits? I'd never forgive myself if-"

Zul, seeming to snag a tenuous hold on confidence in Jau's wake, squeezed her thigh again. "We can't control other lifeforms, Ch'ik. We can only do our best to be happy as a cluster. And let that warren-wrecker show his beak in my quadrant again - I'll knock him out of the sky and carve your name on his corpse." There was a dull thud, muffled by layers of blankets, as he kicked out underneath himself before regaining composure.

Violence was at least one of Ch'ik's love languages, and the swell of emotion in her chest warmed before she shook her head again. "If I let myself get complacent here and something goes wrong, I'm just-" she sniffled, the tears welling behind her eyes the rare, organic sort that couldn't be whipped up by holonovellas. "I don't know if I can recover. So isn't it better not to want at all?"

Roz murmured softly beside her, brushing the side of his softly-furred foot against her bare one. "No. Hope is all we have. Wanting might make us vulnerable, but it also opens us up to so much more beauty and possibility."

Jau laid his cheek on her shoulder, nuzzling softly. "We all do the best we can, sweet Beta of our kits. And if it doesn't work, then we'll figure it out. Now, what do you want, Ch'ik? Not what you think we want. Not what you think you can have. What do *you want?*"

Ch'ik opened her mouth. Closed it. Opened it again. The thoughts were in her head but she couldn't force them out. From the camp-wranglers that always had the back of their hands ready to the succession of sneering, shitty males that saw her as little more than a docking port, she'd always been a crew of one, mid battle. She'd never had a safe spot to land, to *really* consider what she'd been criss-crossing parsecs for.

"I *want.* I don't -" Ch'ik squeezed her eyes shut, struggling to keep her voice steady, her thoughts organized. "I just, I want -" it was as if there was a stone lodged in her throat. She held it back, mind spinning through how to refuse them, and then it happened. One of the kits kicked inside of her, a tiny push that was somehow strong enough to pierce the hull of her hesitation.

"I want to *stay!*" She sobbed, crying hard for the first time in cycles as it all came pouring out. "I want to stay with all of *you*, alright? I *love* you and I *hate* myself sometimes because I know that you deserve better-"

She tipped her head up, a fruitless move to stem the flood of tears that ran hot down her cheeks. The nebula and the whales smeared into a luminescent blur as the warm weight of all three Lapann clustered around her.

Zul pulled her into his chest, letting her inhale deeply against the soft blue fur in the open vee of his coveralls. His scent was all him - clean and warm, an appealing contrast to Jau's faint metallic hints from mech-work and Roz's undertones of earth and greens from hydroponics.

She sniffled and rolled her cheek against his chest to catch a breath. "I keep telling myself to run and break my own heart now, rather than sticking around until I manage to screw something up." Her heart thudded, feeling wildly unmoored. She'd said *the* word. The L word. It was both freeing and terrifying, a simple word that brought the protective walls around her soul crashing down. Gentle flurries of kicks descended across her belly as the kits responded to her emotions and heartbeat.

Zul cupped her head against his chest as his cluster-mates gently stroked her back. She felt his voice rumble through his chest, against her ear, as he spoke. "Ch'ik, you aren't going to screw up anything. We've got our own issues, if you hadn't gathered from our history. But it's like Jau always used to tell Roz and I - when you bring the right broken pieces together, you get something stronger than all of them apart. We knew when you agreed to carry our eggs that we were going to have a family. It started with this." He slid his hand down to brush her stomach, tilting her head back to kiss her forehead gently. "But you're the one that completes it."

She blinked away more tears, touched by the eloquence coming out of the most awkward of the trio. Zul cradled her face in his palms, kissing her gently, running his cheek along hers.

Roz nuzzled her shoulder, scent-marking both she and Zul at the same time. "We're all in, Ch'ik. We've talked. We want you here with us for good."

She reached behind her, sliding a hand through Jau's hair as he kissed her other shoulder. Out of the corner of her eye, Ch'ik caught the sinuous starry-black grace of the entire void whale pod as they glided by the nebula: a beautiful stellar family, joined by their journey.

"Man, are you gonna regret that." She gave a tearful little laugh at the self-deprecating humor, tucking her head under Zul's chin.

Their protests and reassurances poured over her like a warm sonic shower, settling her heart and their kits all at once. She squeezed Zul, breathing deeply against the fur of his collarbone. "...but yeah, ok. Let's do this."

CHAPTER 28
- ZUL -

SHORTLY AFTER THEY'D DRIED CH'IK'S TEARS, THEY cuddled together and finished off the snacks. After betting with sook sticks on how many kit-kicks each bite of melon would elicit, Ch'ik had come down with a craving. Kildi Pies certainly were a *choice*, nutritionally-speaking. In fact, they were so devoid of anything healthy they were famously only available as a counter-mounted afterthought at Starpass Fuel Stop.

Run by one of the largest Con-Glom lines in the quadrant, each Starpass was eerily similar, branded up to the eyeballs, and unnervingly well-lit. Due to some hideous combination of low prices and uninterested robotic staff that were not equipped with enough artificial intelligence to judge the life choices of their clientele, Starpasses had spread throughout the galaxy, driven largely by a profitable sponsorship deal with the

Night Beats holonovella broadcasts. Soon enough, there wasn't a station in the quadrant that didn't sport the familiar three-eyed alien logo.

Lucky for Ch'ik's cravings, the nearest one was less than a sleep cycle away and it wasn't long until Zul looped down into the landing zone of Plarm Station.

Zul guided the *Koton* to one of the smaller ports, waiting for the auto-clearance to launch the ship tether and dock to the station. Ch'ik seemed to be in a big hurry to get them inside - was she really that hungry? They'd had all the snacks not that long ago, and she'd drank plenty of water. Jau had really been on her about the water - a holdover from the days when he used to fight more often. The healing vats would dehydrate the hell out of you if you weren't careful.

Ch'ik seemed very excited about something, pointing in the distance and tugging on Jau's arm as she aimed for the spot. A clear glass tube waited by the beverages, an inner spiral sending up a nauseating churn of opaque, greenish liquid. "Oooh look, Jau! They have titbeast juice here!"

Roz and Zul shared a look and disgusted twitch of their noses as their Beta dragged Jau closer to the font of nightmarish green sludge. Roz lowered his voice as Ch'ik moved out of hearing. "Zul, I'm half-worried that stuff is going to liquefy our kits." Zul snorted as his Omega grinned back before ambling towards Jau.

Zul twitched an ear as they rejoined the other half of the cluster, Ch'ik gesturing with a curious tilt of her head towards Jau, mid-conversation. "...No, I really do want to know! Come on, it can't be *that* bad. You've seen my...yanno." She tapped the back of her shoulder with a raised brow, indicating her third nipple.

Roz, bemused, turned to Zul to explain. "She finally asked about the eye."

Jau rubbed the back of his neck, wrinkling his nose. "Well, I mean, you gotta understand that it was a whole *thing* when it happened, and-"

Ch'ik's eyes went wide and she pressed a finger to Jau's lips. "Oop. Hold that thought. I gotta pee *right now*."

She pressed a hand to her stomach, vanishing hurriedly down a corridor. That had been happening a lot lately, Ch'ik leaving mid-conversation to pee. He and Roz hadn't been around many pregnant Betas in their time, but Jau knew a few from the shipyards and said the constant bathroom trips were normal.

Zul leaned on the counter nearby, eyes roaming over aisles of brightly-colored snacks. Everything was more vivid here, and it was hard not to notice. The Scrum had its bright neon holographs, but was mostly filled with duller-colored lifeforms; it was visitors like his pastel-hued cluster and the occasional botanical that stood out, rather than vice-versa.

Here at the Starpass station, however, the mix of people was a much brighter palette. Vivid green saurines looked through bins of sweet orbs, murmuring in their untranslatable hissing language. A small cobalt-blue lifeform, covered in feathers, frowned over preserved jugs of extra chunky titbeast juice, setting them on the floor as they reached in a cooler for the freshest one. It seemed like a futile effort, to Zul: even if they found the best one in the store, the prize was still titbeast juice.

Roz went to the counter and bought a half-dozen Kildi Pies, holding one up to his cluster-mates with an unimpressed wrinkle of his nose. A light purple slime oozed from a broken corner of the pastry, an unappealing smear against the plastic film. "I'm going to harvest extra vegetables tonight to balance whatever...this is."

Zul held up a brightly-colored package from a nearby shelf between thumb and forefinger, as if he'd caught a venta-rat on the ship. The wrapper was identical to the ankle-deep pile of discards that they'd seen around the *Hawk's* command chair. "These things are *half a credit*. What in pulsars name are they made with to be that cheap? I genuinely want to know. Hey, hasn't it been awhile?"

"Hm?" Jau looked up from where he'd been flipping through an issue of *Mechmarvel Monthly*. "Oh, Ch'ik? Yeah, now that you mention it." He frowned, stuffing the magazine pad back in the holder haphazardly, eyes on the corridor.

Roz's ears dropped as his brow creased. "I'm...not picking up her scent. You guys?"

Zul shook his head, the three of them moving as one to the corridor, storming through the door to the restroom. A weasel-like species at the sonic sinks chittered irritably, drying their hands and shoving past the three Lapann huddled in the doorframe on their way out. Roz pushed the two stall doors open, finding them both empty. He spun back to them with panic in his eyes. "Where is she? Zul, *where's Ch'ik?*"

Roz's scent - earth and greens - filled the room as his Omega instincts went into overdrive: his protective nature had been expanding steadily along with Ch'ik's stomach. Zul knew he had to dial Roz back or his mate was going to start dismantling walls - and any unlucky lifeforms too slow to evade him - in a blood frenzy. "Roz! Let's check the ship, maybe she went back and we just didn't see her."

Jau, usually his dependable backup in crisis situations like this, looked absolutely haunted. He stared at the sonic sink like it was a black hole as his tail twitched spasmodically.

"Jau?"

"I did this." He shoved his hands into his hair, ears wildly askew. "She's second-guessing everything, Zul. I should have told her about my eye sooner, about your family. I was trying not to scare her off, but maybe I shouldn't have pressed her about staying with us. What have I *done?*"

Zul grabbed Jau's shoulders, spun his body to face him, and gave him a firm open-palm slap to the cheek. Predictably, Jau groaned and pawed at his own crotch, whispering angrily. "*Zul*, not *now-*"

Zul gripped his fellow Alpha's shoulders. "Now that I have your *attention*, Jau, help me get Roz back to the ship before he melts down, please? We need weapons. Ch'ik would have had to walk right by us, and she's unpredictable sometimes but she wouldn't worry us like this. Something's happened to her." Jau nodded slowly, extending a hand to Roz, who took it, still looking around the empty bathroom wildly.

It took a few minutes longer than Zul would have liked, but he finally got his cluster back to the *Koton*. Jau matter-of-factly popped the weapons locker open and tossed Zul the plasma rifle. He snatched it out of the air and slid the strap up over his shoulder as Jau strapped on his favorite thigh holster. Zul watched as Jau tried to hand another holster to Roz, but their Omega was so close to overloaded that he just growled and batted the weapon away. Zul caught Jau's eye and shrugged - there was no point in arguing it when Roz was like this, seemingly moments away from tearing the Starpass Stop apart with his bare hands.

"We're going to find her." Zul said, and he wasn't sure if he was trying to calm his cluster mates or himself. "Let's head back to the station and -"

The shrill sound of a hail alert cut through the quiet bridge.

CHAPTER 29
- ROZ -

Zul dove for the controls, slamming the button to answer, and the holo display pulled up a face Roz had hoped his cluster would never see again.

"Marr. What the fuck do you want? I'm busy." Zul's ears had gone Academy-straight, his voice clipped. Roz knew Zul's cousin Marr had been instrumental in getting his cluster exiled, and whatever bad blood he had with the warren-wrecker, Zul had considerably more.

The *laht*-brown Lapann that filled the screen was the picture of arrogance, staring haughtily down his nose at them through the screen and smiling unkindly. "Now, now, *cousin*. Is that any way to talk to someone that picked up your broken toys for you? You've been rather careless with the container holding your kits."

Marr stepped to the left, revealing a scene that made Roz's blood run cold. Ch'ik was pinned against a stack of crates by a snarling Lurquer with a plasma rifle. The barrel of the rifle was pressed so hard under her chin it forced her head up and back against the boxes behind her. She opened her mouth - to scream, spit, or shout, Roz didn't know - but she never got the chance. The Lurquer shoved the barrel of the rifle up, forcing her teeth to close with an audible click.

Her expression flickered with pain, and Roz stomped so hard he was glad for the reinforced welding on the *Koton's* bridge floor.

Zul snarled, flashing teeth. "Marr..." Roz watched as his Alpha's blue fingers flexed uselessly around the edges of the console. "Don't you *dare* hurt her."

"Oh, so this *is* yours." Marr sighed as he glanced over at Ch'ik. "Really, Zul? I had hoped my information was mistaken, but I guess you always were desperate. Stop your posturing - I would never endanger your unborn kits, even if they are going to be growing inside some disgusting little hybrid." he wrinkled his nose, revulsion clear on his features as he stared at the swell of Ch'ik's belly. "Do I even *want* to know how you pulled this off?"

Roz and Jau clutched one another's hands as they watched from outside the viewing field. Zul peered at the screen, looking desperately at Ch'ik, his tone one of cold fury. "What the *hell* do you -"

Marr waved his hand in a vague gesture, rolling his eyes. His sleek brown fur was combed into perfect whorls across angular cheekbones, fluffed out at his neck before it disappeared into the neckline of a pair of crisp coveralls that looked like they hadn't seen a single fraction-cycle worth of wear.

"Oh, you know. Nevermind. All faults aside, you're still *family* - at least now that you've gotten kits off of that Omega runt of yours. I'm sure that however you *found* this Beta and *convinced* her to carry for you was all perfectly above board, right?"

Roz's blood surged with helpless rage, Marr's implication clicking in his brain. Zul and Jau had understood as well, if the sudden deep tinges of their fur were anything to go by.

"How *dare* you-" Zul hissed the words, slamming an open palm on the console emphatically.

"Don't bother with your veneer of propriety. I don't care. Whatever you did, it's fine. Once these kits can survive on their own, we'll even help you solve this little *Beta problem* you seem to have gotten yourself into. Think of it as a gift for your new little ones, even. I know plenty of worlds where an inconvenient Beta can get...misplaced. Nobody ever needs to find out what you did, and I'll vouch that you used a contract Beta that wanted to stay anonymous. All you have to do is bring me those pods."

"What... what pods?" Zul was even worse at lying than he was at basic communication; Roz and Jau caught each other's eyes and shared the same wince. "I don't know anything about any *pods*."

"Oh *please*. You think that a rogue Lapann could pay for an assassination job with broma and it wouldn't get back to the homeworld council?" Marr laughed, folding his arms across his chest. Roz's stomach dropped.

"I don't have any idea what you're talking about." That, at least, didn't sound like a lie; Zul's confusion was genuine.

Roz immediately regretted the decision to leave his cluster out of contracting with 'Ghi back at the Scrum. He knew they wouldn't approve, but he couldn't let Dr'ec's treatment of his Beta go unanswered. But his assassin friend was highly valued for discretion, and vetted new clients with maniacal precision. In addition to worry over Ch'ik, a concern about 'Ghi's safety added to his anxiety. *How the hell did this happen?*

Marr scoffed. "Scouts intercepted one of your broma pods before it could be processed into that despicable dust-substance. Did you know that your pods are a genetic wildtype? If even *one* of those things made it back to Oster, generations of our family's genetic engineering work would be negated. *With* it, however, generations of *our* kits will be financially secure and healthy. That despicable purple *ooze* managed to damage them all beyond repair before he escaped, which means we need the whole pods you're still hoarding to start propagation."

"...Oh." Zul's brow was furrowed in confusion. At least part of that had to be due to the Alpha's complete lack of understanding about anything agricultural, but Roz knew he'd have to come clean eventually.

Zul's cousin shot a withering look at Ch'ik, who'd started hissing curses under her breath until the gun reasserted itself under her chin. Turning back to the holo display, his fingers flicked across a screen, a new coordinate glowing on the *Koton's* nav as the signal transferred. "Meet us at the station's infrastructure zone. As soon as you hand over the Broma, I'll call the homeworld council and -"

As Marr explained the details of the meeting, Jau waved his hand slightly to get Roz's attention out of the camera's angle. Over the top of Zul's head, his smaller Alpha gestured at Ch'ik in the background.

At first Roz wasn't sure what he was supposed to be seeing, other than the look of naked fury on her sweet, familiar face. Then he saw it. While Marr was talking, Ch'ik cut her eyes towards him and blinked twice. Then she shifted her glance right, towards the Lurquer, and blinked three times, slow and deliberate. Roz watched as she repeated the signal again and again, a steady repetition.

Marr droned on about Zul finally redeeming himself in the eyes of their family but Roz had long since tuned him out. All he could hear was the pounding of his own pulse, every cell howling for vengeance against the scumstain who'd dared to lay his hands on their Beta.

CHAPTER 30
- JAU -

JAU SNARLED AS THE HOLO CUT OFF, TIGHTENING the strap on his thigh holster. "Okay, so I think we can all agree that we're going to murder the fuck out of Zul's cousin."

Roz still glared at the dark screen, as if he could beam his anger through space. "Yes."

"Agreed." Zul's terse addition made one of Jau's ears tilt towards him with curiosity. Usually his fellow Alpha was the reluctant one when it came to the overtly-illegal. The last time he'd seen him this all-in on something questionable was when they lifted the hydroponic equipment from Zul's Uncle Bron. His hard-headed cluster mate really was head-over-heels for their Beta.

If Jau wasn't on the verge of absolutely fucking *losing it* with worry, he might have smirked. "That thing Ch'ik was doing with the blinking. I'm willing to bet the kidnapping crew is probably two Lapann - Marr and probably Bourge, if I had to guess - and three Lurquers."

"Agreed." Roz snapped again, taking up a track of furious pacing that took him back past Jau.

Zul leaned back in the command chair, a dumbstruck expression on his face. "Oh. Oh! Shit, that makes sense."

Jau raised an eyebrow as he double-checked the release straps on his chest holster. "What the hell did you *think* she was doing, Z?"

One of Zul's sky-blue ears drooped. "I, uh, I thought she was trying not to cry."

Jau slid a hand down his face with an aggrieved sigh, whiskers springing free around the edge of his palm. "I swear to pulsars, you're as dense as a neutron star. If I'm ever kidnapped I want Roz to rescue me."

Zul huffed. "I'm sorry, okay? I never thought I'd have to see my piece of shit cousin ever again, but here he is, *abducting our Beta.* Implying that we, I don't know, somehow *forced* her..."

Jau scoffed. "As if we could force Ch'ik to do anything. She'd have our knots in a handbasket if we even thought about -"

"Focus." Roz's harsh command rumbled across the bridge, and Jau and Zul snapped to attention at the uncharacteristic outburst. "How do we get her back?"

Chastised, Zul spun back to the nav screen and pulled up visitor schematics of the station. "Marr wants us to meet them at the infrastructure zone security checkpoint. So we, uh, obviously can't do that."

"Yeah. There's no way that's not a trap." Jau patted his coverall pocket, producing a raw sook from when he'd been prepping snacks earlier. He always thought better with something to tear apart. Crunching into it and closing his eyes, he chewed, thinking. A symbol he'd seen on the screen suddenly pulled up a long-forgotten memory from the shipyards. "Hey, Roz - did you see those boxes in the background on the comm call?"

Roz worked his jaw angrily. "No. I was busy thinking about how I'm going to disembowel that brown fuck."

"Yeah, me too. *But* I still noticed the crates of substrate." Jau took another bite of the sook, crunching on it loudly as Roz and Zul stopped to stare at him.

He gestured at the screen with the half-eaten vegetable. "We've been assuming they left with her, but I think they're holding her here, in the fungus farm."

"That tailless, stub-eared *fuck*." Roz ground his teeth together loud enough for Jau to hear if from across the bridge. "He *knows* we can't grapple onto the outside of the infrastructure zone. We're going to have to fight our way through that security checkpoint."

"Just hold on. Hold on." Zul frowned, swiping through console commands until he brought up a detailed holo-projection of the station interior. "Let's think this through. We're no good to Ch'ik or the kits if we're dead."

Plarm Station was, essentially, a *very* large dome balanced on a platform. The long, wide fin of the landing terminal where the *Koton* was docked jutted out of the side of the dome. On the top side, commerce franchises like the Starpass served travelers. Underneath, however, there was a kludged-together mix of plasma fuel filling tanks and other station-oriented equipment, the IZ, or infrastructure zone.

The IZ wasn't labeled on the directory graphic - after all, there was no reason for travelers to visit that part of the station - but it was easily recognizable as the industrial hub. Complex arrays of sensors and stabilizers jutted down around the necessary core components that kept the station orbiting and habitable - gravity, electric, atmosphere.

One of the more profitable functions of IZs, waste management, meant they were well-guarded at stations like Plarm. Passing ships could get discounts on docking fees by dumping their waste at the station's receiving tanks - a win-win for credit-strapped space travelers. The waste was funneled to an on-station biomass plant - a *fungus farm* in common slang - where it was filtered and used to grow massive mushrooms. Once harvested, the caps were used for everything from fuel to food.

Jau stared at the directory diagram for a long moment before Roz reached over. He tapped the squared end of a long, bulky block, tucked in behind the rounded stacks of the reactor cores.

"There." Roz said. "That's gotta be it."

Jau nodded, but none of them spoke as they stared mournfully at the holo. Sure, they could see exactly where they needed to go, but it was what they couldn't see that stood in their way.

Stations all maintained a strict no-fly zone around their IZs. It wouldn't be smart to allow lifeforms with unknown intentions to access integral life support systems that kept station visitors alive and, more importantly, paying docking fees.

The space-side exterior of IZs were always protected by swarms of security drones. There was no reasoning with drones, no second chances. They were programmed to tackle any ship that ignored the boundaries, contaminating them with a flood of nanobots that would disintegrate the interloper from stem to stern. It was a brutal system, as inflexible as it was deadly, but stations weren't willing to take chances with their atmosphere recyclers and gravity drivers.

Or, incidentally, their fungus farms.

Zul tapped the blocky outcropping with a finger. "If that's where Marr is holding her, that's where we go in."

Jau rubbed at the tension between his eyebrows with the heel of his hand. "Z, I don't know what chance you think we have here. You know as well as I do that the drones will dissolve us as soon as we cross into the no-fly zone."

"Not if we disable them first." Zul smiled grimly, kicking a toe at the beat-to-shit duffle bag under the console.

Jau snapped off the last bite of sook, dropping the chewed stub into his pocket with the others he'd stashed earlier. He was a habitual snacker, even more so when he was stressed. He let the remaining root's weight against his thigh settle his nerves.

Pulsars help them, this just might work.

CHAPTER 31

- ZUL -

Z ul quickly maneuvered the *Koton* out of
the docking bay, swinging around the station to the
other, lesser-used traveler entrance that Marr had
indicated. His earless shithead of a cousin had said to
meet before the end of the sleep cycle, which didn't
give them much time.

Zul hefted the black duffle bag with its silver X's out
from under the peripheral console. "Once I disable the
drones, we'll just grapple onto the biomass plant
outcropping and hull-pierce it, grab her, and get the
hell out of here. If we punch it, we'll beat Marr to Oster
and get to the council first." He consciously kept his
voice steady - as Captain, he was the *de facto* leader of
their cluster, and they didn't need to know how badly
he was freaking out right now.

"Have you ever used one of those things?" Jau sounded doubtful from his spot at the control array, eyes full of concern.

Zul huffed a laugh. "No. Not exactly required reading at the Academy, but I'll figure it out. We'll know soon enough if it worked, anyway."

Before seeing Ch'ik use it, Zul's only exposure to Prox-Hack tech had been a brief primer at the Command Academy. The curriculum had lightly touched on the illegal devices, but had focused mainly on how to seize and destroy said equipment on enemy ships. Zul had watched his Beta use the proximity hacker twice, and liked to think of himself as technologically savvy. He knew his way around a user interface, after all.

How hard could it be?

Roz plopped down on the crash couch, widening his thighs with a pat. He'd taken to coaxing Ch'ik to sit in his lap more frequently since the Scrum, and Zul smirked to see the habit extended to him, an Alpha. Roz's color darkened slightly as he realized how bold he'd been, ears dropped in submission. "Just for safety, Alpha, that's all."

Zul dragged the bag over and sat down between Roz's legs without complaint, leaning back to cheek-mark him. "No fur off my ears, my sweet Omega. You're my mate, and I trust you to guard me." Reaching down to unzip the bag, Zul smiled softly to himself at the feel of Roz's fur bristling happily against his arms. He would always be grateful to Jau for patiently teaching him how to love Roz properly: his Omega deserved nothing less, and he'd gone about courting so poorly in the beginning.

Loosening the drawstring, Zul bent down and slid his arms into the gauntlets - left, then right, just as Ch'ik had done. The lights along the device flickered to life and a soft humming began. The benign sound was all the warning he received; the shackles tightened and a thousand whisker-thin needles pierced down into his muscles.

"Ah! Fuck!" Jau had tried to explain his love of pain once, and Zul didn't understand it at all. This just reaffirmed that pain was something to be avoided, not sought out.

"Zul?" Roz patted awkwardly around Zul's shoulders, avoiding the areas where the wires had pierced clean through the fabric of his coverall sleeves.

Damn, he was going to need a new pair of coveralls.

"You okay, Z?" Jau's voice wavered from the controls, eye fixed to the exterior view screens to see if and when Zul's efforts succeeded.

"Fine. I'm fine. I'll be -" Zul started to reassure his mate, but then he realized that the low hum of the device wasn't just a hum any longer. It was a feeling inside of him. It was a noise in his blood, a color in his mouth, a smell in his brain like burning bread.

Zul opened his mouth to scream and fell backwards into the abyss of the mainframe.

At first there was only darkness.

An absence of light and sound so complete that Zul felt as if he were floating in a sensory deprivation tank. He felt himself blink but there was no difference between when his eyes were open and closed - until there was.

A ball filled with crackling orange light had appeared in front of him and Zul had no way to tell if it was very small and very close, or very large and very far away. There were no frames of reference, no lines of perspective to help him judge distance in this between-space. Zul reached out towards the orange light. He was shocked when he saw his hand in front of his face, doubly so when he realized that - instead of coming up from the bottom of his field of view - his fingers seemed to reach down from above his head.

Vertigo lanced into Zul's brain and he was suddenly overcome with nausea. He tried to close his eyes, to steady himself, to figure out what the fuck he was supposed to be doing, here, but even when he felt his eyelids squeeze shut the scene in front of him remained in perfect detail. Shit. There was no escaping his upside-down fingers and the crackling orange light.

Zul realized, too late, that he truly had no idea what he was doing.

He didn't know what he had done to activate the proximity hacker and he didn't know how he was supposed to exit this bizarre abyss, either. Back in reality he was just laying there, useless, and here inside the system he found himself in the same nightmare of uncertainty. Zul knew that he needed to shut down the station's security system, but he had no idea how to.

When the thought of the security system flickered across his brain, Zul started to fall. He didn't know how he could tell - really, there was no difference in sensation, but he knew. *The light rushed up to meet him and his stomach dropped, careening down through empty space and towards the orange energy. Zul fell into that vast framework at breakneck speed, realizing in awed horror that he wasn't staring down an energy ball at all.*

It was a tower of code that stretched forever, both above and beneath him: a labyrinth that extended out into every dimension. Like a garden of flesh, it was a living thing that twisted and merged together into a shimmering tangle. Somehow, he understood this was a representation of the systems that controlled the station's digital infrastructure.

It was all there at Zul's mercy, right at the tips of his nauseatingly-misaligned fingers. He could have done anything, anything at all, if only the pulsating guts of the station weren't senseless to him.

He felt the miserable shadow of failure pass over him, somehow darker than the abyssal void of the mainframe. How was he supposed to find what he was looking for? He'd blithely assumed it would come naturally to him for some reason.

Wait. What was it Ch'ik had said, something about slipping math into a system?

What the the fuck was math? How was he supposed to slip it anywhere if he didn't even know where to get it?

As soon as the thought crossed his mind, Zul was wrenched sideways into a deep chasm within the mass of data. Fear froze him momentarily as he watched the incomprehensible display rotate around him. When everything stopped again, he realized something. He couldn't parse a shred of the code in front of him, but the sequence of events made clear what had happened, as well as where he was within the labyrinth.

Oh, *Zul thought.* I'm an idiot.

Then, he thought of one concept as hard as he possibly could.

Math.

Nothing happened.

Zul threw his incorporeal hands up in frustration, sending his misaligned fingertips brushing down into the glowing code, branched like so many sook tops. At his touch, the code exploded into a cascade of twinkling crystalline shards. The tiny projectiles flew out away from him in every direction, some of them harmlessly cutting through the projection of himself until they winked out of existence.

Zul finally saw the path to success laid out before him, and he would pave it with as much shattered code as it took to bring his cluster back together. He had never thought of himself as being particularly skilled at organized dismantling, but wanton destruction?

Just fucking shit up?

That he could do.

CHAPTER 32

- CH'IK -

APPARENTLY A GIRL COULDN'T PISS IN PEACE.

She'd no sooner finished her bathroom trip at the Starpass when someone jumped her from behind, pressing a cloth to her mouth. There was a faint huff of something sweet, then blackness as her limbs abruptly stopped supporting her.

Ch'ik came to on an unfamiliar ship, mouth dry as dust, a headache pounding at her temples. As her consciousness slowly floated to the surface, she registered her arms being brusquely tugged behind her back, her body propped on some kind of trunk or bench. Stiff plastic cuffs tightened around her wrists with ratcheting clicks that echoed through the silent room - some kind of hold or storage room. She acted more out of it than she was, and her kidnappers had lapped up the bait, thinking it was fear and disorientation keeping her quiet.

She had shown them just how wrong they were.

Ch'ik had kicked out as hard as her swollen belly allowed, boot soles connecting with a satisfying thud into at least one of the lifeforms holding her. She'd made it halfway to the door before a Lurquer with bright blue eyes wrapped his grubby arms around her arms, pinning them to her sides. He hauled her back, kicking and screaming, to where a dark red Lapann spit a tooth and a mouthful of blood out onto the floor.

"That's *right* you dusted-out *fuckhead*. Try to put your hands on me again! That's just a taste! When my Omega shows up you're gonna die *shitting teeth*." She twisted her body, spitting at him and narrowly missing his foot as the Lurquer holding her pulled her away.

The red Lapann snarled at her as he wiped at his mouth, streaking the blood across some weird symbol that had been short-shaved into his cheek fur. Ch'ik suddenly understood what Roz had meant about being a runt. She had to tilt her head way, way back to glare up at her captor - presumably an Omega too. If this furry wall of a lifeform was an Alpha, she was in even more shit than she thought.

"What a *charming* turn of phrase." Her attention snapped to a smaller Lapann, roughly the size of Zul and Jau, with rich brown fur. He perched primly on one of the substrate crates on the other side of the room, his angular face distorted in disgust as he ran a hand through his sleek black hair. "And why haven't we gagged her yet?"

"She says she's got acid spit, Marr." The Lurquer with the plasma rifle supplied with a growl. "It wouldn't make a difference and she'd probably bite us. Bitch is practically feral."

"Hmm." Marr tilted his head and seemed to consider the problem. Gracefully dismounting the crate, he crouched to put himself eye level with Ch'ik, who had been forcibly sat back onto the bench. "I don't think that's true. And at this point I'd be willing to sacrifice a few of your fingers to get this bitch to shut up."

"Come over here and try it then you rangy-looking scum sucker! Look at these salivary glands!" Ch'ik tilted her head back, baring the long column of her throat and grinning wildly as she lied. "I'm so caustic it'll dissolve your *dad's-*" She supplied the word the translator had tripped over, back at the bar. They wanted feral? She'd *give them* feral. The kits kicked little flurries, spurring on her righteous fury.

The largest of the Lurquers actually stooped closer to check, the tail end of his striped scarf dangling down across his chest. Ch'ik didn't plan to give him a chance to call her bluff, and loudly hocked a loogie in the back of her throat.

The Lurquer's eyes widened, then narrowed. "She's bluffing."

"*You're* bluffing. Why the fuck are you even wearing a scarf?" Ch'ik tried to deflect as she eyed the accessory with disdain, swinging off the bench and getting to her feet. She couldn't fight sitting on her ass, and by the pulsars, she was going to *fight*.

Before the Lurquer could answer, Marr strode across the small space and swung one powerful leg up towards Ch'ik's body, across the bench. Fear for something beyond her own hide raced through Ch'ik, but Marr carefully avoided her pregnant belly as he planted his soft-soled shoe in the middle of her chest and shoved her backwards.

It was a gentle kick - Ch'ik had seen the strength of the Lapann, she knew that Marr was holding back. But it was still a fucking *kick* to the *chest*. Ch'ik staggered against a rack of shelves and cried out when the hard metal edges jabbed into her bound arms and the back of her head. It stunned her, but even through the pain and rage she made sure that when she fell, she fell to her knees. Underestimating her was going to be the last thing these idiots ever did.

"They're not going to come for you." Marr hissed in her face, obviously too smart for the old acid-spit lie. He was not, however, smart enough to realize what Ch'ik already knew in her soul: her cluster would never, ever abandon her.

That didn't mean she was going to sit around twiddling her thumbs, though.

With her legs folded back under her, Ch'ik was in the perfect position to stretch her fingertips out and pinch the hilt of her boot knife. Ch'ik pretended to be more dazed than she actually was as she tilted her head back against a shelf, panting dramatically. She blinked slowly at Marr's contorted features, drooling on herself a little bit for effect.

Marr pulled a cloth from the pocket of his coveralls - was that really a fucking *ironed crease* in the legs? - and swiped it over his shoe, as if her body had contaminated it. "Leave it to my deadbeat cousin to breed the trashiest Beta in the quadrant. Zul always did love to throw his goo into the worst possible holes. First that runt, then the one-eyed wonder, and now *this*. Ugh. Bourge, can you please-"

The huge Omega stepped towards Ch'ik, his red rimmed mouth twisting in sadistic glee. Before Marr could complete the order, a low drone hummed through the room. It ratcheted up in pitch, shrieking its way up the scales in a whooping alarm. The sound howled through the room, which Ch'ik just now noticed opened up into a biomass plant - a fungus farm.

That meant she was probably still on the station!

Hope flooded through her, as well as a need to pee again. That was getting really annoying. She was going to spend the seventh fraction-cycle of the pregnancy entirely in the damn bathroom at this rate.

As quickly as it had begun, the alarm cut out. The ringing silence that followed didn't last for long, replaced by a series of garbled musical snippets colliding with one another. Finally, a discordantly calm voice rang over the speakers.

"Plarm Station is experiencing technical difficulties. Please stand by. Plarm Station is experiencing technical difficulties. Please stand by. Plarm Station-"

Ch'ik's kidnappers had huddled together across the room - out of spitting distance, she noted with fierce pride. From Marr's harsh, clipped tone and overly dramatic hand gestures, it was clear he was giving them orders to do something or go somewhere. Whatever. They had stopped paying attention to her, and that meant that Ch'ik could start to wiggle her knife free of its holder.

The angle was painful, and definitely not the way those tendons were meant to stretch, the plastic cuffs digging sharply into her wrists with every twitch. She had to move slowly so as not to attract their attention, and tingling fingertips told Ch'ik that her circulation wasn't doing well, but she wasn't going to let something as unimportant as a little blood flow stop her from protecting the kits. And her own ass, of course.

The harsh overhead lights flickered and went dark. The storage room was plunged into darkness and Ch'ik made the most of every single second of it. By the time the lights blinked back on, she had freed the knife from her boot and rotated the handle in her hand so that she could slide the blade up between the cuffs that bound her wrists together.

She did her best not to dull the blade more than was necessary as she sawed through the plastic in slow glides. *It still had plenty of work to do.*

CHAPTER 33

- ZUL -

AN ENDLESS CASCADE OF SHATTERED CODE EXPLODED
out around Zul as he tore his way through the station's
security system.

He hadn't figured out how to coordinate his body any
more skillfully amid the accidental destruction, but it
hardly mattered. Every jerk and twitch of this
visualization of himself sent sparks spraying away into
nothingness. It reminded Zul of some long-ago trip that
his family had taken to one of their vacation homes, to
the beaches of a hospitality planet. He lingered in
memories of the way he and the other kits had run
giggling through the splashing surf, kicking up sparkling
fans of seawater. That had been the last trip that he had
played carefree in the sun and he had spun in the sand
like he spun now in the code, graceless and -

Free.

Free.

Zul sat up. He tried to rub at his face, to shove some sense back into his bedazzled brain, but he forgot that his arm was swathed in hardware until he accidentally knocked himself in the nose with a heavy coil of copper wires. For a second he saw stars, then beyond the stars the wide and terrified eyes of his clustermates. "What hap-"

Without warning the proximity hacker disengaged. It slid off of Zul's arms and slumped to the floor of the bridge, but the sound of metal on metal was drowned out as Zul screamed.

Roz was there in an instant, holding Zul close to him as Zul clung back, hissing through his teeth at the pain. His weakening scream was cut off by a hoarse cough as he grabbed at his newly-freed arms, bare but for his fur and the multitude of tiny blood spots that had started to mat it.

"Z?" Jau's attention bounced between Zul and the exterior view screens, filled with activity.

"That *thing!*" Zul's teeth were clenched as he tried to breathe through the pain, to handle it without further distressing his mates. He wasn't succeeding all that well. "That shitty *thing* is full of needles, Jau. How the *fuck* does Ch'ik use that? It's *torture!*"

"She's tough." Roz rumbled, steadying Zul as he helped him to his command chair. Jau frowned at the console, carefully navigating through a large, confused crowd of ships around the periphery of the station. Roz squeezed his shoulder, pulling Zul's attention back off the screens. "She's ours, and she's tough, Alpha. Are you gonna be okay?"

"Yeah. It's getting better already. Sorry, I- I was just surprised." Zul absently palmed the base of his own ears, seized by a sudden need to make sure they were still there, and facing the right direction.

His mates' concern didn't seem at all abated by his reassurance, but Zul wasn't sure what else he could say to make things better. He was awake, wasn't he? Upright and undamaged, for the most part, just some blood on his arms and some drool, from the feel of it.

Zul swiped a hand across his nose and mouth, attempting to clear away most of it. Looking down at the mess on his fingers, a chill flashed through him at the thick white rime of frothy spittle, tinged pinkish-red. "Oh."

"Yeah, *oh*. What the hell did you *do*?" Jau grumbled as he rose, nudging Zul towards the *Koton's* visual field.

"Ouch!" Zul yelped as Jau's hand closed gently on his blood-pricked forearm, instantly withdrawing at the exclamation of pain. "I don't -" Zul's whiskers twitched as he wiggled his nose. "I don't know for certain. This thing is so hard to use, I just tried to mess up as much of the system as I could."

"Pfft." Jau snorted, cheek-marking Zul firmly before plunking back down at the control array. "Yeah, I'd say you managed to do that just fine. Look."

All three of them watched the screens, slack-jawed at the display of chaos that had unfolded outside.

The space around Plarm Station was thick with ships and escape pods, with more joining the mess as everyone scrambled to get off the station. Whatever was going on inside the station itself was hardly visible through the few viewports, but from what Zul could see it looked as if the lighting system had gone haywire. Rapid flashes inside strobed between bright white, blood red, and pure darkness.

Zul stared at the mess of queries that scrolled through the general comm channel for the station. The tone seemed to be more amused than panicked, which gave him some confidence. At least he hadn't accidentally opened all the airlocks, or ejected the gravity drive, or something else truly disastrous.

"We should dump the *Aeon Hawk* before we circle around to the IZ." Jau suggested as he brought the thrusters online. "The scrappers might not realize it's abandoned with all of this shit going on, I mean, it might even still be here when we get back."

The three of them shared a look. No one wanted to say it, especially not when Ch'ik was in such terrible peril.

It was finally Roz, usually the sweetest of them, who cracked. "Or...maybe...not?"

Zul nodded. "It - uh - it would be a *real shame* but we can get her a new ship, right? We can get her a *hundred* new ships. We just have to get her back."

Jau backed the *Koton* away from the dock and opened the cargo bay doors to shed the Aeon Hawk like so much spare baggage. It spun gently, drifting in empty space. If the station had been up and running properly, they'd have been cited by the security system for dumping outside of the waste tanks - ships weren't allowed to drop such huge cargo here anyway, waste or otherwise. Jau swung around towards the underbelly of the station, down into the infrastructure zone, as they all held their breath on the bridge.

The fleet of defense drones around the IZ were non-biological in origin, but something about the way the bulbous white orbs moved seemed almost sickly now. Instead of maintaining their protective formation around the no-fly zone of the station's hull, they drifted and staggered into one another like fluid particles in a seasick wave. Jau shot towards them, all adrenaline at the impending fight, riding a lightning bolt of terror and exhilaration as he plunged the *Koton* into the roiling drones.

Drones bounced harmlessly off of the hull of the ship like stellar flotsam. The drones ricocheted with enough force that a few broke free of their prescribed pattern and spun out into space with their deadly nanobot cargo still stowed safely within.

The voice of the automated station security system broke through their comm channel, a screeching electronic voice at decibel levels particularly irritating to Lapann hearing.

"*Lucky Leprechaun* return to the designated docking zone at once. *Lucky Leprechaun* return to the designated docking zone at once. *Lucky Leprechaun* -"

It was unfortunate that Zul had somehow managed to miss that particular facet of the security system in his path of destruction. The message was harmless, but unable to be muted and something of a distraction at a very tense moment.

Zul wrestled a brief moment of crushing guilt. If he'd have swiped the wrong way in the hacker, he might have taken the announcement system offline instead of the drones themselves. The *Koton* would have been swarmed and vaporized before they even realized anything was wrong. It would have been all his fault that their kits would have grown up without a cluster and...and...

...and none of that mattered. His efforts, no matter how slapdash, had been successful enough and *that* was all that mattered. He'd weigh the what-ifs later. A quick shake of his head to clear out the tech cobwebs, another swipe across his nose to remove any remaining blood, and his focus settled once more on getting Ch'ik back home with them.

CHAPTER 34

- ROZ -

JAU GAVE A PRACTICED FLICK TO THE CONTROL array as they pulled up alongside the station, turning the *Koton* to face their instruments of piracy against the bulkhead. Once they were in place, Roz bounded off the bridge, long strides carrying him to the cargo bay. The once-again cavernous space was filled with the metallic, ozone-laden smell of a recently vented atmosphere. He took a few inhales, getting used to it: there would be more of that to come once he'd done his job.

The high hydraulic whine of the grapplers echoed through the bay, the *Koton* shuddering from stem to stern as it latched onto the side of the station. Roz placed one heavy boot against the lever that engaged the hull-to-hull sealing mechanism and sprang up into the open space that had so recently housed the *Aeon*

Hawk. His powerful leap allowed him to sail through the distance, body curved back like a bow string, rising to twice his own height. He grabbed firmly onto the handles at the edge of the hull piercer, letting his own weight drag it down.

The articulating arm that kept the hull-to-hull mech attached to the ceiling of the bay extended with the movement. Climbing arm over arm, he hauled himself over the three massive roller cones, edged with a new set of tiramite-tipped cutting teeth. He swung easily onto the ladder, welded directly into the bright yellow enamel of the exterior facing. Clipped to one of the rungs was his drilling helmet, right where Roz had left it after the last real job that they'd done.

His helmet was a custom job, specifically made to fit his head since even a runty Omega had a skull much too large for standard gear. It was a full face style that protected his entire head, from the rear that covered the base of the skull down to the section that wrapped around his mouth and chin. It was hell on visibility, but it had an auto darkening face shield and a built in air filtration system and a wireless link to the ship's internal comm system.

Buying that helmet had been a major milestone for him, after the first few grappler jobs where flying shards of white-hot metal had ripped at the edges of his ears, but now it seemed like a lifetime ago. Even the fraction-cycles before Ch'ik had come into their cluster seemed like a distant memory.

Roz had loved that life as much as any of them, but things had changed. With Ch'ik in their family and the kits coming soon, he couldn't imagine going back to it. He didn't *want* to.

The younger, sadder version of himself who had scrawled BORN TO DRILL above the visor after another lost season of eggs was gone. That empty part inside of him had been filled in ways he had never imagined could be his, all thanks to a rowdy Beta with zero sense of self-preservation.

With a final look at the slogan, Roz tucked his ears down as he slipped the helmet over his head for what he hoped was the last time. Then, he got to work.

Setting the tricone bit on its course to drill through the station's exterior hull, the liquid crystal filter in the visor lens darkened instantly. Protected - visually, at least - from the blinding shower of white hot sparks that fountained up, Roz rode the hull piercer like a mechanical titbeast, rocking and swaying his body to counteract the rhythmic rises and falls. Toxic fumes darkened the air and the screech of rending metal engulfed everything, drowning out any doubt he'd had left in him for the plan. No going back, now.

A red light flashed in his periphery and Roz reached out to engage the cooling system. He was an old hand with the hull piercer, which meant he *never* turned away from the guidance system. He knew too many Lapann who'd made that mistake, and it was an error in judgment you only made once. Reaching out, he flicked a line of switches and spun the dial that sent jets of cooling gas hissing down the lines. Coolant flooded out around the heated metal, setting the edges of the new, surprise entryway the *Koton* had so thoughtfully installed in the side of Plarm Station.

Soon, the screech dropped down to a deep grind as the bit found purchase, chewing its way through the interior layers of the hull. Roz tapped a button in the lower half of the helmet to let Zul and Jau know that it was almost go time - he may never have pierced a station hull before, but he knew what that sound foretold. He knew the drill - literally and figuratively. Soon, they would be together again. All of them. Roz would do whatever it took to make that happen, even if that meant he had to slaughter every single member of Zul's extended family.

"We're on our way down!" Jau's voice came over the tinny helmet intercom, not a moment too soon.

All at once the hull piercing mechanism broke through into the station and dropped down to the furthest extension of the articulating arm.

Roz braced himself for the jarring deceleration as it came up short, but he had failed to account for the sudden shift into the station's gravity field. In an instant everything recalibrated - down was front, back was down, and Roz managed to hang on to the control panel just long enough to pull the pin that triggered the emergency shutdown before he slipped loose.

The high whine of the motor cut out in an instant and in the next his boots were thumping down against what felt like a springy rubber floor.

The soft ground absorbed most of his fall, but Roz still folded down to his hands and knees to lessen the brunt of the impact. Above him, the cutter cones were still spinning, but without any power behind them they slowed, eventually going silent as vision-distorting plumes of heat leached off of the heated metal cones. Roz hooked his fingers under the edge of the helmet and flung it behind him as he rose from his crouch. As Roz's eyes adjusted to the darkened room, he could just barely make out the ominous-looking shadowed edges of massive mushrooms, each as large as - or larger than - the *Koton* itself.

He was inside the fungus farm.

CHAPTER 35

- JAU -

Zul leaned through the hull-hole, careful to keep his hands and feet clear of the edges. The coolant helped structural integrity, but the metal was still glowing white-hot from the piercer's friction. He cupped a hand to his mouth, yelling into the dark, cavernous space while Jau waited to jump. "Roz! Coming through!"

"No hostiles yet! Big jump, watch the gravity!" Roz's voice sounded far away but it wouldn't be for long: with both their Beta and Omega out of sight, Alpha instincts were riding both he and Zul particularly hard. *Find. Hunt. Secure.*

Jau didn't know what awaited him on the other side of the breach. He only had his Omega's word, but that was more than enough.

Powerful muscles coiled in his legs when Jau crouched, preparing himself for a huge jump. He sailed through the air above the hole, but only a few seconds later, he started dropping like a stone. Tensing into a controlled fall along the fully-extended articulating arm of the hull piercer, he shoved himself forward with as much force as his own mass could give him.

The border between two gravity fields was always a precarious spot. Apprentice pirates were often overwhelmed by nausea and vertigo when crossing that invisible threshold, but the crew of Lapann were far past those early errors. Jau breathed deep and let the disorientation surge through him without allowing it affect his balance. The pull of 'down' instantly shifted 90 degrees, but he twisted gracefully into it. The glow of the *Koton's* cargo bay vanished behind him as he dropped down into the underbelly of Plarm Station.

For a moment he was airborne, suspended in a space so vast and cavernous that he couldn't get his bearings. It was warm and dark and then, once he had landed, soft. That last detail threw him for more of a loop than any gravity shift could have, leaving him wobbly-legged and confused.

Jau staggered to the side to clear the landing zone, acutely aware of how close Zul had been behind him, but before he could go too far he heard Roz behind him. "Nope. No, no, no, Jau, *stop.*"

Jau froze when a huge, familiar hand tightened on his elbow to hold him steady. The dimness in front of him gradually resolved into a vast network of suspended walkways. When his depth perception finally kicked in, Jau realized that he was standing on the edge of a cliff.

No, not a cliff. A *mushroom*. A huge tower of wide, flat caps, all forming a terraced hill of fungal flesh with Jau at the apex. He was shocked into silence as he hastily stepped back from the beveled precipice that he'd nearly plunged from.

There was a muffled thump from behind them as Zul came through the breach, followed by a short yelp and a muttered curse. Jau stayed where he was when Roz patted him on the shoulder and went to check on their captain, awestruck at the sight of the massive fungus farm.

Jau craned his head back and saw that Zul had grappled them on one of the side walls of the farm, high above the floor. Roz had actually drilled *through* one of the ladders that were bolted along the wall for access to the suspended walkways above. In an extreme stroke of luck, they had positioned the breach directly above the enormous mushroom at the far end of one of the rows of grow tanks - any further to either side and they would have fallen straight down to the riveted steel floor, likely to their deaths.

It was a *long* way down. The true distance was difficult to judge given the lack of light - the only illumination came from red lights in recessed tracks that ran along the sides of the grow tanks far below. Jau wasn't sure if Zul had shut most of the lights off during his little hacking escapade or if it was the usual operation of the fungus farm. What was that saying, about how Imperium Investigators were like mushrooms? Feed them shit and keep them in the dark? From the looks of it, these mushrooms ate a whole lot of shit. It only made sense that the lighting was also kept to a minimum.

Jau blinked his eye as he scanned the surrounding area, searching for any hostiles that might be hidden in the ghastly red glow. The huge mushrooms made it difficult to take in the entire scope of the biomass plant; there were far larger and less inviting-looking shrooms than the one he stood on, and that was just within Jau's line of sight. His *worryingly limited* line of sight. This fungus farm would be a tactical nightmare if Marr's crew was able to effectively ambush them.

"Jau. We've gotta go. This thing's pretty stable but I don't like trusting it to support all three of us." Roz's voice was pitched low but not panicked. When Jau turned he saw that Roz was standing next to a new, jagged edged hole where they had all landed on the top of the mushroom cap.

Zul was next to him, scowling as he plucked stray bits of shroom off the barrel of his plasma rifle. His coveralls were flecked with the stuff, all the way up to his waist, and Jau had to bite back the urge to cackle at his cluster mate - this was neither the time nor the place. Still, Zul was lucky Roz had been the one to help him out of the mushroom hole - Jau wouldn't have been able to hold back from laughing, no matter how dire the situation was.

The three of them descended the towering mushroom with ease. The way that the caps were stacked made a kind of enormous soft, squishy staircase, each "stair" taller than Jau's entire body. They stayed together as they cycled through dropping down and keeping watch for any hostiles, ears on alert for any sounds of danger.

It had been near silent at the top of the mushroom, but by the time they dropped down to the floor level, the noise of the biomass plant was almost overwhelming. Long tubes bolted to the sides of the grow-tanks hummed with all of the sounds of moving liquid as all of the station's waste gurgled and churned and rushed along the thick substrates from which the mushrooms towered. They would have had to yell if any verbal communication was necessary.

Zul scanned up and down the row of tanks before he gestured to the same wall that Roz had drilled through and made a series of quick gestures with the hand signals that they used to communicate in hostile situations.

Check along the perimeter. Look for doors. High alert.

That last part was, in Jau's opinion, a little redundant. He started to roll his eye at Zul but found his gaze arrested yet again by the enormous mushrooms. It shouldn't have awed him as much as it did - after all, Jau had piloted the *Koton* through the roots of the *Ygg* back at the Scrum plenty of times, and that tree was orders of magnitude larger than these shrooms. But Jau had never actually stood next to the tree-ship like this. He had never climbed down the side of it and gawked up at where the top of it disappeared beyond sight.

Far above them, in the tiny lattice network of catwalks, something moved.

Jau narrowed his eye at the slow moving speck, but before he could distinguish anything his vision was disturbed by the twinkling sparkle of a red targeting light.

In a moment of panic, Jau abandoned hand signals and yelled at the top of his lungs. "Sniper!"

Roz's hand grasped him by the front of his coveralls and yanked him to the side, the three of them stumbling under the nearest mushroom shelf. A ruby explosion of plasma rifle fire rained down around them. Wide red laser rays glanced harmlessly off of the floor and tanks but cleaved through the flesh of the mushroom on the other side of the aisle. Those rails of merciless energy left singed scars in their wake as they sliced chunks from the edges of the shelf-like fungus. Severed slabs from the body of the dense mushroom crashed to the floor of the farm in dull, station-shaking thuds. Jau could feel the vibration in his teeth as Zul caught their eyes and gestured.

Roz was the only one of them that had to actually duck so that the tops of his ears didn't drag along the prominent gills on the underside of the mushroom cap. Together, the three of them hugged the side of the grow tank, sneaking along along the edge of the tank towards the wall.

The air was filled with the delicious smell of sizzling mushroom - would have been better with a little fat in the frying pan, Jau thought hysterically. Unfortunately for Marr and his shithead crew, he wasn't about to volunteer his own.

By the time they reached the end of the row of tanks, the attack had relented. Still under the cover of the mushroom, they peeked around the corner. A long, narrow alleyway ran along the bulkhead of the station; the other direction had a much wider access path along the wide flat ends of the tanks, row after row of them, stretching out to the other side of the biomass plant.

Eye contact. A gesture from Zul. A nod. Then, they ran.

Jau expected to feel plasma rifle fire singe his tail as he sprinted between tanks, but nothing happened. The only red lights were the red facility lights lining the floor, and the faster they moved the harder it would be for the lifeform up on the catwalks to target them. With ears laid back to dampen the all-encompassing roar of the pumping equipment, Jau and his mates darted from row to row of giant shelf fungus. He was starting to feel more confident until, all at once, the topography changed.

There were no more towering mushrooms in front of them, instead they were flanked by shorter rows of fungus in all sorts of bizarre varieties. These fungi were still large but ranged closer in size to small shuttles or massive buildings like the stacked caps they'd just left behind. Brown leathery sails that looked like giant ears grew beside hills of lumpy white boulders, oozing with black ochre. Wrinkly toadstools glowed with a faint green bioluminescence further down the line. The sheer variety of huge fungi, however awe inspiring, didn't soothe his panic at the lack of cover.

Zul stepped back from the corner of the tank and pulled Jau and Roz into a huddle, his arms thrown over their shoulders so he could be heard over the din of machinery.

"There was an access ladder a few rows back. I'm gonna climb up to the catwalks and see if I can flush out our sniper buddy. Once I have them distracted you can go for it. Don't let anything stop you. Get Ch'ik, kill whoever gets in your way or hurts her."

Jau and Roz dipped their heads together in acknowledgement, and Zul's arms tightened around

them for the briefest of squeezes before he spun away.
He took off at a dizzying pace, traveling back the way
that they'd come. Jau watched his plasma rifle bouncing
on his back as Zul disappeared under the thick shelves
of mushrooms.

There was nothing to do but wait.

The waiting was difficult, and seemingly endless. Jau
did his best to keep his breath steady and deep, priming
his body for a burst of activity when it was needed. He
kept a calming hand on Roz's shoulder; he didn't need
the flood of hormones coming off of Roz to tell him his
Omega wasn't doing well. The longer they were
separated from their imperiled Beta, especially this late
in the pregnancy, the more his mate crested the edge of
barely-controlled violence. Roz seemed dangerously
close to shattering into an incandescent and
uncontrollable rage. Secretly Jau hoped one of the
fucking idiots in Marr's crew would make the
undoubtedly-fatal mistake of going toe-to-toe with Roz.
It'd be good for his Omega to literally bleed off some of
this looming aggression.

The sharp hiss of plasma fire erupted from the catwalks
overhead, pulling both he and Roz from their waiting
crouch. Zul must have finally made it up the ladder.
Deadly plasma blasts strafed overhead, spurring them
onwards. Jau muttered a short Osterian prayer for the
safety of his mate, and tried to take peace in knowing

Zul had Academy training in marksmanship to keep him safe.

Roz tapped Jau's arm, nodding to where a blue-eyed Lurquer was just barely peeking around a corner. Gun already out, their enemy sent a few wild shots their way as he ran towards them with a chittering curse.

As Jau and Roz braced themselves for combat, a plasma blast lanced down from the distant catwalks, too poorly aimed to be anything but stray fire. The wide red plane of rifle fire, even though it missed their bodies, still caused issues. It cleaved through the body of a lumpy, bulbous mushroom, covered in swaying white tentacles thicker than Jau's arm. Those soft clumps of spores shivered and swayed precariously. With a soft *whump*, the slice widened to a jagged crack, sending a fungus avalanche slumping over he and Roz.

The toe of Jau's boot caught on a grate and he stumbled as it fell toward him, leg twisting as he fell to a knee before he could get clear. He had just enough time to look up and grin as he watched Roz rear back and kick the charging Lurquer in the face as hard as he could. Jau silently thanked the pulsars his Omega was safe before the wide wall fungus folded over, slamming Jau down into the floor.

All of the air was knocked from his lungs, abruptly. The deceptively heavy, soft crush of the mushroom's fuzzy tentacles pressed him flat, pinning down most of his body. Even when he finally managed to clear a small cavity around his face with the one arm he worked free, his nose was blocked with blood - his recently-healed fight injury inconveniently reopened. Jau struggled to extricate himself, but it was nearly impossible under the inexorable weight of a mushroom slice ten times his size.

If Jau would have been knocked unconscious by the impact he would have smothered to death for sure. Even so, the lack of air circulation, coupled with the humming vibration of the floor beneath him, created a morbid temptation of warm, dark weight. His body begged to close its eyes, to surrender to the inevitable.

Fuck that.

Jau shoved two fingers against his broken nose, letting the lance of pain beat back the cruel temptation of rest. He wasn't going to let anything stop him. He was a *fighter*. He had always *been* a fighter. He had never fought against an opponent as large as this mushroom, sure, but Jau wasn't going to go down without making this fungal sonofabitch *work* for it.

Spitting stray spores and wiping them away from his eye, Jau pushed himself forward and struggled in what he dearly hoped was the right direction. His muscles screamed and burned from the bruising heft of fungus, his head spinning with nonsense as phantom colors swum behind his closed eyes. Zul and Roz and Ch'ik and the lights that were their tiny unborn kits, just out of reach. He reached. He *reached* for them through the mess of broken gills and chunks of spongy fungus. He grasped for his future, for all of his life, lungs still burning like he was sucking void. Just when he thought that he could reach no further, his fingers slid beyond the soft flesh of the mushroom and into cool, clear air.

Jau wanted to scream in triumph but his lungs were preoccupied with sucking deep, unobstructed breaths. He hooked his fingertips around the edge of a grate and pulled himself forward with a bloody groan until he cleared the slice. He rolled over onto his back, dazed, then shoved himself over again as he coughed wretchedly to clear the spores from his airway.

His senses returned to him bit by bit, not nearly as fast as he would have liked, but each gasping gulp of air that he took in was a victory that cleared his head a fraction at a time. Finally, the situation in front of him resolved itself back into a messy whole.

The blue-eyed Lurquer that Roz had kicked in the face twitched on the floor a few paces beyond Jau, dying. His head had been caved in by the force of Roz's frightful strength, chunks of bone and bits of flesh, a ruined mess of gore. It filled Jau with a grim sort of victory, watching the Lurquer spasm and, finally, go still.

Good.

One down, four to go. Jau braced one hand against the slumped shelf of mushroom and pushed himself up to stand. He knew that he would be sore as fuck once the adrenaline wore off, but he had shit to do.

A roar of outrage rang out, even louder than the constant din of the biomass plants's pumping equipment. Startled, Jau looked up beyond the corpse of the Lurquer and saw Roz, engaged in hand to hand with a huge, blood-colored Lapann Omega. *Oh fuck. Bourge.*

Marr's Omega was nearly twice as tall as Roz , muscle-bound and hulking. Jau wasn't surprised to see the special forces chevrons short-shaved into the dark red fur of his cheeks - new lines since the last time his cluster had tangled with the station-sized fucker.

Jau was also admittedly confused at the way that the huge Lapann howled and clutched at his nose like a kit with a skinned knee. Roz, fur sweaty and disheveled from fighting, simply stood there with his fingers pinched together and a smug expression.

Then, the low red facility lights winked off of the single whisker that Roz held between his fingertips.

Jau watched in awe as Roz stepped closer and rained ferocious blows against the soft and vulnerable parts of the other Omega's body. When he staggered, Roz gripped his massive arm at the elbow and turned to throw his opponent up and over his shoulder. Then Roz dropped the bigger Omega down head-first and spiked him hard onto the floor. Whatever sickening crunch there may have been was lost under the din of the pumping equipment, but Jau saw the impact and awkward angle of Bourge's thick neck.

It wasn't over yet, but it would be soon.

The crumpled figure on the ground started to awkwardly move, but Roz planted one big boot against the other Lapann's back and shoved him back down. Roz looked up to Jau with darkened eyes and Jau had never loved him more - this feral, fierce, and absolutely unstoppable Omega in front of him had his heart entirely. Roz's jaw flexed as his gaze swept Jau, checking for injuries, taking in the devastation of the mushroom for the first time as the bloodlust ebbed. Jau shook his head and patted his chest, their cluster's universal symbol of *all good*. Roz nodded, making a few quick, slashing hand gestures just before his gaze cut back to the Omega on the ground, who had started feebly struggling again.

Go. Find her.

Jau nodded and took off along the perimeter again, looking for any sign of a storage room. He sprinted past dizzying amounts of fungus gardens, from tiny white clusters of delicate caps to tentacle-topped wedges that smelled like death. All of them cast unnerving, stuttering shadows that rose and faded in the flickering plasma firefight above.

Streaks of red laser fire lit up trails along the ceiling until they abruptly stopped. Jau feverishly hoped that Zul's gun was the one to fire the last blast. Jau trusted in Zul's ability, but concern for his mate still distracted him and he turned his head to scan the catwalks above. He saw a shadow as a body dropped down and disappeared into the rows of mushroom tanks - too small to be Zul, he hoped.

He was so busy trying to catch a glimpse of Zul's silhouette, he'd let his guard down: Jau didn't see the brown-furred figure until it was too late. Marr stood from his hiding spot behind a clump of yellow toadstools, a laser pistol aimed point-blank at his head.

Jau flinched and dove. The pistol fired.

The pain was sharp and searing, but nowhere near as bad as Jau would have expected dying to be. It was, puzzlingly, less painful than the impact of his knees on the grated floor as he dove for cover. He reached up, patting at his own face and wondering if the lack of significant pain was because he was already dead. His questing fingers found no wounds - beyond the broken nose that still throbbed and bled sluggishly, anyway.

Stray mushroom spores clouded out around Jau as he stood on shaky legs, running his hand up through his shaggy hair. To his immense relief he found no scorched edge of bone, no exposed brain, only a circular hole in his left ear, about a hands width from the base. He winced as two of his fingertips dipped into the open wound of it, then winced again as the barrel of the laser pistol pressed to the top knob of his spine.

"You never should have gotten involved with my cousin." Marr's haughty voice was hardly audible over the pumping equipment but the smug, self-satisfied tone still made Jau's fur flatten with indignation.

The stomp came unbidden, breaking through cycles of pit-fighting instincts that had taught him to stow his emotions. "Fuck you, Marr."

"He would have fallen in line, you know. Zul would have come back around to the family if not for you rough trade idiots whispering in his ear about *right* and *wrong*." Marr gave a sharp humorless laugh before he sighed and continued. "None of you would have been exiled. You could have had a normal little life on Oster, but no. Now you're going to make me kill you on this shithole of a station. I hope it was worth it."

Jau mumbled something under his breath.

"If those were your last words you're going to have to speak up."

Jau mumbled again and Marr heaved another put-upon sigh, dramatic and loud, intended to be heard above the equipment. When Marr ducked down closer, Jau felt it. The current of displaced air that moved ever-so-slightly through the fur of his neck. The way the barrel of the laser pistol shifted, almost imperceptibly, against his back.

Marr growled, breath hot against Jau's cheek. "What the fuck did you just call me, you earless little -"

Jau dropped his shoulder and shifted his body to the side, tapping into his last reserves of strength. When Marr reflexively fired, the shot went harmlessly past the side of Jau's neck, plasma glancing off some distant bulkhead. Calling on pit-fighting muscle memory, he whipped his head backwards and *felt* the crunch of Marr's facial bones breaking - the asshole dealt with military fucks, not down-and-dirty bareknucklers like Jau, who embraced full-contact fighting. With a twist of his wrist Jau disarmed Marr, kicking the pistol away so that it skittered off under one of the rows of tanks. Jau spun around to face his opponent, reaching for his own weapon and finding the holsters empty and torn - chest and thigh both.

Realizing he'd probably left both behind in the mess of mushroom spores, Jau growled with irritation. Then Marr started clawing at Jau's face, presenting a more immediate issue. It didn't matter where his weapons were, ultimately, because they weren't *here*. Marr was, though, and the rage that contorted his features told Jau that Zul's terrible cousin didn't intend to go down without a fight.

It should have been simple. Jau should have been able to settle the matter with a few strong jabs - god knows his Scrum career spoke to his ability. But this wasn't a match - he was sore and exhausted from the ongoing stress of the chase, of the bruising, crushing weight of the mushroom, and now even his old wounds were slowing him down as his last reserves of adrenaline petered out. Jau managed to land a few blows but Marr was a stronger, nastier fighter than Jau had expected. Just as his opponent had underestimated him, Jau underestimated the lengths Marr would sink to - the *laht*-brown asshole hooked a finger through the hole in Jau's wounded ear; the pain that followed was enough to briefly white-out the vision in Jau's remaining eye.

They stumbled and crashed to the floor, a messy struggle that ended with Jau flat on his back, Marr's hands wrapped down around his neck. Jau sputtered and choked as he tried to claw at Marr's face but his arms were too short. He couldn't quite reach and so he thrashed, frantic, hands skimming down his own body as he searched for something, anything to use as a weapon. The edges of his vision had started to go dark, black spots blooming as his lungs ached for air, burning for the second time today. His trembling hands found nothing but empty pockets, until his frantic fingers closed on *something*.

There.

Blood dropped from Marr's likely-broken nose, spattering across Jau's face like a warm, gentle rain. He relished the sign of weakness in his opponent as he finally found what he was looking for: the single sook from the *Koton*, the snack that he had stashed into his coveralls pocket to save for later. Later had arrived and the familiar orange root - woody and unyielding under all but the sharpest knives or Lapann incisors - was now the object of his deliverance.

Perfect, perfect, perfect. Delirium and bloodlust surged into a heady cocktail, firing all the dark, decadent parts of Jau's oddly-wired brain.

Jau moved without hesitation. He pulled the long orange root from his pocket, stabbing it smoothly up through Marr's left eye and into *his* brain. As the light dimmed in the enemy Alpha's unimpaled eye above him, Jau indulged an exhausted, petty urge to sully Marr's final moments.

"Say hi to your dead Omega for me, Marr. I'm going to topple your empire with a smile on my face."

CHAPTER 36

- CH'IK -

CH'IK SHIFTED ON HER KNEES, FLEXING HER TOES in her boots to stay ready. She was getting the fuck out of here and back to the boys, as soon as possible.

After she peed.

Oh, and killed this idiot they'd left babysitting her.

The horrific screech of metal-on-metal had overwhelmed the station's other sounds a few minutes ago, just after the alarms and lighting went haywire. The two Lapann - Marr and Bourge, she'd gathered - had taken two of the Lurquers with them, the entire group scattered and panicked as whatever plan they had seemed to fall apart.

That left only her and Green Scarf staring each other down. The glorified henchman looked at her as if she was leakage from a waste tank, but Ch'ik knew he was on edge. He'd seen how much damage she'd managed to do to Bourge's smug red face before she was pulled away, after all. Ch'ik uncharitably hoped that Lapann didn't regrow teeth.

Oh well, joke was on him. She was going to kill his ass *and* her cluster was coming to kick his corpse.

"Ah!" The tip of Ch'ik's knife jolted a shocked exclamation from between her clenched teeth.

She hadn't expected the blade would part the plastic so quickly. Even though she could feel a hot line of blood dripping down the outside edge of her hand, the cut wasn't too painful. The rush of sensation as the circulation returned was actually worse, making her wince.

Green Scarf's head whipped around at the sound, narrowing his eyes at her. She hurriedly turned the pained gasp to a dramatic sniffle. The Lurquer smiled cruelly at her as the tears welled in her eyes - that shit had stung, but it was already feeling better. *Shit.*

Ch'ik quickly thought about the saddest episodes of Night Beats. She thought about holding the kits for the first time. She thought about watching them grow up, holding them close just before they set out on their own.

Ch'ik sniffled again, the tears flowing more reliably now. The Lurquer loomed over her and sneered "It's about time you -"

Her voice broke with a soft, tearful sob as she looked up at him through her lashes. "Do - do you have a family?"

He bristled with annoyance at being interrupted, flicking the end of the scarf back around his shoulder. "No."

"Good." She grinned maniacally, savoring the sudden uneasy fear in his expression.

Ch'ik swung the knife around and stabbed it deep in between two of the chitinous plates on the Lurquer's thigh. There was a gristly tearing sensation that vibrated up the blade and through her hand. A little experimental wiggle severed his primary neural cord, sending him crashing to the cold floor in front of her.

The knife had stuck fast in the Lurquer's leg, twisting the handle out of her grip as he fell. With her pulse pounding in her ears, she wrenched it free with a wet pop, scrambling to find a steady spot astride his spasming torso. Ch'ik had a *thing* with a dishonorably discharged Imperium medic a few cycles back, and learned quite a bit from their idle pillow talk. Lurquers had a non-traditional nervous system, but most of their circulatory routes were in the same places as other species.

Ch'ik put her hand on Green Scarf's forehead and shoved down, holding him still and plunging the knife into his neck. He'd threatened her, he'd threatened her *cluster* and something new and strange growing in her was *determined* not to let that stand.

One of the kits started hiccuping inside of her, sweet little repetitive motions, short sharp kicks against her belly at reassuringly regular intervals. As Ch'ik reduced her captor to waste tank fodder, those tiny hiccups became a metronome of violence, keeping time with thrusts of her knife until the Lurquer's green scarf was black with blood and her arm was so sore she worried she would lose her knife into the ruined mess of the body.

"Calm down, you." Ch'ik patted her belly with a satisfied smile as she wandered out of the room, leaving bloody footprints and the crumpled, perforated corpse in her wake. "Don't make me piss in my coveralls now, not after all of that."

The kit only stopped hiccuping once she had made her way with staggering steps to a nearby bathroom, and finally, *finally* peed. With a relieved sigh, Ch'ik cleaned her hands in the sonic sink on the way out of the restroom... not that it did much good. Ch'ik immediately retrieved the filthy knife from her boot holster before ducking out of the bathroom moving further down the hallway - there was no telling if she'd need to stab another nasty dipshit to death.

Ch'ik limped towards the end of the corridor and, heading for where the pumping equipment was loudest. For where she thought she had heard the sound of the *Koton* drilling into the station. She wasn't hurt so much as exhausted, though her hips still throbbed from staying in one position too long with her huge, pregnant stomach.

A door burst open at the end of the hall, a frantic Roz inhaling deeply before locking eyes on her. His face crumpled, eyes flooding with tears as he ran with shocking speed to her. "ZUL! JAU! SHE'S IN HERE!"

His fur was matted and damp with sweat and blood, and he smelled like mildew and rotting dirt, but he was *here*. He didn't even try to hug her around her belly, sweeping her up into his arms and cradling her against his chest. She dropped her knife to the ground, throwing her arms around his neck and hugging tight. He nuzzled her neck, sucking deep lungfuls of her scent, his chest shuddering with emotion.

"The blood, are you - did they hurt you? Are you alright?" He craned his neck to look in her eyes, his expression twisted between grief and gratitude.

She shook her head, running her cheek along his to soothe him. "I'm fine, big guy, this isn't my blood. They knocked me the fuck out with something back at the Starpass, but I killed the one they left guarding me, this is his blood. The kits are all fine and moving. Are *you* okay? What the fuck happened out there?"

A flurry of heavy footfalls brought Zul and Jau swinging into the corridor door frame, immediately closing the distance and forming a giant huddle around her and Roz.

Roz relaxed visibly, holding her slightly away from his body so his mates could reassure themselves she was alright. "She's fine, the kits are okay, the blood is Lurquer, not hers."

Ch'ik swiped a few overwhelmed tears from her eyes. She could stand, but she didn't think she had a chance in hell of convincing Roz to release her. "Marr and Bourge?"

Jau's ears flicked sharply, the left displaying a bloody, roughly cauterized hole that made her breath catch with concern. "Dead as fuck. Station can deal with their corpses, as far as I'm concerned."

Zul shook his head, smoothing Ch'ik's hair back from her forehead and kissing it softly. "We'll dump all of them into the waste tanks. They're shit, they belong with shit, and they're *not* getting a funeral back on Oster. Let Bron lose his mind over his son vanishing. Hope it keeps him up at night."

For being drenched in concerning amounts of blood and sporting a few gory wounds, her cluster was kinda sexy when they got all vengeance-y, Ch'ik decided with a smile. Of the five eyes fixed on her face, not a single one had batted a lash at her admission that she'd offed a guy on the way to the bathroom.

Ah, shit. She really was in love.

CHAPTER 37

- ZUL -

With a stern word to Jau to *SIT DOWN AND rest*, Zul and Roz rigged makeshift stretchers out of a discarded pair of coveralls and two mushroom stalk support rods. It was slow going, and a little awkward between their height difference and Bourge's oversized form. Eventually, however, he and his Omega managed to get all the bodies, including the spattered remains of the Lurquer Zul had taken out with sharpshooting, into the largest waste tank. Enzymes churned, and when the security protocols on the programmed compost nanites failed to find life signs on the masses dumped in, the corpses were quickly mulched beyond recognition.

Clambering up a side support ladder, they managed to crawl back up to the ship, though Ch'ik had gotten powerfully nauseous as they crossed the gravity borders. After taking a moment to rest in the cargo bay, he and his cluster grinned and watched as their Beta, still gloriously blood-soaked and giddily exhausted, grabbed a tube of red hull paint.

A fraction later, **SORRY ABOUT YOUR HOLE** had been scrawled in messy letters, taller than Jau, around a hasty temporary patch that covered their makeshift entrance to Plarm Station. Roz quickly stowed the piercing mech as Zul spun up the *Koton's* systems, and they all got the hell out of dodge and continued the trek to Oster.

Once the course was laid in, they'd all hit the sonic showers hard, removing every trace of mushroom, blood, and regret from their bodies. The Lapann all "helped" Ch'ik with wandering hands that were filled with as much promise as they were breast, or cock, or ass. Those hands, however, wrote a series of sales contracts that their absolutely wrung-out bodies were *not* prepared to cash: Zul barely managed to set the autopilot before they fell into the cluster bed together, naked, and slept like the dead.

Ch'ik half-woken earlier as a back twinge bothered her, but Zul had gently massaged it away until she slipped back to a deep sleep into which he had followed her so quickly that he hadn't even noticed that his consciousness had deserted him until the dreams found him.

He dreamed that he was traveling along a near-infinite system of suspended walkways between Plarm Station and the Megaptera Nebula, that he had watched the void whales as they breached and dove through reefs of gigantic mushrooms, that the stars had been born all around him like blooming flowers and the incomprehensible beauty of it had reduced him to tears that floated and sparkled like orange crystalline raindrops in the abyssal void.

Subtle movement stirred Zul awake fractions later, a powerful yawn cracking his jaw wide as he blearily took stock of his cluster. He missed the warmth of Ch'ik curled against his side, but his grogginess fell away and his cock stirred with interest as he realized the other three were definitely *not* still sleeping. Jau was up on his knees at the edge of the bed, Ch'ik wrapped around his back, her arm disappearing down his hip. They were facing Roz, kneeling on a pillow tossed on the floor, ears dropped in submission. The lasciviously wet sucking sounds left little to the imagination, even if Zul didn't have a front row seat yet.

He crawled closer, nuzzling Ch'ik's thigh to let her know he'd woken too. She grinned down at him with sharp fangs, relinquishing her grip on Jau's cock and settling back on her heels to grab Zul's instead, giving it a teasing squeeze before gliding up and down. Zul's knot swelled and he sighed in appreciation as her clever fingers went to work.

After Ch'ik and Jau had jumped each other after the Scrum, they'd all talked about mating bites, as well as her impossibly-sharpened teeth in the heat of the moment. At the time, she seemed uncomfortable with the idea of bonding with his cluster - but since Ch'ik had agreed to stay with them now, Zul hoped that her mind had been changed on that too.

The *how* still baffled them all, but the working theory was that her consistent exposure to so much broma pod dust had unlocked something in her latent Lapann DNA. That was a puzzle for Oster geneticists to unravel, though: Zul just wanted her to claim them, and to claim her in return. Every time she got turned on, her sexy little teeth sharpened, as theirs had before they'd formalized their cluster with mating bites. They'd all been giving her the space to decide when she wanted to use them, but he personally *ached* for her to sink them into his flesh.

Zul positioned himself behind Ch'ik, holding her hips to anchor her in place, pinning her between Jau's back and his chest. Zul loved this, his entire cluster touching each other, one warm knot of sexual contact that sizzled with erotic energy. His fingers crept down to Ch'ik's slit, gliding and curling, his cock jumping when he found her absolutely dripping with arousal.

He purred as he murmured at her ear, letting the vibration in his chest relax her, hoping it would heighten her pleasure. "Do you want a knot, my beautiful Beta?"

She let out a squeaky little *mmhm* as Zul dipped two fingers into her tight channel, scissoring them slightly to tease her. She dropped her head back on his shoulder as he inhaled deeply against her neck, savoring her aroused scent. Her voice was low and husky with desire, and Zul wondered idly how long the three of them had been playing before he woke. "*Yes* Alpha - please, *need* you."

He chuckled and guided her onto all fours beside Jau so they could watch the action as they fucked, tugging over a pillow so Ch'ik could hug it comfortably and balance her stomach. Zul was a watcher, and he made no apologies for it - seeing his mates get each other off like this was hotter than the twin suns. Getting to do it while he was knot-deep in Ch'ik? That thought nearly undid him before he'd even started.

He notched himself against her entrance, intending to go slow for her sake, but she shoved her hips back and took nearly half his length at once. He exhaled sharply, struggling for control and gripping her shoulder, giving a soft hiss of pleasure as he pushed in further. "Easy now, you little minx. I've got you."

Jau stretched out on his side to put his face below Ch'ik's, tugging her down for a long kiss as Roz worked his Alpha's shaft over with a lashing tongue and lust-hooded eyes. Zul reached out, running his fingers along

Jau's ribs in a slow caress, feeling his back muscles tense as his fellow Alpha began to thrust into Roz's waiting mouth.

Zul matched Jau's thrusts with his own, Ch'ik's lusciously thick thighs parting even further to welcome him in. He wanted to hold out for longer, but between the silky feel of her body and the mind-bendingly erotic sight of Roz latched onto Jau's cock, his knot was swelling, demanding entrance. As Ch'ik grabbed a fistful of Jau's hair and sunk her teeth into his ear, Zul shoved forward, wedging his knot into the tight embrace of her body with a ragged groan, coming so hard he nearly passed out.

CHAPTER 38
- CH'IK -

FINALLY GIVING INTO INSTINCT, SHE REARED BACK and bit Jau's ear. Blood on her teeth, she braced and rode out the firm jerks of Zul's hips as he filled her with his cum, gasping her name. Something primal and fierce in her purred with satisfaction, clenching her body around one Alpha's knot as she claimed another.

Jau jerked, giving a surprised yelp that quickly stuttered out into a moan. Heat rushed between her legs at the sound of that desperate, strangled noise. Looking down Jau's body, Ch'ik's gaze was riveted by the sight of Roz on his knees, the way that his hand was wrapped around Jau's swelling knot as his wet, open mouth worked expertly on the length of his cock. She nipped at Jau's ear again, held him down firmly as he moaned.

"I can tell how much you like this. I can *smell* you, Ch'ik. Oh, oh *fuck.* I'm going to bite you, I'm going to *mark* you -" Jau's fingers clutched at Roz's hair, his thrusts going erratic, the promise seeming to push him to the edge.

"Oh yeah?" Ch'ik grinned against Jau's cheek, feeling Zul slump against her back. Zul was holding his own weight up and massaging her lower back with slow, lust-hazed sweeps of his palms as he watched. "I'm gonna make you *taste* me too. Once you give it up for Roz I'm gonna sit on your face."

Jau groaned another curse and seized like a clenched fist. His flushed cock - what little of it Ch'ik could make out between Roz's hand and eager mouth - jerked and twitched and Ch'ik pulled his hair again, giving his ear another cruel bite that was too much for Jau to take: his restraint snapped. Ch'ik could feel her blood buzzing everywhere - the soles of her feet, the palms of her hands, the swell of her cunt around Zul. She watched hungrily as Jau came with a desperate whine and Roz swallowed. She loved the way his big pink hands clutched Jau's cock as he knotted, a line of his pale yellow cum spilling between the Omega's lips.

She softly pinched the bitten edge of his ear with a knowing smile as he rode out his peak, delighting in the way his involuntary grimace melted into a dazed look of lust. Jau was hers now, and soon the other two would be as well. "Was our Omega good, Jau?"

"Good. *So* good." Jau nodded, still shivering through the aftershocks, reaching down to stroke Roz's hair fondly. When Jau tilted his face back up to her, his expression was dazed and dreamy. "Can you sit on my face now?"

Ch'ik grinned, made sure to show him the sharp point of her tooth. "You don't gotta ask me twice. I'm ready as soon as Zul's knot goes down. But -" she used her light grip on Jau's bitten ear to direct his attention to her. "- what about Roz?"

Roz hadn't moved from his position on the floor, eyes wide and glassy. Ch'ik saw that his hands were still clasped around Jau's knot, working it in a slow massage. The tentacles on the Omega's cock writhed and rubbed along his pink, wet cockhead, seeking and eager.

Jau reached out and swiped a thumb across Roz's chin to collect some of the stray drops of jizz, tucked his thumb back into Roz's mouth to suck clean. "Roz, baby, what do you want?"

Roz released Jau's thumb from his mouth with a filthy wet pop, his words a heated rush. "I want a knot, Alpha. I *need* it. I need to come but I want something inside of me so bad." He whimpered pitifully. "So bad. But I can be good. I can wait."

"Why wait?" Ch'ik stretched her torso down against the bed, working out tension in her shoulders. Zul clutched happily at her hips, trying his best to stay still so his knot could ebb.

All eyes swung to Ch'ik. Roz's expression was one of pure, simple need but Jau had some of the dashing cockiness that Ch'ik had come to expect from him.

Jau smirked. "I appreciate the vote of confidence, but it's gonna be a while before I can pop off again. You too, right Z?"

Ch'ik felt the slight movement against her ass as Zul nodded.

"Didn't say anything about you two, did I?" Ch'ik snorted as she worked her hand free of Jau's hair. She wiggled her fingers at Roz, giving him a grin. "Do you only like to take dick or can we get creative?"

It took a moment for the two of them to process her suggestion, but Ch'ik could tell the exact instant that they put it together because it was as if a bomb had gone off. Ch'ik gave a shocked yelp as Jau twisted around, burrowing between both her legs and Zul's legs as if he was about to work on the underside of a shuttle.

Zul barked a laugh at Jau's eagerness, adjusting a little to better kneel astride his mate's chest. Jau's soft hair brushed the underside of her belly as his tongue happily lapped at where she and Zul were still joined. Zul moaned softly as Jau's tongue curved and curled, tracing the base of his cock as well as Ch'ik's clit.

Ch'ik gripped the edge of the bed with a gasp, grinding down into Jau's mouth and moaning. "*Ohhhh*...that's... yeah, keep that going, Jau." He slowed his rhythm, leaving off of touching Zul so his knot would go down, taking his time and working her up into a slow, delicious state of full-body arousal.

Her body jerked slightly when he felt the familiar tug of Zul's knot slipping out of her - *had it been that long already?* Jau followed Zul's cock out of her, sucking it clean so thoroughly Zul's hips kicked appreciatively.

She settled on her back to watch the Alphas, coaxing Roz up beside her to grip and stroke his cock. Long, soft pink strings of precum threaded down her hand and fingers as he leaked copiously, eyes squeezing shut in pleasure when he wasn't staring wantonly at his mates.

Jau ran his tongue up Zul's cock a final time, the expression in his eye hot and predatory. He gave Zul a deep kiss, cheek-marking him before sliding back between her thighs, laying with his ears towards Roz and the foot of the bed. "Come here, Beta. Give me what you promised."

She slipped one of her shiny fingertips between her lips, sucking it audibly to make Roz whine sweetly with need. Obliging, she knelt upright on the soft bed, putting space between Jau's face and her body. "You know I was joking, right? You don't really have to let me sit on your face."

"Huh?" Jau's forehead wrinkled in confusion as his ears flicked up towards her. "Why not?"

"I'm gonna *crush* you." Ch'ik gestured at, well, her whole self with a laugh. Her thighs had already started to tremble slightly just standing on her knees.

Jau scoffed, rolling his eye. "No you're *not*. Besides -" he tugged her firmly to kneel over his face, darting his tongue at her clit in a way made her legs tremble even more "- that'd be just about the best way to die."

His palms claimed her hips, pulling her down all the way onto his eager, devouring mouth. The breath wooshed out of her as his tongue wasted no time dipping in, tasting Zul's release in her.

It took a minute for her to be able to see straight again, but when she could, her attention was immediately drawn to Roz. He had gone down on his hands and knees in front of her, and as Ch'ik rolled her hips down against Jau's face she stared at his big body and felt her mouth water.

Spread legs, each pink-furred thigh easily twice as wide as one of her own, framed where Roz's dripping cock hung between his legs. His heavy balls were already drawn up high and tight to his body. Though his face was hidden by the sculpted slope of his back, Ch'ik could tell from the tension in his body that he was absolutely alight with anticipation.

As Jau's clever tongue thrust inside of her, Ch'ik reached out and laid one hand on Roz's soft hip, stroking across the deliciously thick swell of his ass. All of Roz's nervous tension melted at her gentle touch and the trembling in his muscles simply disappeared - aside from where his little pink and white tail twitched with every new sensation.

Good, Ch'ik thought to herself as she slid two fingers down the cleft of his ass. Roz being relaxed would certainly make it easier for her to 'knot' him, but she still needed to ask him to pass her the lube if he wanted her to get her entire hand in there. Maybe she'd see what a few fingers could do - she didn't want to hurt her Omega, after all.

All of Ch'ik's thoughts skidded to an abrupt halt as her fingertips found, instead of the tight furl of an asshole that she'd expected, a ready entrance, dripping with slick. Curiously, the feel of Roz's hole wasn't entirely unlike her own cunt. The structure was different, obviously, but the sensation of his open, needy body - hot and wet and yielding - was all too familiar. A shocked moan tumbled out of Ch'ik's mouth as she pressed her two fingers deep inside, encountering no resistance.

"That's - oh fuck, Roz, that's so good. Such a good Omega. You got this wet just for me? Just thinking about taking my fist?" Roz nodded, the reflective bulkhead mirroring his face contorted with lust, mouth slack and panting.

She'd watched the big Omega play with their Alphas several times now, and she knew exactly what kind of praise spun up his engine. Pleasure beyond Jau's mouth coursed through her as Roz's body responded eagerly to her.

Roz's shoulders shuddered as he dropped his face into the cradle of his strong, folded forearms on the bed. Zul gently gripped a handful of Roz's hair, holding the Omega's torso down to the bed, helping him keep his submissive posture. Another wet pulse of slick slid between Ch'ik's fingers as she slipped two more inside of him - nearly her whole hand, now. She had to remind herself to go slowly as Jau returned his attention to laving the flat of his tongue across her swollen clit.

"Fuck." She had to bite back a scream of pleasure at the overload of sensory input, lust boiling through her. "Unh, both of you, I..."

Ch'ik trailed off as she was swept away by the warring sensations, grinding down on Jau as she fucked Roz's dripping hole, but she knew she had to get her head back in the game. Sure, Ch'ik only had five fingers - and her hand was positively *dainty* compared to the massive mitts of the Lapann - but she wasn't going to just fist Roz without a little bit of communication.

"Roz. I'm gonna - fuck, Jau, slow down." She tried to stand up a little taller on her knees to escape his mouth, but he didn't let her budge. He at least stilled his tongue for a moment. "I'm gonna tuck my thumb in now, okay? You have to tell me if it gets to be too much."

"It won't be." Roz sighed happily, the short, downy length of his pink tail flicking up out of her way.

"Roz -" Ch'ik started, and Jau's tongue resumed its dance, scrambling her train of thought.

"Roz." Zul echoed, tipping Roz's chin up with a pair of gentle fingers, his voice hardening. "You'll do exactly as our Beta says. Tell her how to make you feel good, and if you need her to stop. Understand?"

"Yes, Alpha." Roz moaned as his head dropped back into the tangle of bedsheets, body pulsing around her hand in response to his dominant mate's command.

Ch'ik rolled up onto her knees, letting Jau take a breather as Zul instructed Roz. She looked around the swell of her stomach, sharing a smirk with Jau before the one-eyed pirate rededicated himself to licking Ch'ik out like he had a pistol to the head. Her legs trembled on either side of Jau's head, but she vowed not to let the tricky bastard distract her too much, not when she had Roz spread out and needy in front of her.

Ch'ik pulled her hand out enough to fold her thumb against her palm. Then, with her free hand soft on Roz's hip as a gentle anchor for the both of them, she twisted and pressed her folded hand back inside of Roz. He was so wet and open it was an easy glide, but Ch'ik almost forgot to breathe as she focused on staying slow and steady.

The widest span of Ch'ik's hand finally met Roz's body, her knuckles pressing in against the tight rim of his hole. Ch'ik rocked her fingers into him, pushing against the smooth, slick-wet flesh until Roz finally shivered and relaxed completely. As she crossed that last bastion of resistance, she was able to fuck her entire hand inside of him.

Roz cried out. His back arched and a gush of slick dripped out around Ch'ik's wrist as he spread his knees even wider, clutched at his own ears and Zul's gently-stroking hands, babbling and begging.

"Please, Ch'ik. Oh, please, please knot me, I'll be so good for you Beta, I promise, please just give me your knot." He dropped his hand from an ear, curling big pink fingers at the bedsheets as he sobbed with pleasure.

Zul locked eyes with Ch'ik, giving a slow nod. Jau speared his tongue up into her mercilessly, bringing it all to a fever pitch alongside Roz's pleading whimpers. Ch'ik raised up on her knees to get a better angle, too distracted to care that she was probably dripping her own fluids onto Jau's face at this point. She corkscrewed her hand inside of Roz's hole and finally curled her fingers together into a fist.

Roz shouted into the bed, and Ch'ik couldn't see him shooting off from her angle but she *felt* it. The way Zul's eyes glittered with satisfaction as he cooed praise to their Omega added an erotic edge to it all. The muscles inside of Roz's body rippled and tensed and squeezed so hard that Ch'ik felt like the tiny delicate bones in her hand ought to have cracked from the pressure.

Heat flooded through her with each perfect, burning clutch of Roz's body around her fist. Ch'ik rocked it inside of him, just to savor his desperate cries. She dropped her hand from Roz's hip to rub at her clit, so distracted by her Omega's climax that she hadn't even realized that Jau had stopped eating her out. It was only when Ch'ik looked down past where Roz's wet hole fluttered around her wrist and saw his awed eye looking up at her that she realized, but by then she was too far gone to care.

Ch'ik pressed down on her clit as Roz tightened around her fist and that was all it took for her to come. Jau surged up beneath her, hands tight on Ch'ik's hips as he tongue fucked her through her orgasm. The wash of sensations was too much to handle: it shocked another immediate orgasm out of her as she rode Jau's face to exquisite heights of pleasure and power.

Jau turned his head as she came, sinking his teeth into her inner thigh. She cried out, bending forward and unleashing sharp teeth on the curve of Roz's hip, eliciting a cry of delight from the big Omega. She barely had a moment to lap her mating bite on Roz before Zul was on her, gathering her up against his chest as well as he could, nosing at her neck with growling, huffing breaths. She let her own bite offer him permission, nipping the muscular column of his neck just before his teeth found the curve between her neck and shoulder.

When it was over and they had carefully disentangled themselves from one another's bodies, Ch'ik barely had the wherewithal to stumble into the sonic shower in the en suite. Zul helped Roz in to clean himself up, relinquishing him to Ch'ik to lovingly bathe and pamper in the afterglow. Under the warm, pulsing lights of the shower, Roz cradled her arm to his cheek, sinking his teeth in at the side of her forearm at her encouraging nod. It was only fitting his bite adorn her "knot," after all.

After drying off, her freshly-bonded cluster all collapsed back onto the bed together - one cozy warren-nest of affectionate burrowing and sleepy kisses. It was morning, in the daily cycle of the ship, but with Jau curled around her back, her head pillowed on Zul's thigh, and Roz settled into her arms, Ch'ik was helpless to do anything but embrace a warm, dreamless sleep sweeter than any she'd ever known.

EPILOGUE

In a turn of events that would surely disappoint Oovooa, the kits hadn't chewed their way out through Ch'ik's abdominal wall after all. Just a quick incision and some numbing agent did the trick - her cluster's kits came squalling into life in Oster's finest maternity suite, a gift from a grateful, newly *laht*-enriched planetary medical system.

They were the softest, sweetest things she'd ever seen. If there had been any doubt, that first heart-stopping moment in between when they stopped glowing and gave their first grumpy yells erased it entirely - Ch'ik hadn't been able to take her eyes off of them, those patchy-furred, blind, wrinkly little lumps that had immediately stolen her heart.

It made her smile, even now, to remember the way that she had snarled at the med-bot as soon as it had finished suturing the incision, ready to render it down into a bucket of bolts. She hadn't wanted anyone near other than her mates and her three tiny kits after the delivery.

"They're getting so big already." Ch'ik sniffed, and the smell of old milk and baby kits flooded her senses all the way down to the sappy mess of her formerly-hardened heart. "I mean, they used to be so tiny that I could hold each of their little butts in the palm of my hand? And now their little butts are almost as big as my whole hand? I don't know, I just..."

"They *are* getting big. They'll be opening their eyes soon." Roz reassured her with a murmur, nuzzling the short hair at the nape of her neck. He was curled around behind her as he supported Nara, the little orange kit who preferred Ch'ik's third nipple to the exclusion of all others.

Ch'ik smiled to herself as she remembered the way those tiny fists had flailed whenever she had tried to get Nara to take a turn latched on the front, worried that her smallest kit had somehow felt neglected next to Mauv and Vaer. It had been an exercise in frustration until Ch'ik had realized that Nara was just like her - zero tolerance for being told what to do. After that, Ch'ik had just shrugged and let the kits nurse wherever they wanted; she didn't want to worry so much over *those* little things that she didn't appreciate *these* tiny little things snuggled against her.

It was amazing how these fuzzy slips of life already seemed to have personalities, even though they weren't yet two fraction-cycles old. Nara's preference for her third nipple. Vaer's squalling insistence on only sleeping upright on someone's chest. Mauv, the biggest of the three, who would root around and latch onto anything even vaguely rounded - ear tips, fingers, noses.

"Alright, no more stink butt." Jau gently patted Mauv on the bottom as he popped the kit off from suckling his nose. "Nuh-uh. You gotta go back to Beta if you want that."

Ch'ik reached up for the pale purple kit and cuddled him against her chest with a sigh of contentment as he latched. Jau leaned down to press a kiss to the top of her head before settling himself beside Zul, who was drowsing lightly with soft green Vaer curled up on his chest. The low lights in their living quarters flared like fire off of Jau's golden ring, threaded through the healed edge of his plasma shot-pierced ear. Jau looked particularly chipper for a lifeform that hadn't slept for more than a few moments at a time, and had been a gift from the pulsars when it came to minding the kits.

The time had passed in a warm and sleepy haze. Roz, Zul, and Jau were never more than an arm's length or call away. Her cluster - a term that still felt odd, even in her own head - was always there, ready to help. If what she needed was 'a break' then each kit had a parent to cuddle with while she passed out - and the Lapann never, ever shamed her for needing one. Between the four of them, a rough first fraction-cycle notwithstanding, they'd managed to work out a solid schedule and support system for the little ones.

Shortly after the kits arrived, Zul had gotten a hail from an Imperium patrol about the *Aeon Hawk*. The patrol leader explained that the Plarm Station malfunction had resulted in a lot of lost ships they were attempting to reunite with owners, and the *Hawk's* last data upload had been from their *Lucky Leprechaun*, tracked to Oster. Ch'ik had been overjoyed to have the *Hawk* returned, though celebration was oddly subdued from the rest of her cluster. With all the credits earned from selling the broma pods - even though she'd ended up giving most of them away in a fit of altruistic pregnancy hormones - she could afford to outfit her ship the way it deserved. She was already mulling over a pair of those sweet spinning tail thrusters she'd seen in last fraction-cycle's *Mechmarvel Monthly*.

After their exile was reversed with a formal apology, the cluster had agreed that, once the kits were a little older, the *Koton* would start making annual runs between Ch'ik's broma sources and Oster. Even though Zul's extended family no longer had a conspiratorial strangle-hold on planet's agriculture strains, Oster still needed a significant volume of imported broma to keep up with *laht* demand for the next few cycles.

Happily, however, the kit mortality rate had already plummeted to nearly zero after only a few fraction-cycles, just on Ch'ik's broma haul alone.

Oster's largest *laht* producer would go on to name a fan-favorite formula in Ch'ik's honor.

....and their cluster lived happily stellar after.

- THE END -

Hey there, reader – Vera and J.L. here! We'd like to take a moment to thank you for reading our weird, wild, and (hopefully!) wonderful excursion to space via the bunny alien omegaverse. This story was genuinely a delight to write, expanding far beyond its foundations as a little 10k-long novella. We fell head-over-heels for these characters, and we have secret short story/novella plans for everyone's favorite vape-addicted fight promoter. (If you want in on that, make sure you sign up for Vera's newsletter over at ValentineVerse.com!)

Here's the part where we ask for your support. Reviews can make or break a book, so if you liked this book as much as we did, can you do us a solid and let folks know? Leaving reviews on **Amazon**, **Bookbub**, **GoodReads**, and so on help with exposure and getting new readers to check us out. And hey, we're big fans of BookTok / TikTok (**@ValentineVerse**) and Bookstagram / Instagram (**@VeraValAuthor**) too, so be sure to tag us if you'd like to show us some love on there. Thanks again, and have an awesome day!

Hungry for more? Check out these titles!

Book 1 in the Holiday Hedonism Series
Back for Seconds: A Reverse Harem Feast

When your family leaves you to clean up after a busy holiday dinner, you decide to nip future It's-my-turn squabbles in the bud by quietly breaking the wishbone yourself. When a private joke brings your desires to life, the kitchen gets a lot hotter - Trent, Sam, Carter, Pierce and....Gregg, you guess...are the dirty dishes here to satisfy needs that go well beyond that pile of - actual- dirty dishes in the sink.

Back for Seconds: A Reverse Harem Feast is a 8,959 word stimulating short story about the power of leftovers and bringing together strangers for some close and -extremely- personal fun. This tale is written for adults, and intended for 18+ audiences only. It involves explicit group activity, mild MM scenes, and consensual humiliation of a side dish that, let's all be honest here, kind of deserves it.

Book 2 in the Holiday Hedonism Series

Regifted: Ganged by the Ghosts of Christmas

From the critically-acclaimed authors of **Back for Seconds: A Reverse Harem Feast** comes a brand new reverse harem tale of holiday hedonism, Chaz Dickens-style. This filthy, gender-bent twist on a Christmas Carol follows businesswoman Ellie Nadir and four ghostly guests - Jake, Anon, Yore, and Exor - as she learns how rewarding giving can be. She'll be absolutely filled with...joy...by the time they're done helping her embrace the true meaning of Christmas.

Regifted: Ganged by the Ghosts of

Christmas is a 11,355 word stimulating short story about being filled with holiday spirit(s) and learning how to embrace the act of giving. This tale is written for adults, and intended for 18+ audiences only. It involves explicit group activity, unprotected "interactions" with ghosts and their subsequent glowing ectojism, bondage, love taps to the face, the ol' hide-the-chain trick, and consensual humiliation of the female main character, including some degrading terms that sensitive readers may find offensive.

(Also, y'all, there's a *definitive* HEA in this one, okay? Don't come for us this time!)

From the critically-acclaimed authors of **Back for Seconds: A Reverse Harem Feast** and **Regifted: Ganged by the Ghosts of Christmas** comes a brand new reverse harem tale of holiday hedonism, and this time love (and lust) are on the line. They're magical monster-hunting vampires living in a van, she's a fed-up middle-aged divorcee attempting to geocache her Valentine's Day into oblivion. Perfect. Now the question is: can Quintain, Fletcher, and Marcus convince Ruby that the best way to resurrect her love life is with a few guys that are also back from the dead?

Ruby and the V-Day Vanpires is a 9,619 word stimulating short story about the importance of cleaning up public parks, practicing safe archery, and that age - and getting absolutely RAILED in the back of a van by three bi vampires - is only a state of

mind. This tale is written for adults, and intended for 18+ audiences only. It involves explicit group activity, unprotected "interactions" with said undead suitors and their ahem nocturnal emissions, slight kidnapping, the ol' fangy kiss to access liquid vampire chow, being impaled (the fun way, with 2 peens in 1 V), being impaled (the NOT fun way - like, with an arrow), sex pollen/poison (aka have to the deed to survive), as well as brief mentions of Homeowner's Associations (HOAs), and geocaching.

About J.L. Logosz

J.L. Logosz can be found on Twitter as
@JayElWrites. She enjoys going on road trips,
looking at cool rocks, and having a last name that is
truly career-kryptonite. J.L. hails from the frozen
wasteland of North Dakota, where she lives with her
husband and two children in a weird liminal state on
the empty prairie – unknown, unseen, and
incomprehensible to the human mind. Being sincere
about herself on the internet makes her break out into
hives.

Follow her other social media accounts here:
https://linktr.ee/jllogosz

Burning Embrace: A Sexy Fire Safety Skeleton Short Story

You went to sleep one cozy Christmas eve with visions of sugar plums dancing in your head, only to awake to fiery destruction. What happened? And who is this sexy skeleton walking out of your burning tree?

- **Reader(m/f) / Sexy Skeleton (?)**
- **Rated PG-13**
- **Second Person POV**
- **2000 words, short story**

- Content Warnings: graphic depictions of structure fire, imminent death, narrator in danger.
- Pretty much completely in reference to a Twitter meme from the United States Consumer Product Safety Commission.

About Vera Valentine

An unapologetic book-huffer and devourer-of-stories, Vera Valentine has carried on a torrid love affair with the written word for nearly all of her 39 years. Grown in the diner-laden wilds of the New Jersey Pine Barrens and transplanted to North Carolina, she lives with her husband, seven cats, and two dogs, most of whom are house trained. An avid fan of the Paranormal Reverse Harem genre, she tossed her author hat into the ring in September of 2021 and never looked back.

A self-professed chaotic capybara, Vera can usually be found spending too much time on social media, chilling with fellow newbie authors, or scribbling down plot bunny ideas in her trusty paper sidekick, the Bad Idea Book™.

If you'd like to stay in touch and up-to-date on Vera's latest projects, pop by **www.ValentineVerse.com** to follow her on social media, sign up for the ValentineVerse Newsletter, and more! :)

facebook.com/ValentineVerse

twitter.com/VeraValAuthor

instagram.com/veravalauthor

amazon.com/Vera-Valentine/e/B09FRQ6V7V

tiktok.com/@valentineverse

goodreads.com/21809549.Vera_Valentine

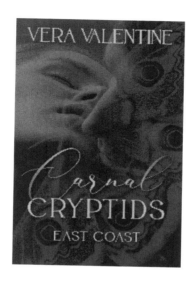

Carnal Cryptids: East Coast

Book 1 in the Carnal Cryptids Series Available in Kindle Unlimited

Desiderata needed a drink. After a long day of dodging darts and heckling tourists from her balloon game booth on the Wildwood boardwalk, she just wanted to forget her looming housing angst for an hour. When heavy flirtation and a cocktail from a suave substitute bartender shakes up her evening, things are looking up.

Until, of course, she catches him making out with a hot

college guy not five minutes later.

In an attempt to forget the sinfully sexy stranger from the night before, Desi agrees to a dinner date with the eyeful of tall, dark and handsome that shows up at her job the next day. There's just one little catch: he's apparently already dating the two guys from the bar.

For JD, a shift behind a Jersey shore dive bar was always the same: predictable, boring, a little bit sticky. So what was it about this gorgeous brunette that instantly had him on the rocks? One look at her brought out the beast in him - and a desperate hope that she might be what he and Penn need to save Will for good. After over a century of struggle, they were due for a win - and someone who really believed in them.

One night.

That's all they'll need to get Desi to agree to.

But it's going to be one *hell* of a night.

Carnal Cryptids: East Coast is a paranormal RH monster romance, which means that the female main character is attracted to more than one male love interest, and doesn't need to (or want to!) choose. The monstrous men that love our heroine - and each other, quite frequently - all bring elements of horror, fear, interesting anatomy, and urban legend / cryptid goodness to the mix. *This story is intended for an 18+*

audience; please review content warnings in the book (available on the Amazon "Look Inside" feature and/or the authors website) prior to reading.

Regret and Redemption: A Carnal Cryptids Short

Book 1.5 in the Carnal Cryptids Series Available in Kindle Unlimited

When the door to her rental place comes crashing in, Jess is ready to fight back and protect her best friend Desi's whereabouts at any cost. Betrayed by her own phone, she's violently pulled into a world full of monsters and mayhem, forced to fight back with the sharpest weapon she has. When one of her attackers emerges as an unexpected ally, Jess is forced to confront not only the existence of mythical Concepts, but some decidedly human emotions too.

Dov has existed for years under the thumb of a man he both despises and depends on, forced to act against his own interests to stay alive. When he's pushed to cross a line, he finds something unexpected on the other side a black-haired beauty with an attitude that could take out a tank. Now it's up to him to make the break he's been longing for, and hopefully some amends while he's at it.

This story primarily focuses on enhancing events that have already occurred in Carnal Cryptids: East Coast, and offers additional insight and backstory that will lead into Carnal Cryptids 2: Southeast. While adult language is used and attraction is definitely present, this tale is just for a bit of backstory and thus does not contain spice (e.g. there's no kissing, no beast-with-two-backs, etc.) - sorry! There will be LOTS in Carnal Cryptids 2, though, so try not to worry too much.

Carnal Cryptids: Regret and Redemption is a short / alternate POV tale intended to be read between Carnal Cryptids: East Coast and Carnal Cryptids 2: Southeast. It is intended for an 18+ audience and contains kidnapping, bondage, brief discussions of self harm / suicide, brief mentions of sexual assault

(concern over, not perpetuated), general violence, gun violence, brief mentions of military PTSD. *Please review content warnings in the book (available on the Amazon "Look Inside" feature and/or the authors website) prior to reading.*

Carnal Cryptids 2: Southeast

Book 2 in the Carnal Cryptids Series Available in Kindle Unlimited

With another summer on the Jersey shore coming to a close, Jess was more than ready to hang up her water park vest until next year. Still recovering from the shock of being kidnapped and nearly killed, she's barely had time to process the fact that monsters are real.

The impulsive offer to let her repentant abductor-turned-protector crash on her couch is going better than anticipated. So well, in fact, that inviting him along on her annual road trip is a surprisingly easy choice. But when old acquaintances, unresolved desires, and ancient impulses enter the mix, their straight shot down I-95 is suddenly full of dangerous curves.

A threat from the past in their rearview mirror.

Raw hunger, hot and heavy as a swamp.

Sharp, vicious smiles, sinuous as a river.

1400 miles to go.

Carnal Cryptids 2: Southeast is a paranormal RH monster romance, which means that the female main character is attracted to more than one male love interest, and doesn't need to (or want to!) choose. The monstrous men that love our heroine - and each other, quite frequently - all bring elements of horror, fear, interesting anatomy, and urban legend / cryptid goodness to the mix. This story is intended for an 18+ audience; please review content warnings in the book (available on the Amazon "Look Inside" feature and/or the authors website) prior to reading.

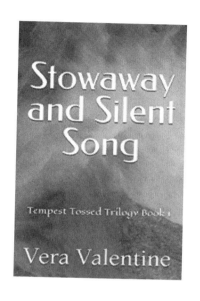

Stowaway and Silent Song

Book 2 in the Tempest Tossed Series Available in Kindle Unlimited

A selkie, a siren, and a sea captain walk into a tavern...

After building a reputation for herself as one of the best cargo-runners in the Winding Way, Captain Miranda Cardonna finally feels at home on the deck of her own ship, the Tempest Tossed. But when a tempting stowaway with one hell of a secret ends up in her cabin, she's plunged headfirst into a world of shifters, waveborns, and prophesy that pulls her in like the tides.

As selkies, sirens, and assassins seep into her once-mortal life, can Miranda find her footing in a new world where magic, love, and lust flow freely?

Stowaway and Silent Song is the first of three books in the Tempest Tossed Trilogy, with the additional two books slated for release by late 2021 / early 2022. This is a fantasy paranormal reverse harem title, which means the heroine has multiple love interests and doesn't need (or want!) to choose between them. There are also many M/M scenes woven throughout, so enjoy!

This story is intended for an 18+ audience; please review content warnings in the book (available on the Amazon "Look Inside" feature and/or the authors website) prior to reading. Contains explicit content / potential triggers, including but not limited to BDSM / Power Exchange, General Violence, Alcohol, Cursing, Knives, Murder, Drowning, Allusions to Past Assault, and Group Sex.

COMING SOON FROM VERA VALENTINE

(NOW AVAILABLE FOR PREORDER)

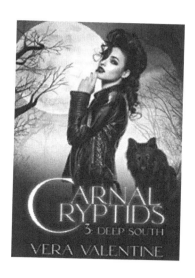

Carnal Cryptids 3: Deep South

Book 3 in the Carnal Cryptids Series

Available in Kindle Unlimited

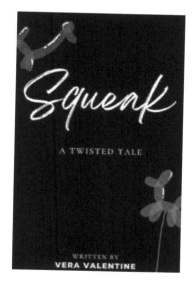

Squeak : A Twisted Tale

A Balloon Animal Shifter Omegaverse Novella

Available in Kindle Unlimited

Made in the USA
Middletown, DE
12 August 2024